MADOC'S MOTHER MET his gaze, and even from three ships' lengths away, he could see her smile.

She would kill all these people—kill Ash—for him.

It didn't matter if he wasn't ready or trained. He couldn't let that happen.

Raising his hands, he drew every bit of strength from his own soul and reached toward her. His fingers, white with cold, shook as he forced the power rising in his veins to stretch across the water.

Stop.

She deflected his attack like a slap, and his focus crumbled. Beside him, Ash's flame faltered. Tor shouted his name, but he didn't listen. He anchored his hips against the vessel's rail and reached for Anathrasa again, pulling her into the net of his need. He would drain her like he had Ignitus and Geoxus, and then she would suffer a mortal's death like all those she'd taken as tithes.

Anathrasa's scream filled his ears, so shrill he nearly clapped his hands over them. It rose, silencing Tor's shouts for him to stop. In seconds, Madoc felt as if his bones were cracking under the pressure of that scream.

Panic twisted through his anathreia, freezing it like the wall that blocked their escape.

Then every frozen vein of his soul shattered, and the world went black.

Also available by Sara Raasch and Kristen Simmons

SET FIRE TO THE GODS

RISE UP
FROM THE
EMBERS

SARA RAASCH
& KRISTEN SIMMONS

BALZER + BRAY

An Imprint of HarperCollins*Publishers*

To those of us who must now

rise from the embers.

Rise Up from the Embers
Copyright © 2021 by Sara Raasch and Kristen Simmons
Map Illustration by Leo Hartas
All rights reserved. Manufactured in Lithuania.
No part of this book may be used or reproduced in any manner whatsoever without
written permission except in the case of brief quotations embodied in critical articles
and reviews. For information address HarperCollins Children's Books, a division of
HarperCollins Publishers, 195 Broadway, New York, NY 10007.
www.epicreads.com

Library of Congress Control Number: 2022934038
ISBN 978-0-06-289160-0

Typography by Jenna Stempel-Lobell
22 23 24 25 26 SB 10 9 8 7 6 5 4 3 2 1
❖
First paperback edition, 2022

ONE

MADOC

MADOC HAD SAVED lives, altered thoughts, and drained the power from gods—but he could not stop the knife swinging toward his gut.

With a grunt, he twisted away, but the steel sliced through the side of his sweat-soaked tunic, a breath away from his skin, and came to a stop beneath his left arm, beside his pounding heart.

"You're not trying," Tor growled, his long, damp hair clinging to his jaw, his tunic stretching across his broad shoulders. He may have matched Madoc in size and build, but that was where the likeness ended. Tor was hardened by years of training; his reflexes were quick as flames. He was a seasoned Kulan gladiator—or at least he had been before his god was murdered.

Now he was an accused traitor, on the run from a vengeful goddess—Madoc's mother—just like the rest of them.

Madoc shoved Tor back and wiped the sweat from his brow with his forearm. They'd been training every day since they'd sailed out of

Deimos's war-ravaged capitol, Crixion, two weeks ago. They hoped to find refuge in the Apuit Islands with the goddess Hydra's people, who they'd heard had allied with Florus, the god of plants. But with the gods of fire and earth both dead and Deimos in the grip of Anathrasa, the Mother Goddess, they had no idea how they'd be received. For all they knew, Hydra would think them spies and send her warriors to destroy them.

That was, if Anathrasa didn't hunt them down first.

"This isn't working," he muttered. Though Tor had taught many fighters to use igneia, fire energy wasn't the same as the anathreia Madoc himself possessed. If he was going to be any use to Ash and the others, Madoc needed to learn how to effectively manipulate soul energeia. But whenever he'd used it before, he'd either lost control or nearly killed himself in the process. Even with Tor's lessons, Madoc was no more ready to face Anathrasa now than he had been when they'd fled Deimos.

"Excuses." Tor tucked his blade back into the leather sheath at his belt and wiped his palms on his reed leggings. "I've seen you make a seasoned gladiator cry for his mother. Rip the energeia from a god like a rotten tooth. If you're going to drain the Mother Goddess before she finds a way to claim the other five countries, you'll need to be ready for anything. You're holding back."

Behind him, the ship's rail bobbed against the horizon, churning Madoc's stomach.

He tripped over the hatch cover leading belowdecks as another wave hit the stern. The swells had been bigger the last two days, the air cooler. He could feel it now, needling each bead of sweat on his temple as the sun sank low in the pink sky.

They were getting closer to Hydra's islands.

"If this boat would stop moving, I could concentrate." He staggered to stand, glaring at Tor's steady, wide-legged stance. Maybe he had saved Madoc when Geoxus's palace had fallen, but Madoc was really beginning to hate him.

"Anathrasa doesn't care if you're on the land or sea."

"She'll care if he throws up on her."

Ash lounged on the wooden steps to the upper deck, waving five flame-tipped fingers in front of her face. Since Madoc had returned her igneia—transferred it through the conduit of his body with his soul energy—the fire she created was blue.

Like the dead fire god's.

Madoc had heard Tor whispering with his sister, Taro, and her wife. They thought Madoc had accidentally given Ash the power he'd taken from Ignitus.

He wasn't sure they were wrong. None of them knew exactly what it meant, but if anyone was strong enough to figure it out, it was Ash.

She was wearing two tunics to fight the cold, but her shins were uncovered, and his gaze had fallen to her bare ankles, crisscrossed by the leather straps of her sandals, when another wave knocked him sideways into the foremast.

She laughed, and he couldn't stop his grin, even as the small crowd that had gathered near the helm above her snickered. Every Kulan on this ship had their sea legs, but Madoc still spent every morning and night with his head over a bucket.

"I'm not going to throw up." *Probably.*

"Focus," Tor ordered. "Anathrasa will be ready. She'll have protection. Aera and Biotus were allies of Geoxus—they'll likely join her now that he is dead. And who knows how many of the god of earth's centurions will rise to her aid once they realize what she can do?"

Madoc shivered. His mother was cunning. She'd survived for centuries by tithing—sucking the souls out of the gladiators Geoxus had offered her. She would not be defenseless now. Those who stood against her would be tithed, and the rest would suffer in silent allegiance for fear that she'd turn on them next.

"You know my intention," Tor continued. "Now stop me."

"Maybe that's the problem," Ash said, snuffing out the blue flames in a closed fist. "You don't really mean to hurt him. When he used anathreia to fight before, there was always a threat to his life." Her dark eyes flicked to his. "Or mine."

Madoc's shoulders drew together as he thought of the Deiman guards dragging Ash out of the preparation chamber at the arena after Anathrasa had taken away her energeia. A new sickness twisted his stomach as he remembered the palace, the tithes—his hollow soul, needing to be filled. His mother had forced him to take Petros's power, even if it meant killing him, to make himself strong. He'd taken Ignitus's power next, then Geoxus's, and it had nearly destroyed him.

If he hadn't been able to give that power to Ash, it would have.

Now a hunger for those same feelings, for the taste of another's energeia, was with him all the time, pressing against his lungs with every breath. But he refused to give in, not when this ship was filled with people who'd risked their lives for him. Not when he knew what tithing had done to Ash. To his sister, Cassia.

If he was going to be strong enough to drain whatever power his mother—the mother of all gods—had left, he needed to find another way to sate this growing need.

"I have no problem making him bleed if that's what it takes," Tor said with a sharp smile.

Madoc winced in Ash's direction. "Has he always been like this?"

"Oh, no." She grinned. "He used to have a training room and full armory at his disposal."

Madoc sighed through his teeth as Tor drew his knife and advanced again, a driven look in his eyes that made Madoc suspect he hadn't been kidding about making him bleed.

He was close enough to strike, and Madoc raised his hands— empty, at Tor's insistence—to defend himself. As they circled on the deck, Madoc reached out with his anathreia, feeling for Tor's emotions, finding the same intense frustration as always.

But it was laced with something else. A thin, pulsing warmth that reminded him, with a jolt of pain, of Ilena.

He blinked back his last image of his adopted mother, holding his face in her hands, telling him they would see each other again, just before she disappeared into the riots outside the temple to find Elias, Danon, and Ava. It was better this way—the farther Madoc was from Deimos, the safer they were—but he worried for them all the same.

Tor's head tilted. "What was that?" When Madoc shook his head, Tor stepped closer, dropping his weapon to his side. "What were you just thinking of?" Warmth spread across the space between them, driving a new spear of hunger into Madoc's soul.

Madoc glanced to Ash, who was now leaning forward, elbows on her knees.

"Home," he said quietly.

He didn't feel comfortable discussing this with Tor—his family was his to protect, even from friends. But if mentioning it helped him control his anathreia, he would do it.

Tor breathed in slowly, his eyes lifting to the horizon. "When Ash was a child, we often traveled for matches and wars. She grew up on ships like this."

Madoc glanced at her, watching him with a confidence he didn't deserve. If she knew how much he wanted to draw that confidence out of her, she wouldn't be so steadfast.

"When she missed Kula, I would tell her that Kula had come with her." Tor stepped closer, resting one large hand on Madoc's shoulder. The warmth was undeniable now, separate from the igneia in his veins, and Madoc held his breath, not trusting himself to swallow the air without a taste of it.

"Home is here." Tor moved his hand to Madoc's chest, where he softly pounded his fist twice. "Not there." He pointed behind them, to the sea. "The things that matter live inside us, and we protect them as we protect any other part of ourselves, with the power we've been given."

Madoc thought of Ilena and Elias. Danon and Ava. Even Cassia. And Ash, because she belonged with them, too. Only now he didn't picture them fighting or running. They weren't being hunted by Anathrasa or tortured in some prison cell as he'd dreamed every night these past two weeks. They were surrounded by a wall higher than those outside the grand arena. One fortified with the hardest, heaviest stones Elias had ever moved.

He locked them safely behind his ribs.

"Igneia is pulled from flames. Geoeia from stone." Tor shook his head in wonder. "You already have a fine source to pull from—your own soul—you're just afraid to do it."

Anathrasa had told him he needed other energeia to feed his power. He'd felt it work when he'd taken energeia from Petros and when he'd warped Jann's mind in the arena. Though he thirsted for it now, he'd never considered taking anathreia from himself.

Whatever soul he'd possessed himself had been broken a long time ago by Petros's hands and Crixion's streets.

"Don't be afraid," Tor said, meeting Madoc's gaze.

When he breathed, he felt the fondness behind Tor's frustration, but he didn't take it. His hunger had changed; it solidified the walls around his fortress. A knot of muscle in his neck relaxed as his anathreia whirled to life inside him for the first time in two long weeks.

Without warning, Tor lunged, knife aimed at Madoc's heart.

Stop.

Tor's hand froze in midair. He looked at it as if baffled, just before the knife dropped from his grip and embedded into the deck with a *thunk*.

"Good." With a grin, Tor spun, reaching out a hand to draw igneia from a lantern posted on the ship's mast. The fire balled in his palm, then sliced across the air beside Madoc's left shoulder. The sleeve of his tunic was charred; the heat seared his skin.

Excitement raced through Madoc's limbs as he rolled aside, then leaped to his feet. The next attack came just as fast, but this time he was ready. Tor wasn't just coming after him, he was coming after Madoc's family, his home. This wasn't about fighting or training. It was about defending what was his.

Madoc raised his empty hands, clutching the cold air as the energeia raced through him, ready for orders. *"Stop."*

The red flames licking Tor's skin suddenly went out. He stumbled back as if hit by an invisible punch, then went straight over the side of the ship.

Madoc's anathreia retreated like a kicked puppy. For one second he gaped at a wide-eyed Ash before they both raced to where Tor had fallen. Madoc's fingers dug into the splintering wooden rail as he searched the white-tipped waves. A moment passed, and then Tor sputtered to the surface, his arms circling as he treaded water.

"Was that really necessary?" Ash asked, unable to hide her grin.

Madoc laughed weakly.

"Man overboard!" From the helm rushed a flock of sailors, including Taro, Tor's sister. She wore the same glare Madoc had come to recognize from her, though now her eyes sparkled in amusement.

"Can that soul energy of yours give you wings?" she asked. "Because you'll want to be somewhere else when he gets back up here."

Ash giggled, but Madoc only winced.

Following Taro's lead, he reached to grab a thick coil of rope lying on the deck. With the help of Ash and Spark, Taro's wife, they succeeded in dropping one end down to the ocean below and fastening the other around the nearest mast.

Tor grabbed the end and began heaving himself up. Madoc didn't need to see his face to feel the bolts of anger flying off him.

"Maybe we should leave him down there a few minutes to cool off," he suggested.

"Just delaying the inevitable," Taro said. "It was nice knowing you, Madoc."

He groaned as they laughed. They were joking, of course. Tor wouldn't really kill him.

He hoped.

"Get him up here." Behind them, Spark's voice had dropped. Her worry prickled against Madoc's skin even before he saw it etched into her face. He followed her gaze up to the crow's nest, where a Kulan sailor was shouting to the crew at the helm while he watched the horizon through his spyglass.

"What is it?" Ash tensed beside him, peering into the distance. The sun had dipped below the horizon now, painting the sky an angry scarlet. She snagged the arm of a sailor, a boy no more than fifteen, who was sprinting toward the mast.

"Ships on the port side coming on fast." The sailor's voice cracked. "Too fast for a mortal crew. They've got help."

Madoc's pulse quickened. "What kind of ships?"

Please be Hydra's or Florus's fleet, he willed. Surely the goddess of water had the ability to make her ships cut through the waves at an accelerated clip.

"Black and silver sails." The sailor slipped free of Ash's hold and raced toward the mast to uncoil the lines. "Three of them!"

Madoc turned to Ash, a roar filling his ears. Only one country boasted the black and silver flag: Deimos.

Anathrasa had found them.

Shoving past Taro, he grabbed the thick corded rope Tor was climbing and heaved, straining to get the older man aboard as quickly as possible. Taro and Spark took up the slack behind him as Ash raced to the quarterdeck to see what was coming.

"Next time," Tor ground out between ragged breaths. "Try to keep my feet on the deck."

Madoc managed an apologetic shrug.

"Deiman ships spotted on the port," Taro barked at her brother as he clambered over the deck. He was soaked straight through and shrugged off his tunic with a violent shiver.

"Can we outrun them?" Tor asked.

Taro shook her head. "They're coming on too quickly."

The mainsail cracked as it filled with air, and the Kulan ship sailed faster than an arrow. Madoc gripped the rail to hang on as sailors rushed around him, securing lines and shouting orders. Below him, the hull slapped against the waves, driving hard to the west, into the last smear of daylight.

Anxiety snapped through the air. It mixed with a cold, snaking dread that pressed through Madoc's skin, chilling him to the bone. He couldn't think with all the emotions screaming around him. He could no sooner drown it out than quiet the crowds in the grand arena during a war.

He caught sight of Tor exchanging tense words with the captain, then Ash, pointing behind them into the night. He carved a path around the twin masts toward her, peering into the failing light and focusing on the heat of Ash's skin as she wrapped her fingers around his wrist. Warmth rippled up his arm, through his chest, steadying him. Without thinking, he curved his other hand around the slope of her waist.

"There!" she shouted. "Do you see them?"

He squinted, and soon he could make out a flash of silver in the dark sky. As he stared into the gloom, another joined it. Then a third. Three Deiman ships, flying over the waves, the heavy hulls skimming the surface of the water as the sails above stretched to full capacity. The sight of them filled him with equal parts dread and wonder. He'd never seen ships move with that kind of effortless speed.

"How are they going so fast?" he asked.

"I don't know," Ash said. "Earth Divine sailors can't move a ship like that. They must be either Water Divine or . . ."

"Air Divine." Madoc blew a tight breath through his teeth. He'd once seen a gladiator with aereia create a tornado during a match—it wasn't a stretch to imagine one manipulating the sea winds to their advantage. If there were Air Divine sailors aboard those ships, that would mean that Aera, who had been Geoxus's ally before his death, had come to Deimos to join Anathrasa.

Ash nodded, her brows drawn with worry—not just about who the ships carried, but what trouble they might bring. He hadn't been the only one training these past two weeks. Her new igneia was different, more intense—she could pull the blue flames without a source but had trouble controlling them. This was the burden of possessing a god's power in a mortal body.

Sometimes he wondered how it hadn't killed her.

"Slow down!" called a sailor above them. "There's something ahead!"

They spun to search the darkness lying before them.

"Land?" Hope lifted Ash's voice. "Is it the islands?"

Ash and Madoc dashed toward the bow of the ship, past the captain at the helm. Tor was already there, shooting a stream of fire into the night to light the way. Spark and Taro stood beside him, squinting ahead, to where a gray, shapeless mass expanded in the distance.

"Fog?" The air had taken on a frigid chill, and the word puffed steam from Madoc's lips.

With a quick shake of her head, Ash lifted her arms and heaved a spray of blue flames ahead, twice as far as the others could manage. Taro, standing closest, fell to her side with a cry, the heat of the blaze too intense even for a Kulan.

The beacon illuminated a sparkling gleam ahead, rising into the sky, disappearing into the clouds. Fear raced through Madoc's blood.

Not fog. Ice.

A solid wall of ice.

"Stop!" Madoc shouted. "It's a blockade!"

The ship heeled as the captain turned hard to avoid the wall of ice. The change in course brought them closer still, and in dreadful awe, Madoc stared up at the gleaming wall, veined with a scaffolding of blackened vines. They'd heard that Hydra and Florus had created a barrier to anyone from the outside, but they'd assumed it was a barricade of ships, or dignitaries who would take their claims to the gods.

They hadn't expected a wall.

Ash's fire died as the starboard side scraped against the blockade, chunks of ice falling onto the deck. One hit a sailor, and with a stunted scream she toppled down the ladder.

"They're closing in!" shouted Spark. More calls rose around them, shifting Madoc's attention.

Then, snaking through the chaos, a golden thread of silence.

It pushed through the wood, through the cloth and flesh and blood. Through the night and the water. It lifted the hair on his arms and the back of his neck, and as he breathed it in, he knew this curiosity was directed at him.

Anathrasa.

"She's here," Madoc murmured.

Ash's fierce gaze heated the side of his face.

"Then we fight," she said.

He took her hand, squeezed her fingers in his. He wanted to look at her one more time. He wanted one more night of her sneaking into his bunk belowdecks, lying together in the quiet so they didn't wake the other sailors. One more frantic kiss behind the mast when Tor wasn't looking.

There was no time.

He'd known from the moment they'd left Deimos that his mother would come for him. He had what she wanted—the ability to drain the power from gods and transfer it, as he had with Ash. To give Anathrasa the energeia of the six gods and make them mortal so she could harness anathreia again and take over the world.

He needed to stop her before that happened.

"We fight," he said.

The ships were closer now. Their sails snapped in the wind. Their hulls smashed against the waves. Madoc made his way to port side, facing the closest ship that carved a line toward them, its silver bow like a battering ram, ready to shatter them against the monstrous wall of ice.

The captain was still trying to push the ship faster, but they'd lost the wind beside the blockade, and their speed had slowed to a crawl.

"Ready?" Tor called, somewhere to Madoc's left.

He tried to focus on his family, on protecting his home, but his concentration evaporated as Ash lit up the night with blue flames, revealing the old woman standing at the helm of the approaching ship, flanked by Earth Divine soldiers in silver armor and Air Divine warriors in pale, thin wisps of fabric.

Madoc's mother met his gaze, and even from three ships' lengths away, he could see her smile.

She would kill all these people—kill Ash—for him.

It didn't matter if he wasn't ready or trained. He couldn't let that happen.

Raising his hands, he drew every bit of strength from his own soul and reached toward her. His fingers, white with cold, shook as he forced the power rising in his veins to stretch across the water.

Stop.

She deflected his attack like a slap, and his focus crumbled. Beside him, Ash's flame faltered. Tor shouted his name, but he didn't listen. He anchored his hips against the vessel's rail and reached for Anathrasa again, pulling her into the net of his need. He would drain her like he had Ignitus and Geoxus, and then she would suffer a mortal's death like all those she'd taken as tithes.

Anathrasa's scream filled his ears, so shrill he nearly clapped his hands over them. It rose, silencing Tor's shouts for him to stop. In seconds, Madoc felt as if his bones were cracking under the pressure of that scream.

Panic twisted through his anathreia, freezing it like the wall that blocked their escape.

Then every frozen vein of his soul shattered, and the world went black.

TWO

ASH

UNPREDICTABLE IGNEIA DURING training was one thing—no one's lives depended on Ash countering Tor's moves. But in a battle, with Anathrasa's ships bearing down on them and the other Kulan sailors already streaking fire across the night sky—Ash's chest constricted with equal parts fear and dread.

She had been training for years. She could control her igneia.

Only this wasn't *her* igneia.

Ash shoved aside the thought and thrust out her palms. A funnel of blue arced over the waves. The heat in it came straight from her heart, stole her breath with the searing intensity of the white-blue flames.

From one of the Deiman ships, an Air Divine warrior let loose a column of wind that slammed into Ash's fire. She flinched and her fire arc missed the lead ship, slamming into the water with a hiss that clouded steam into the air.

Cursing, Ash shook her hands out by her sides and shot another stream of blue fire into the night, chasing the orange ones sent by the Kulan sailors. Sweat beaded along her hairline, racing in trickles down her neck. She focused on bending the fire stream toward the lead ship, toward Anathrasa.

Anathrasa, whose alliance with Geoxus had caused Ash's mother's death on the sands of Kula's arena, and who had drained Cassia of her energeia before Petros killed her, and who had drained Ash's own energeia.

Anathrasa, who would force Madoc to destroy the world—or force Madoc to murder her himself in order to stop her.

However demented she might be, Anathrasa was still his mother—and beyond that, *could* he even truly hurt her? Or would she just rip the anathreia from his body before he could do anything and leave him an empty, aching shell while she went about siring other Soul Divine mortal children who would actually obey her?

The fire pouring from Ash's hands wavered, then shot out even stronger. It burned so hot she saw the wood rail at her hip start to glow red. But it wasn't just the fire that was hot—it was *her*, her body, and if she hadn't been wearing fireproof Kulan reeds, she'd be bare in the night.

Ash clamped her eyes shut, every nerve aching with conflicting emotions.

Burn it all. Kill her.

Stop! It's too much—too much—

Then, a scream.

Ash peeled her eyes open. Images blurred in sweat, flashes of firelight, and movement on the Deiman ships.

Anathrasa, bent over on the forward deck, her lone figure flickering in the light from the Kulan fires.

Hope tasted bitter. Had Ash done that? Had she truly hurt—

But then she saw Madoc reaching for his mother, his face set with vicious intent.

He had been trying to take Anathrasa's soul. Were they close enough to each other?

Who had screamed?

Madoc's knees cracked onto the deck. He let out a strangled moan and Ash's resolve tightened.

There could be no more pretending that Madoc had given her her own igneia back. The night they'd left Deimos, Madoc truly had given her Ignitus's power. The fire god's body was gone, but his energeia lived on. It was why the Kulans were still able to use igneia—it hadn't vanished into nothingness. It was in *her*.

No longer did Ash have to pull igneia from a source. It was always just *there* now, inside her, ready. And she could make orange flames, sure—gold and yellow and scarlet. But the first one that burst out of her was always a startling turquoise flicker of scalding heat.

She had the god of fire's soul inside her now. She had power, and damn it all, she would *use* it.

It terrified her. It twisted her stomach into knots and had her choking down food she couldn't taste and falling into fitful sleeps, because she was *terrified* of what having this much power meant. What was she now? *Who* was she now?

But she was more terrified by how much it *didn't* terrify her.

And seeing Madoc on his knees, clutching his head, made all Ash's worries seem trivial.

This ended *now*.

Ash stepped up to the rail, her nails biting into her palms. The Deiman ships twisted through the obsidian waves, a trio of matching wooden bows. Their masts flew the flag of Deimos, a pearly column against a silver background, and the orange flashes of Kulan fire gave the flags a vivid glow. Across the decks, Ash caught sight of Deiman centurions with their fingers splayed, using geoeia to keep palm-sized knots of pebbles aloft, while the Lak warriors funneled coils of wind over their heads. All of them waited for Anathrasa's orders.

Anathrasa was now clutching the wooden rail. Was she gasping? Had Madoc done something to her?

She's weak, Ash's warrior instincts barked. *Attack!*

"Attack!" Anathrasa's gravelly voice filled the night air.

For weeks, Ash had been stacking rage like kindling in her soul. Cerulean fire streamed out of her, charging from the Kulan ship to the lead Deiman vessel. Anathrasa's face was pale in the coming light, and she dropped behind the rail as the scalding flames raced across the ship. The fire washed into the Deiman centurions and Lak soldiers behind her, who stumbled back.

Ash didn't hear their cries of pain. The sear and churn of the fire swallowed her up.

A lifetime ago, Ash had practiced with other fire dancers before performing for Ignitus, and she'd trained with her mother in igneia fighting techniques. She'd thrown fire whips and sustained flames and had spun fire in interlocking circles over and over and over, until she had complete control.

She didn't want control now. She wanted Anathrasa to cower knowing that Ignitus's energeia lived on. She wanted the Mother Goddess to know that, for all her centuries of planning her revenge against her murderous children, she could not extinguish Kula.

Sweat beads tumbled down Ash's temple as she bent her arms, remembering her dancing, all elegance; and her mother, all precision.

Her fire coiled around one, two, three remaining soldiers, and she squeezed. The flames contracted and her victims shrieked.

These weren't the screams she wanted.

Ash's concentration broke and she dropped the soldiers. Where was Anathrasa?

"The God Killer! Attack!" shouted one of the men she'd released. "Avenge Geoxus!"

Ash huffed an empty laugh. She remembered Geoxus's body dropping limply onto the marble floor of his throne room, the knife in her hand wet with his blood. She'd been suppressing her satisfaction at killing him just like she'd suppressed Ignitus's power. She'd thought she should feel guilt, or regret, or reverence for killing something immortal—but all she'd felt was glee.

God Killer. She liked the sound of that.

More centurions used geoeia to hurl rocks into the air. More Air Divine sent powerful winds to carry the rocks higher, faster. A wave of stones vaulted through the star-speckled sky, a shower of rocks as vicious as arrows.

Time slowed. There was only the burn of fire in Ash's limbs, the taste of salt and sweat on the air, the vague awareness of Spark tending to a barely conscious Madoc.

Ash's heart gave a hard lurch, horror almost yanking her to her knees next to him—it was only by sheer force of will that she kept her feet. Then that will turned to fury.

Anathrasa had hurt him.

Tor shouted something, but Ash couldn't hear through the noise in her mind.

She thought she'd feel some release after finally breaking the restraints she'd placed on herself. But the more igneia she poured out of her fingertips, the more a different need built. Pressure welled up in her throat, something that had sat under her igneia these past two weeks, waiting, waiting, waiting.

The stones came closer. Kulans across the deck sent up a cry.

Beyond them, Anathrasa sneered.

You will not touch him, Ash promised. *You will never touch him again.*

She lifted her arms. Her blue fire raged, hurtling up from the deck of the Deiman ship and washing through the air after the stones. Some of the rocks she could simply burn up before they did any damage; others she redirected with quick flashes of heat.

Fire and earth.

It made Ash dizzy, seeing the flames twist around the rocks. Each bump of fire against rock *hurt*. She could feel the singe, a sharp jab of awareness that made her recoil.

Ash sank back to her own body with a jolt and gulped scorched air. Her nerves felt deadened. She was raw and drunk and dizzy. It was so sweet, so simple, to use igneia—

But she wasn't using only igneia.

She could feel the rocks. She could *feel* the grit of porous sandstone, the razor-sharp edge of shale. They were like fire, but they were nothing like fire, and Ash felt a part of her soul sigh, stretch, and burst forth.

"Ash!"

A voice, calling her. Something bucked beneath her—the very foundation of the earth.

"Ash—*stop!*"

The world pitched again. No—the ship.

Reality broke over her. Her heart hammered as though she'd run twenty laps around Kula's largest arena, and when she peeled her eyes open, she saw rocks.

Rocks all around her.

Boulders, chunks of marble, granite—they filled up the deck of the Kulan ship.

Tor's fingers bore into her arms. "Ash, you have to stop! You're sinking the ship!"

You're sinking the ship.

"No." Her mind tripped. "I'm trying to stop the assault—"

But as she spoke, a rock filled her open palms, then clattered to her feet. Another followed, and another, stones pouring out of her hands.

She was Fire Divine, not Earth Divine. She couldn't be—

The night they'd fled Deimos, Madoc had taken Ignitus's igneia—and he'd taken Geoxus's geoeia, too. Madoc had been nearly unconscious, unable to walk on his own, from the pressure of holding two gods' souls in his body. Then, belowdecks, he'd given Ash igneia. Afterward, he'd been his normal self.

No one had asked where Geoxus's geoeia had gone.

Ash's senses widened and she felt every grain of sand on the Deimos ships. Geoeia pulsed through her body, heavier than igneia, but in a sturdy, immobile way that Ash suddenly craved.

Impossibly, she felt herself smile.

She was the god of fire now, and the god of earth.

She had *both* powers.

Tor shook her. A look of horror crossed his face, and it was enough to break her out of her euphoria.

"You're sinking the ship," he repeated. "You have to get rid of these rocks."

Behind him, Taro and Spark knelt next to Madoc, the three of them gaping at her.

The Kulan ship groaned as the great vessel lowered, dropping closer and closer to the thrashing ocean waves. This boat was built for speed, not to bear the weight of stones.

Ash's mouth fell open. "I—I don't know how I'm doing this."

Burn it all—she had no idea how to use geoeia. Where had these rocks even come from, except her own subconscious will? Panic heated her body, and columns of blue fire surged out of her hands.

Tor wrenched back, hissing in pain as the fire licked his ankles. Only Ignitus's fire could burn a Kulan. *Her* fire. When she'd sparred with Tor in the past two weeks, she'd tried and tried to keep her flames away from his skin. Still, she saw red burns on his shins and arms. He had never mentioned it. Neither had she.

She buckled, dropping onto a boulder. "I'm sorry! I'm sorry—"

Her apology died. Sorry for *what*? Burning him? Sinking the ship?

Tor's face was sympathetic but scared.

Their ship was in chaos, Kulan sailors hefting stones overboard, while in the distance, Anathrasa's ships sat still and watchful, likely confused as to why their prey was suddenly sinking.

Ash had doomed them.

Stomach clenching, she gagged and stared down at her traitorous hands, now wreathed in flame. She shook her fingers, curled them into fists.

Geoeia, she willed. *Control it, control—*

The ship lurched to starboard before rocking back to port. The crew wailed, grabbing for purchase on wood or stone as the ship rose through the water and came to a trembling stop.

They had been sailing for so long that the sudden immobility made Ash dizzy.

Had they hit the blockade? She and Tor stumbled for the rail and he shot fire over the water.

Not water now. Ice.

The whole of the ocean around the Kulan ship had solidified into a sheet of foggy ice that matched the barricade at their backs. Only the Deiman ships, rocking in angry waves, were still free. And Anathrasa, now upright again, was calling orders for her centurions to regroup.

"What happened?" Ash panted, her breath a cloud in the chilly air. Even with igneia living inside her, she was so cold here.

"Hydra," Tor guessed.

Madoc, now standing, shot his eyes to the wall of ice and vines. "Or Water Divine guards on the barricade."

Madoc. He was all right.

Ash lurched toward him, not caring about anything else. She had been furious at Tor for playing the role of overprotective father and for trying to keep her and Madoc apart on this voyage, as though she was a child who'd given her heart to the first boy she'd seen. She threw herself around Madoc now, Tor's glower be damned.

"What did she do to you?" she whispered against his neck.

His arms clamped against her back, weaker than usual, but still resolute. "I'm not sure. I tried to take her anathreia."

Ash stiffened. She wanted to tell him he shouldn't have done that, not yet, he wasn't ready. But how many other chances would they have? She would have done the same thing.

"And it hurt you somehow?" She touched the back of his head.

He shuddered. "I don't know—"

"What. Did you bring. *To my home?*"

The voice was melodic even in its obvious fury.

Ash twisted in Madoc's arms, unwilling to let him go just yet.

On the deck of their ship, amid the rocks Ash had summoned, was a woman who had to be the goddess of water. Behind her, Apuitian soldiers were climbing over the rail, dressed in glistening furs and skins, their arms wrapped in pulsing streams of water they could easily flick out in attack. And within that water, small particles glowed—some sort of algae, maybe? It gave off a subtle light that Ash's igneia couldn't touch, much like Geoxus's phosphorescent stones.

Ash had seen the water goddess long ago in Ignitus's palace. She had been only a face made of water then, as she'd been communicating with Ignitus from afar via her element, but Ash saw the same features in her now.

Hydra was tall and pale, with thin eyes that were narrowed in suspicion. She wore only a skintight layer of what looked to be sealskin around her torso and upper thighs, and her long black hair hung to her lower back, as shimmering and straight as an undisturbed pond. When the soldiers on Anathrasa's ships called out another attack, she flicked a long, slender hand at them and Ash heard a splash of water, followed by a mingled chorus of coughing and shouts.

Her attention jerked back to the fight.

Ash whirled, her body tense. Could she risk attacking again?

His arm still around her waist, Madoc tugged her closer. "Don't." His voice was gruff.

Ash looked at him. In the Kulan firelight, he was gaunt and gray, his eyes bloodshot. He was upright and conscious, but only just barely, and when her eyes met his, he exhaled and let his forehead drop against her jaw.

He'd tried to take Anathrasa's energeia—had she managed to take his instead?

Ash's heart kicked with dread. "Sit." She tried to lower him to the deck. "You should—"

"Hydra!" Anathrasa's voice cut across the waves. "My daughter. I have missed you."

Hydra went rigid and her glare cut to the Deiman ships. "Anathrasa?" Her lips barely moved.

"Surprise, darling," the Mother Goddess returned. There was a warble in her tone, almost as though she was in pain. "My death was a fiction created to protect me as I regained my strength. The time has come, Hydra. Tell your brother—this barricade you and Florus created will not protect you."

"From what?" Hydra scoffed, but Ash saw that the goddess's skin had taken on a sickly hue. "Geoxus's navy doesn't scare—"

"Geoxus is dead. Ignitus, too. And you have your brothers' murderers before you."

Ash's grip tightened on Madoc, protective, terrified. She would kill Anathrasa if she touched him again.

"Think carefully before you pick a side, daughter," Anathrasa said. "I will give you and Florus one month to show yourselves in Deimos and surrender to me. I'll even leave you these traitors—bring them with you when you return, or I will consider you complicit in their crimes."

Ash eyed Anathrasa's ship. Its sails snapped in the breeze, the wind curving the vessels around as Anathrasa limped across the deck.

She was leaving. Madoc *had* wounded her.

Any joy Ash might have felt dulled as Madoc's weight dropped heavier against her. She eased him onto the wood planks.

A rock clinked. Hydra flicked a small particle of gravel from a boulder to the deck, her nose wrinkling in disgust. Around her, the Apuitian soldiers seethed with eagerness to attack.

"Anathrasa. Two gods *dead*. A mortal who can use both igneia and geoeia." Hydra analyzed Tor, then a few Kulan sailors, before landing back on Ash.

Horror filled Ash's body. It stoked both the igneia and geoeia in her soul, and she had to clamp her jaw shut, her muscles wound to suppress the roiling power.

"So let me ask again," Hydra said. "What did you idiot mortals bring to my home?"

THREE

MADOC

MADOC FELT AS if he'd been taken apart and roughly shoved back together. His body ached in a dozen different places—his head, his back, his knees and eyes. Ignoring the pain, he stood and focused on Ash's hand centered between his shoulder blades, and on the goddess before them.

Hydra's pale eyes assessed them as she picked her way around the boulders on the deck. Her face and dark clothing were lit a pale blue by the glowing algae in her warriors' water. It was quiet enough to hear the soft groan of the wood beneath her steps, and the waves lapping over the ice that now cradled the ship.

"Speak!" she ordered, lifting a single finger. "But know that if any of you so much as thinks of using igneia, I'll sink this ship to the bottom of the sea. Is that clear?"

Madoc dipped his chin, as did the others. But Ash was trembling as she withdrew her hand from his back. Was she hurt? He tried to reach for a sense of her emotions, but his anathreia was raw and beaten. Guilt sharpened the pounding in his head as he glanced over her for injuries but found only scrapes and bruises. If he could have stayed on his feet, he could have helped her. She'd needed him—they all had—and he'd been useless.

Her voice faded in Madoc's ears, and he blinked back a wave of fatigue. He didn't know what had happened when he'd attacked Anathrasa. One moment, he'd been reaching for her soul, intending to wrench it free the way he had Geoxus's power. The next, anathreia had exploded inside him. Now he could barely keep upright.

"We came here to bring news of your brothers' deaths, goddess," Tor said, ignoring the wound that painted a thin, scarlet line across his tunic's chest. "To tell you that Deimos has fallen, and Anathrasa intends to claim the six countries as her own. We didn't anticipate her tracking us down before we reached you." He knelt, his head bowed. "This ship's crew and her passengers are not at fault for Anathrasa's attack tonight. The blame for that rests with me alone."

Ash opened her mouth to object, but Tor shot a glare her way, silencing her.

Tor would take the fall for all of them—for Madoc, though they'd known each other only a short time—in order to win Hydra's favor. Tension sharpened the pressure at the root of Madoc's neck. This man owed him nothing yet risked his life for him again and again.

Hydra stopped before him, one hand over her stomach. "How did my brothers die?"

"Geoxus killed Ignitus," Tor said, intentionally vague. "He was siding with Anathrasa."

Madoc's eyes briefly closed as he recalled the throne room at the palace. The boulders falling from the ceiling. The screams of the centurions and Kulans as they'd battled.

The manic glee in Geoxus's smile as he'd rammed a jagged shard of his throne through his brother's heart.

"She made them mortal?" Hydra glided fluidly across the boards, closer to Tor. "She didn't look very powerful to me just now."

Tor's jaw clenched. "I don't—"

His words were cut off by a choking gargle as water began streaming from the corners of his mouth.

"Tor!" Taro dropped to his side, slapping his back, but the water was leaking out of his ears and nostrils now. Madoc's heart kicked against his ribs.

"Please!" Ash lifted her open palms to the goddess. "We came to help you!"

"Then it would be a pity to drown on your lies now," Hydra said.

"I did it." The words scraped Madoc's already-raw throat. He refused to let Tor die protecting him. Not when he'd pulled Madoc out of the palace, where'd he'd been tortured by Geoxus, Petros, and Anathrasa. Not when he'd trained Madoc on the ship.

Not after he'd tried to save Cassia from her indentured servitude in Petros's villa.

It didn't matter that Tor and Ash had failed, or that Cassia was dead. Few people had stood for Madoc when he needed them, and he would not lose one of them now.

Ash's worried gaze met his, her hands fisted in the sleeves of her tunic.

Madoc sucked in a breath, hoping it would last if Hydra filled his lungs with water next.

Hydra stepped before him, her clear blue eyes aligning with his. After a moment, she blinked, and Tor gasped. He spread his hands over the boards as Taro ordered him to breathe.

Hydra assessed Madoc's dark hair and square jaw. "Why is a Deiman on a Kulan ship?"

"Half Deiman." Madoc squinted to focus on her flawless face as his vision wavered.

Hydra's brow quirked. "*You* rendered my brothers mortal?"

"Yes," said Madoc. "But Ignitus was an accident. I was aiming for Geoxus."

She huffed, a cold laugh that Madoc was sure would end in his drowning. But there was no point in hiding the truth now. It was just a matter of time before she learned who he really was, and if she didn't hear it now, from him, they would never earn her trust.

"And how did you do that?" she asked, amusement curling her lips. Around her, the Water Divine warriors shifted uneasily.

"Anathreia," he said. "Soul energy."

"Madoc," Tor warned.

Hydra's mouth flattened into a thin line.

"Madoc," she said tightly. "Only a descendant of Anathrasa herself would have soul energeia."

"She's my mother," Madoc explained. "We're not exactly close."

Hydra's chin lowered. Her hands flexed. Madoc siphoned in another quick breath, unsure what she would do next.

"So she's not just alive," the goddess mused darkly. "But mother to a mortal son."

Madoc nodded. "Geoxus had been feeding her human tithes in exchange for bearing a Soul Divine child—someone to help him take over the six countries. I was the only one who survived."

Hydra lifted one hand, and a drop of water rose from her palm, gleaming in the dull light. It was a tiny thing, barely the size of his pinky—but he didn't know what she intended to do with it, and that drove a spike of fear through his chest.

"Why should I believe you?" she asked. "If you can do what you say you can, you could destroy me right now."

The drop of water floating above her hand swelled and narrowed to the shape of a spear tip aimed at Madoc's eye.

"I wouldn't do that," Madoc said quickly.

"Why not?"

"You heard Anathrasa," he said. "If you don't surrender, she'll call for war—not the kind with gladiators. With armies. If you're going to fight her and win, you'll need me."

Hydra flinched, and the arrow spun in a glittering tornado into the shape of a clawed hand.

"Because you can defeat her?" Hydra huffed. "Then why didn't you do that tonight?"

He spread his feet. Lifted his chest.

"You lie, Madoc. And I detest liars." In a blink, the clawed hand had turned to an icy knife, which Hydra grabbed and held against Madoc's throat.

He went still, the sharp, frozen point digging into the thin skin over his jugular. Beside him, Ash cried out in surprise, but he held her back with an extended hand.

Believe me, he willed Hydra. *Trust me.* But she was as much a wall as her blockade of ice was. Too strong for his weakened power.

In desperation, he reached for the next best thing. The nearest Water Divine warrior—a man in a sealskin hide and a fur hood.

Help, Madoc willed.

The warrior twitched, the icicle in his grip dropping lower.

Now, Madoc screamed wordlessly to him as Hydra's knife nicked his throat.

The man shook his head. "Goddess . . . I think . . . I think he may be telling the truth."

Hydra blinked back at him in surprise. "You do, do you?" Her voice was ice and challenge.

As the other man's soul broke free from his hold, Madoc's breath came in a hard rasp.

"I'm sorry, Goddess." The warrior raised his weapon again, his eyes confused. "I don't know what came over me."

Hydra's teeth clenched as realization hardened her features. "I've seen these tricks before." She eased closer to Madoc until he could feel a trickle of blood sliding down his neck. "Maybe you are Anathrasa's son. Maybe you can sway a mortal mind. But my brothers were gods. If you did what you said, you would have absorbed Geoxus's geoeia, and Ignitus's fire. You would be a gladiator fit to take down Anathrasa."

He hesitated, unwilling to answer for fear of putting Ash in more danger, and in that moment, Hydra lunged.

"He gave them to me!" Ash cried, stalling Hydra's advance. "Ignitus's energeia. Geoxus's as well."

Hydra turned her glare on Ash.

"He *gave* them to you," Hydra repeated. "What a nice gift."

Ash wrung her hands before her. What was she doing? She had Ignitus's fire, but the geoeia had dissipated. He couldn't feel it in his blood anymore.

What had happened to it?

"I did this," Ash said, motioning to the boulders on the ship. "Madoc only intended to give me back the energeia Anathrasa took from me. But he gave me Ignitus's power. And he must have given me Geoxus's power, too."

Madoc eyed her carefully, wondering if this was the truth, fearing what it meant if it was.

With a forced swallow, Ash reached toward a boulder on the deck behind Hydra and shoved it away, knocking two men to the side as it tumbled off the broken side of the ship.

The icy knife at Madoc's throat turned to water, splashing down his front. He drew in a quaking breath.

Hydra straightened, the wall of ice gleaming behind her. She glanced from Madoc to Ash.

"A conduit who possesses anathreia," she said. "And a gladiator who can bear the power of gods."

"We can help you," Madoc said.

Hydra gave a thin laugh.

"Yes," she said. "I think you can."

She turned, and with a wave of her hand, the ice wall began to melt, a hole rising from the sea, growing broader and higher, until it made an arching waterfall large enough for a ship to pass through.

With a lurch and a loud crack, the ship began to move. Not just the ship, Madoc realized, but the entire block of ice it rested upon. The Apuitians lowered their hands and weapons, awaiting their goddess's instructions as the ship moved forward through the falls, into the night beyond.

"Look," Spark whispered, and Madoc glanced behind them, finding that the arch was already lowering into a solid sheet of ice again.

Madoc lifted his gaze to where a million tiny lights flickered in the distance. As they glided forward, the lights pulled into groups, and Madoc made out the vague shape of the mountains they outlined.

The Apuit Islands.

Soon they'd reached a dark dock, where a dozen more Water Divine soldiers waited in thick fur coats.

"Rest," Hydra ordered without looking back. "We'll talk in the morning."

With that, she lifted a bridge of ice from the sea below and stepped off the side of the ship, into the darkness.

Madoc woke in a fur-lined hammock to the sound of footsteps creaking across the floor. He jolted upright, remembering his sore body and pounding head too late.

Biting back a groan, he whispered, "Who's there?"

"Shh. It's me."

Ash's soft voice eased his nerves, and he swung his legs off the side of the hammock, his last memories returning in a rush. The Apuitian guards had brought them down the dock to a wooden lodge scented by smoke and salted fish. There, they'd been given water and food, and then been escorted to a series of huts along the shore. Ash had joined Taro and Spark in one. Madoc, Tor, and a few of the sailors were sharing another.

They hadn't had a chance to talk about what had happened with Hydra, or the fact that Ash appeared to have two energeias instead of one. Tor had probably wanted to wait until they were alone to discuss it.

"How'd you get in?" Madoc whispered. There had been guards posted outside the doors.

He could barely see Ash's silhouette creeping toward him, outlined by the moon's glow through a skylight. He wasn't sure how much time had passed—a few hours at most. The sky outside was still dark, with no sign of the impending dawn.

"Window," she said softly. He glanced across the room, past the hammocks hanging heavy with Tor and the other fur-clad sailors. They hadn't been permitted a fire in the central hearth due to Hydra's concern that the Fire Divine were hiding their true intentions, and though the cold bothered Madoc, he found it more manageable than the Kulans, who were used to scorching temperatures.

Her hand found his knee, sending a wave of heat up his thigh. He took her fingers, dragging her closer. He wished he had this hut to himself. If Tor woke up, he'd be lucky if he only tossed Madoc into the frigid ocean outside.

Tor still owed him for their training mishap earlier.

"Come with me," she whispered, her breath a warm cloud on the side of his face.

He pushed quietly off the side of the hammock and followed her through the netted beds, toward a closed window. She lifted the hatch and, after a quick glance outside, pulled herself up and over the edge.

He followed, less gracefully.

"Quiet!" she whispered as he picked his beaten body up off the ground.

Hand in hand, they ran down the rocky path toward another hut, this one smaller and unguarded. She pushed through the sealskin flaps over the entrance, clearly having already scouted out their path.

"What is this place?" he asked as she lit a small bundle of sticks on the floor with a blue flame from her fingertips.

"Storage, I think."

With the dim light flickering in the room, he could make out the stacks of furs and pelts and barrels of supplies lining the walls.

She stood, her teeth chattering despite her reed pants and extra tunics. Reaching for one of the furs, he wrapped it around her shoulders, then spread another on the ground in front of the fire. He sat on it and patted the space beside him.

With a grin, she sat, sliding close.

For a minute, they didn't speak. She leaned against his side, and he pressed his cheek to her hair, reveling in the feel of her warm body against his, even through the fur. But as they watched the flames, he thought of what had happened with Anathrasa, and how he'd failed Ash in the fight.

He'd been training so that she could count on him—so all of them could. But he'd fallen apart, like always. He could barely manage his own energeia, while she was somehow hosting two.

"Are you all right?" he asked.

She looked up at him, brown eyes sparkling. When her gaze dropped to his mouth, it took a moment to remember what he'd asked.

"I'm all right," she said.

"It doesn't . . . hurt or anything?" He couldn't help reaching for the silky ends of her hair and winding them around his finger.

She shook her head.

"How do you do it?" he asked. "When I had both Geoxus's and Ignitus's energeias in me, it felt like I was being ripped in half."

He could still feel his bones stretching, his blood too thick for his veins. He'd wanted to crawl out of his skin.

"I don't know," she said with a small frown. "Maybe Hydra has some idea."

His teeth dug into his top lip. Maybe the goddess of water would know of something to help Ash. Or maybe she'd try to exploit her, like Geoxus and Anathrasa had done to him.

"Do you trust her?" he asked. If Hydra had seen Ash fight with geoeia and igneia, then surely Anathrasa had as well. It wouldn't be long before the Mother Goddess realized how Ash had become that way. A God Killer with god powers and a God Maker with soul energeia were even more of a threat than who'd they'd been before, and Madoc could not fathom what that might mean without Hydra's protection.

"I don't know yet." Ash shifted to look up at him. "Are you all right? You're not hurt?"

A scowl pulled his brows together. "Just my pride."

She chuckled.

He smirked, but the lightness inside him grew heavy again. "I thought I could take Anathrasa. Pull out her energeia like I did with the other two."

"It took six gods to defeat her before."

"And?" he said.

She smirked. "Good point. Why couldn't you kill her?"

He reached around and squeezed her side where he knew she was ticklish. He'd found that out last week, when they'd been sparring. It had been his favorite way to beat her ever since.

"Enough!" she squealed. In her attempt to get away, her leg had slid up his thigh, and it didn't matter how often they'd sparred, or kissed, or that he'd seen her nonstop for two straight weeks. Her leg made his mind go completely blank.

"You have that look again," she said.

"What look?" He tried to keep his voice even, but her foot was brushing the inside of his calf and he was starting to think about a lot of things that Tor would murder him for even considering.

"Like you like me." She bit the corner of her lip.

She had no idea what that was doing to him.

"That's strange, because I don't," he said.

Her grin widened. "Too bad. I was going to suggest sharing this blanket."

He cleared his throat. "Well, in that case, I like you very much."

With a snort, she pulled away, just enough to hand him the side of the fur, so he could wrap it around both of them. Inside that soft cocoon, he could feel her hand spread over his chest, her knee hiking dangerously high.

Tor will kill you, he told himself.

He lowered himself to his back, one arm behind his head. She curled up against him, her cheek on his chest, a perfect fit.

Just a little while, he thought. Then he'd get her back to her bunk. Tor would never know.

He willed the minutes to slow as he listened to her breathing, watching the rise and fall of her shoulder. She had to hear his heart thumping in his chest. His thoughts returned to the home Tor had told him about in training. The place he kept inside him to protect the things that mattered.

He wanted to protect Ash, but he had failed today. She needed to be able to depend on him.

He wasn't worthy of her otherwise.

With a frown, he pushed up to his elbow. He needed to get her back. Tomorrow would be a big day, and she'd need all her strength if she was going to prove her value to Hydra.

She looked up at him, her eyes sleepy, her hair a mess. "Not yet."

Tor and the gods be damned. Madoc wasn't going anywhere.

As he settled back, she pressed her lips to his collarbone, and then the slope of his shoulder. She kissed his jaw, and his breathing grew unsteady. He pulled her closer, pressing his lips to hers, for once glad that his anathreia didn't hunger for the power of her igneia, and that his own thirst wouldn't pose her any harm.

He kissed her slowly. An apology. A promise. His hands found her narrow waist and slid up her back, tracing each winged muscle over her shoulder blades. When his fingertips reached the nape of her neck, she gasped, and he had the sudden urge to kiss her there.

So he did. But there was a place she liked more, right beneath her ear, and when his teeth grazed that spot her moan speared him to the core.

Their pace quickened. Their hands grew more urgent. The past two weeks on the ship crashed through them—every stolen kiss, every knowing glance. The fear, the loss, the need, all overpowered by fighting, all coated with bruises. And then the chaos of the war was breaking through—gods and blood pushing them faster and faster, until her palms seared his side, and he could barely catch his breath.

She whispered his name and he was done. Done with arenas and war and the constant, infernal rocking of ships. Done with energeia he didn't understand. Done with everything but her.

He knew in some small part of his brain that he needed to slow this down. To think. They'd kissed and shared a few frantic moments, but this was different. He could feel himself on a precipice—one he wasn't sure she could see.

She needed to know she was safe with him. Even if he couldn't protect her in battle, he could make sure she felt safe now.

He pulled back. Kissed the long lines of her throat, her jaw.

"Is this all right?" he asked, his mouth on her collarbone.

She nodded quickly.

"And this?" His hand climbed the rise of her hip over her leggings, then down the lean muscled length of her thigh. Tracing the soft, warm skin beneath her knee, he pulled her leg over his hip.

She pressed against him in answer, and when her dark, hooded gaze held his, he felt anchored for the first time in weeks.

Another shift. Another question. "Yes," she told him, again and again, until she was over him, reaching into her pocket for a small pouch, which she emptied into her hand.

A dark-red powder spilled out, smelling vaguely of spice and earth.

"Taro gave me this a while ago," she said, her cheeks taking on the faintest blush. "It's . . . um . . . sellenroot. For—"

"I know what it's for," he said. Sellenroot was a contraceptive, meant to make a man temporarily infertile. Ilena had given some to him and Elias the day their voices had stopped cracking, along with a stern lecture about respect and not carrying on like cats in heat.

He sat up, enjoying the way her calves curled around him. "Are you sure?"

She nodded. Smiled.

His heart thudded in his chest.

"Are you?" she asked.

He wanted to tell her yes, but the word felt too small for all the feelings now raging inside him. He wanted to tell her he was honored she'd chosen him, and that she was the most beautiful thing he'd ever seen, and that if she changed her mind and wanted to stop, that was all right because holding her was enough.

He wanted to tell her that he'd be here tomorrow, and the day after that, and the day after that—as long as she'd have him. Because this wasn't the kind of infatuation that softened with time. She had wrapped herself around his bones. She'd become part of his home.

But he didn't say any of it. Instead, he reached for her hand and licked the powder from her palm, swallowing the bitter root and every last doubt that he wasn't good enough for her.

Her lips crashed against his, and soon the taste was on her tongue too. Their clothes were shed, their hands woven. And when the last barrier between them was past, he held her, shaking, and whispered all the things he'd been afraid to say before.

But he knew that for her to believe them, really believe them, he'd have to prove himself to her.

And somehow, starting tomorrow, he would.

FOUR

ASH

ASH WOULD HAVE slept forever if not for the thin sliver of light that cut under the sealskin door. It flashed over her eyes on a brush of wind and she burrowed deeper under the fur blanket.

Thoughts started to push through. Morning. She wasn't in her hammock—

Then the arm that was draped over her waist curled, dragging her closer to the cozy heat at her back, and rational thoughts drifted away.

Ash grinned and wriggled under the blankets until she was face-to-face with Madoc. He was still asleep, one arm bent under his head, the other now loose around her hip. His lips parted in slow, steady breaths, his brow furrowed in a dream.

Gods, he was beautiful.

Ash pressed her thumb to the wrinkle between his eyebrows. It softened, and she trailed her hand over his ear, down his jaw, reveling in the fact that she could touch him here, and here, and here, as much as she wanted. The muscles in his neck that had gone corded with exertion last night. The soft black hairs across his chest. The lines of his abdomen—oh, he had a truly striking stomach, and even though she had already traced these muscles over and over, the feel of them still made her body seize. Her fingers trailed lower, to his navel above another line of hair—

Ash looked back up at Madoc's face now, and he was smiling.

He cracked one eye open to peek at her.

"Hello," she said, as innocently as she could muster.

Madoc sighed drowsily and rubbed his thumb against her back. "What time is it?"

"Early."

He winced. "We should go back to our bunks."

But he made no move to get up, and neither did Ash.

She kissed his chest. His neck. Nipped at his earlobe, sucking it between her teeth, and his throat rumbled with a moan. He rolled her onto her back, pinning her against the fur they'd made a bed of, the top blanket wrapping them in a cocoon of heat and sweat and Madoc's mouth on hers, her arms around his torso, their legs knotted.

Ash arched up against him, pressing her bare chest to his, utterly consumed—

Just as a figure burst through the sealskin door.

All pleasure died. Ash actually felt it drop dead on the ground around them.

Instinct yanked her to her feet as she hastily held a blanket over her body.

Tor stood in the doorway, the flap peeled wide. Behind him, Taro and Spark were breathless—frightened, even.

She hadn't been in her hammock, so they'd been out looking for her.

Ash went immobile as she watched Tor take her in. She was holding the blanket up, but she was clearly naked—and Madoc was sitting behind her, pulling the bedding to cover himself.

"What—" Tor's mouth dropped open.

Ash had never seen his pupils so wide, his face so purple. A matching panic rendered her mind blank.

Tor waved his hands like he was trying to keep Ash from fumbling any explanation. "Get dressed," he ordered, his voice like iron. "Hydra summoned us half an hour ago."

He spun on his heels and marched out into the morning light.

Ash lowered to her knees, unable to support her own weight. Out of the corner of her eye, she saw Madoc fold forward, his face in his hands.

"Even when I was at the mercy of Anathrasa, Geoxus, *and* Petros," Madoc said into his palms, "I didn't feel as close to death as I did just now."

Ash sputtered with laughter. Madoc looked at her and gave an exhausted grin.

She pressed her eyes closed. "Get your clothes on before I build a stone wall around us and refuse to ever come out again."

Because apparently I can do that. Call stone as easily as fire.

And Anathrasa saw me do both.

Horror ripped a jagged hole in her joy.

Ash started to stand again when Madoc's fingers closed around her wrist.

She stared down into his dark eyes, speechless at the raw way he always looked at her. As if he was baring himself to her and her alone. Like he'd tell her all his secrets if she only asked.

"Whatever happens today, I'm with you," he told her.

She nodded. "And I'm with you."

Madoc kissed the inside of her wrist, then began searching through the furs for his clothes. Ash mirrored him, fighting hard to focus on the feel of his breath on her skin, but already the future was chipping away at her happiness.

Only Taro was still outside by the time Ash and Madoc were decent. She motioned toward a long, curved boat on the shore. Two Apuitian sailors stood within it.

"Tor left already," Taro explained as they took seats on a bench against the side rail.

Ash heaved a sigh of relief, instinctively reaching out to steady Madoc when the Water Divine flared their arms and the boat launched away from the shore.

Taro smirked at her. "Just focus on this meeting with Hydra."

"I plan to." But hesitation churned in her stomach. Doing so meant focusing on how she had both Ignitus's and Geoxus's energeias in her body. And on the fact that the last mortal who had had the power of gods inside them had been someone the six gods had united to create—and who they had used to combat the Mother Goddess.

Had Tor made that connection yet? Had Anathrasa? Was Ash the only one who was horrified at the prospect of standing before Hydra, knowing what kind of weapon she herself now was? What would the water goddess do with both Madoc and Ash as threats?

The boat followed the green-brown shoreline of the island where they'd spent the night. Huts littered the ground, not a tree in sight on the sloping rise of the otherwise barren hills. This was the northern-most island, closest to the ice-vine barricade, and from what Ash had found as she explored yesterday evening, not many Apuitians lived there. It seemed to be a docking place for outsiders, which until their arrival had only meant people from Florus's country of Itza.

Ash leaned into Madoc, half for his warmth, half just because she wanted to. As the boat turned south, she heard him gasp, and her eyes leaped to his face.

A look of pure wonder overtook him. Ash shifted to follow his gaze.

The waterway had opened up and was ushering them deeper into the Apuit Islands.

Any details that had been lost in the darkness last night were vivid now in the morning sun. Dozens, maybe hundreds, of islands dotted the ocean off into the horizon, large and small, flat and mountainous, stark and lush. Ash had seen glimmers of fire and candlelight in the midnight shadows last night, but they had looked warped somehow, like flames encased in multifaceted lantern glass. Now she under-stood why.

Unlike the visitors' island, every structure, from the houses to the docks to the grand, arching bridges that connected the islands, was made of ice.

Feathered ice arched to form a long tube-shaped house into which fishermen hauled crates of their catches. Walls of clouded ice made up clusters of villages, with smoke somehow puffing out of chimneys. Great ice spears vaulted up into the sky, holding delicate buttresses that supported bridges between the closer islands. Everywhere was green grass, brown earth and sand, and crystalline ivory-blue ice.

"This is incredible," Ash breathed.

"Do you notice what's missing?" Madoc asked. "Arenas."

She cut her gaze over the islands again. He was right. Not an arena in sight.

That was more disconcerting than the relentless cold, just because of how *unusual* it was, but Ash reminded herself that it was good. She and Tor had entrusted Kula's safety to Brand, another of Ignitus's champions, until they took care of Anathrasa—but for a moment, Ash saw beyond the impending war. She saw the sort of future she wanted for Kula, for every country.

Unease still grated against her heart, and she edged closer to Madoc.

The lack of arenas wasn't threatening—she knew Hydra and Florus were used to being peaceful. But in Kula, Deimos, Lakhu, and Cenhelm, fighting was ingrained in each person. What would those countries look like with no arenas, no outlet for that foundation of battle?

Ash pressed her lips together. Honestly, she didn't much care. Questions like that put the victims of this brutal world second, and *that* was what she and Madoc were truly undoing—stopping gods and bloodshed from taking precedence.

So let the rest of the world burn their arenas to the ground. They would find peace in the embers.

Hydra's palace filled a whole island.

Sheer columns of ice twisted into the air, showing people walking up and down ice steps within. Blue-white walls towered between clear ice balconies that must be alarming to actually stand on. Razor-sharp turrets gave subtle reminders that water could be wicked as well as lovely.

Their boat docked and the Apuitians led them ashore. Ash stared up at the glittering palace, and even though she had the power of two gods in her body, she felt small.

As they entered the towering halls she swallowed, steeling her expression. The air itself felt frozen, grating Ash's throat with each breath, and the floor was thankfully lined with a fur runner to counter the slipperiness. She tried to dredge up confidence. She thought of her mother, walking into arenas with her head held high. She thought of how it felt to use igneia. She thought of—

Madoc's hand found hers.

She clamped down on his fingers, both their hands frigid.

The God Killer and the God Maker, she thought. *What a doomed pair we make.*

The Apuitian guides led them through doors already open into a long, wide throne room. Either side of the ice floor was gone, showing lapping water. Courtiers gathered at the far end of the room around a throne sculpted of spears of ice every bit as deadly as Geoxus's obsidian throne back in Deimos, the same one he had broken apart to murder Ignitus.

Ash swallowed, unable to feel her hand in Madoc's anymore.

The moment they entered the room, Tor and Spark met them from the side. They wore the same layered tunics and furs as Ash and Madoc, desperately trying to stay warm while still having a range of motion. Tor adjusted and readjusted a cloak over his chest, refusing to look at Madoc.

The crowd around the throne parted. Hydra was seated on it, her hands on the armrests, her back straight. She pushed herself up to stand, showing the gown she now wore, a long, trailing cascade of blue silk lined with fur at the wrists, throat, and hem. Her black hair lay in a series of braids around her shoulders, a crown of ice atop her head.

She crossed the room halfway before stopping, her hands loose at her sides, her sparkling blue eyes going from Ash to Madoc to their clasped hands.

They both jerked apart at the same time. Too late, Ash realized they should have kept their relationship hidden.

"Goddess." Tor stepped up. "We didn't introduce ourselves properly last night, nor thank you for your interference with Anathrasa. I am Tor Tsea from Kula. This is my—"

"You talk too much." Hydra lifted her hand. Tor clamped his mouth shut, likely remembering the way she'd filled his lungs with water with only a glance.

Ash shot forward a step, panic welling. "Wait. Goddess, I'm Ash Nikau, of—"

Hydra flipped her hand in a circle. "Of Kula, daughter of Char Nikau, great-granddaughter of Ignitus, and so on and so on, and did you really think I wouldn't already have found all this out? Madoc, Anathrasa's son, also the adopted son of a poor stonemason family in Deimos; Taro and Spark, married, Undivine; a whole contingent of Kulan sailors with unimpressive histories but who are still being watched closely by my soldiers. And another of Ignitus's gladiators is in Kula trying to assert order in the chaos of Ignitus's absence—which I'm hoping is something you know about, and not another problem?" She waited only long enough for Tor to nod and mumble Brand's name. "Good. See how easy that was? Damn you mortals, for creatures with such short lives you sure do like to waste time with pleasantries."

Ash's mouth dropped open. "Well. All right."

Hydra whirled, banishing the courtiers. "The topics we're about to discuss aren't exactly common knowledge," she explained when they were gone. "Mustn't panic mortals when it can be avoided."

"With all due respect," Taro said from behind Ash, "the mortals are *already* panicked in the rest of the world."

Hydra ignored her and swept her gaze over their group. "The Mother Goddess is back. She's taken over Deimos, and soon enough Kula, you say? If Ignitus is dead."

Ash tried to object, to tell her that they had sent Brand to ready Kula's defenses to stop that very thing, but Hydra talked as quickly as water tumbling over a cliff.

"And I think it's a safe assumption that Aera and Biotus are either tied up in her plot, or soon to fall themselves? They always were predictable. Glory! Bloodshed! Riches! *Boring.* Now, what is your plan to defeat Anathrasa?"

Madoc pulled back his shoulders. "I'm her son. Soul Divine. I've been training to steal the rest of her anathreia. I—" He swallowed. How badly Ash wanted to take his hand again. "I tried to last night.

I think I injured her—or something happened, at least. We were hoping—"

Hydra frowned. "Why would you try to attack Anathrasa?"

Madoc's mouth dropped open. "To take her anathreia. To defeat her?" It came out as a question.

Hydra looked from Madoc to Ash and back again. "You have anathreia the same way all my Water Divine children have hydreia. They can control water, but their control of it poses no threat to *me*. Even in Anathrasa's weakened state, you could never actually kill her. You, born of her, will always be inferior to her as far as energeia goes. You can manipulate souls, which puts your power *slightly*"—she paused for emphasis—"above those of the six gods. But you are not equal to Anathrasa's power." Hydra pointed at Ash. "She is."

Painful silence gripped the throne room.

Ash's eyes peeled wide. She couldn't breathe. Couldn't blink. "I'm sorry," she managed, her throat dry, "what did you say?"

Hydra squinted at Ash, then at each confused, gawking mortal face in turn. "Wait an ice-cold minute." She smiled. *Chuckled.* "You mean to tell me you don't realize what she—Ash, is it?—what she is? You didn't do this to her *on purpose*?"

"Do *what* to her?" Tor growled the question.

"Do you know the full story of how we brought down Anathrasa the first time?" Hydra arched one thin eyebrow.

Ash's heart was tight in her chest. "Ignitus told us about the gladiator that the six gods used to defeat Anathrasa." Her mouth was still bone-dry; it hurt to talk. "By transferring pieces of their energeias into her."

"The same way Madoc transferred my brothers' energeias into you," Hydra finished.

Ash felt the blood drain from her face. She'd suspected it on her own, but hearing a goddess confirm it nearly pushed her unconscious, black spots dancing across her vision.

"What?" Tor frowned. "No. No, that isn't what—"

But his voice trailed off. Ash could feel everyone around her putting together these same realizations, their silence shifting to stunned horror.

"Do you think Anathrasa knows?" Ash whispered. Her whole body was numb.

"Of course she knows," Hydra threw out. "Why do you think she had her ships flee? I'm terrifying, yes, but I wouldn't have put up much of a fight to save you if they'd kept attacking. Not my battle—well, it wasn't at the time. No, Anathrasa ran because Madoc here must have surprised her with that anathreia attack—maybe she underestimates him?—and then you, Ash, rattled her while she was unexpectedly weakened. But I doubt that will last for long."

"How?" Madoc gasped the question. "I didn't turn Ash into anything!"

"You're lucky you didn't kill her." Hydra leveled a stare at Madoc. "When my siblings and I united to stop Anathrasa, we went through forty-seven mortals before we figured out how they can tolerate god powers. The rest—" She made a choking noise, her tongue out, eyes bulging.

Horror pinned Ash in place. Ignitus hadn't told her they'd had to murder people to find one who could handle their powers. And it made the fact that Ash *hadn't* died the moment Madoc gave them to her that much heavier.

"How am I alive?" Ash managed.

"Because you died," Hydra said matter-of-factly, "but someone brought you back."

"I think I'd remember dying and being resurrected."

"When we did it the first time, we were able to resurrect the gladiator through her connection to energeia. Did Ignitus rip you back from death after an arena fight?"

Ash spun a look at Madoc, and she knew he was thinking the same thing.

Elias had pummeled her with geoeia on the arena sands in Crixion just after Cassia's death. Ash had refused to fight him, even as he strengthened his attack. But Madoc had saved her.

"You didn't die, though," Madoc said, his voice thin. "You weren't . . . I didn't . . ."

He faltered, and Ash choked. Neither of them really understood what he had done to save her.

Had Madoc really brought Ash back from death?

Hydra smiled. "And then, either after or before, your energeia was taken? Figuring out *that* part was a complete fluke—when we practiced it on our gladiator, her goddess brought her back to life through their connection to the same energeia. It was tricky and terrible and damn near killed them both—but when it worked, the gladiator had no energeia at all. Which actually made her the perfect vessel for pieces of *all* energeias."

Tor huffed—whether in disbelief or fear, Ash couldn't tell. "You're saying that being brought back from death and drained of energeia is all it takes for a mortal body to hold a god's power?"

Hydra nodded, her hair flipping around her cheeks. "Yes. It blurs the lines between gods and mortals. Ash should be dead, but she's alive; she was made for energeia, but it was taken—you are exactly what we need to kill Anathrasa. Which I should be thanking *you* for, for not making me scramble to find some other way to avoid her war. In only a month! We'll need pieces of all the energeias. But for now, you're willing to fight her?"

Ash started. Was Hydra asking her? Could she actually say no?

She wouldn't, though.

She saw the future spiral out from this moment, one where she would need to embody not just fire and earth, but also water, plants, air, and animals. A future where she would become Soul Divine. Not like Madoc, who could control anathreia but couldn't hold other divinities in himself. No—Ash would have pieces of the six gods' energeias, Soul Divine like Anathrasa herself.

She would become the Mother Goddess to defeat the Mother Goddess.

"Yes," Ash heard herself say. It burst out of her from somewhere dark and wounded.

Yes, she wanted that. To know that she was more powerful than this cast-off Mother Goddess. Ash had seen what Anathrasa was capable of firsthand—she had watched her drain the geoeia out of Cassia's body in Petros's villa. She had sucked the energeia out of gladiators tithed to her by Geoxus. She had taken Ash's own igneia with a flick of her hand.

Ash wanted to watch Anathrasa cower and die for all the suffering she had inflicted. She wanted to know that Kula would be safe. Tor, Taro, Spark, everyone she loved—*safe*.

And Madoc wouldn't be the one to stand before his mother and deal the fatal blow.

"Yes," Ash said again.

Hydra faced Ash completely, her eyes piercing into the depths of Ash's soul. "Good. Then I want to try something. This might hurt."

She shoved her palm flat against Ash's chest.

A bolt of ice shot into Ash's body, freezing her inside out. She gave a startled gasp as the whole world crystallized into ice.

"What are you doing to her?" Madoc shouted. Distantly, Ash was aware of his hand on her arm, and him jerking back with a sharp yelp of pain.

All she could see was Hydra's face, blurring into a circle of color as her vision narrowed, a window clouding over with crawling tendrils of frost.

Hydra pulled back, her grin not dimming, even as Tor stood by with flames in his hands and Taro had a knife drawn. Tor must have pulled igneia from one of the fires they'd passed on the islands, arming himself. As if he could fight a goddess.

Ash's attention dropped to Hydra's hand. Age spots speckled her skin, and as Ash watched, more climbed her wrist, maturing her otherwise immortal flesh.

The same way Ignitus had had gray hair, and Geoxus had had wrinkles around his eyes.

Each time they gave pieces of their energeia, it drew the gods a little closer to mortality. And Hydra had freely given some of hers to Ash.

It instantly softened what remaining distrust Ash had toward her.

"You gave me hydreia?" Ash whispered.

"Ash, look at me." Madoc grabbed her arm. His other hand was at his side, clenching and unclenching against the fur lining of his tunic. The tips of his fingers were white with frost.

"What happened?" she managed.

Madoc shook his head. The frost was already dripping off his fingers.

He might have said something else, but Ash looked down at her own hands.

Water.

She splayed her fingers, and liquid spurted into the air before splashing against the icy floor.

No one responded. Madoc didn't let her go, and she felt his muscles tense, shocked fear radiating out of him.

"Three down," Hydra declared. "Three to go."

Impossibly, Ash felt her lips lift in a grin that matched Hydra's.

She had hydreia. She had never, in her wildest dreams, thought of controlling water.

In one hand, she pulled the heat from her chest and palmed a small blue flame. In the other, she focused on the chill in the air, on the ice beneath her feet, and an orb of water formed.

Oh, this would be *fun.*

Tor, fire still raging up his arms, stomped toward Hydra. "You have no right to put this on her. What will happen to Ash once she's as powerful as Anathrasa *and* has drained Anathrasa of her powers? Can a mortal—even one who can hold a god's power—endure all that anathreia? This could kill her. Or worse."

With a snap, Ash got rid of both the fire and water. "Whatever this might do to me, it's a risk we have to take. What's the alternative? Our plan to have Madoc face her wouldn't have worked."

Tor whirled on her. But after a moment of silence, he closed his mouth, resignation on his face as he put out the flames on his arms.

He shook his head, and Ash could see the strain on his face. "Florus may help us," Tor said softly, "but Aera and Biotus will side with Anathrasa if they haven't already. They won't willingly give Ash pieces of their energeias. What you did to her was unnecessarily—"

"I can get them."

Ash's heart jolted as Madoc stepped forward.

"I can get aereia and bioseia the same way I took Ignitus's and Geoxus's powers," he continued, confidence strengthening his voice. "If Anathrasa wants the energeia from all the gods, she'll probably be trying to get Aera and Biotus to Crixion too. Odds are good they'll both be there, so I can go back to Deimos and get aereia and bioseia"— he interlocked his fingers with Ash's—"and bring it to you, and you can . . . you can face Anathrasa."

"Smart," Hydra agreed. "That might work."

"No!" Ash shouted. She lowered her voice. "No—Madoc, you aren't going back to Crixion. Anathrasa has to know by now that you gave me igneia and geoeia. She saw me fight on the ship. It isn't safe for you to go to her—she'll kill you for betraying her."

Madoc licked his lips. "What if I'm the one who was betrayed? I'll tell her you tricked me into giving you Ignitus's and Geoxus's powers. I'll tell her that you and Hydra came up with this plan to defeat her, and once I heard it, I realized my error and ran back to her."

Ash blanched. "Madoc—"

"No, listen." He pushed closer to her, lightness in his lifted eyebrows, his half smile. "If I surrender to her and tell her I've rethought betraying her, I'll be at the center of her plans. I can get information, and I'll know exactly where Aera and Biotus are. Better than sneaking around Deimos—if I get caught doing that, there's no lie that will save me."

Ash *hated* this. She hated all of this.

"We'll get you on the first ship to Crixion," Hydra announced. "I'll have some of my Water Divine give you fast sailing waters. We can get you there in a few days."

"Wonderful," Madoc said, his teeth clenched, likely at the thought of being on a ship again.

"Won't Anathrasa be suspicious of how he got back so fast?" Ash tried.

"Tell Anathrasa you escaped when I sided with the Kulans," Hydra said. "Tell her you manipulated the anathreia in my Apuitians to get them to help you travel faster. Gods can't sense their people when they're being controlled by anathreia."

She spoke from experience, no doubt when Anathrasa had first tried to destroy the world.

"She'll still come for us in a month," Tor added. "We need to set up a meeting with Florus to get him on our side—how quickly can we get to Itza, or get Florus to come here?"

"Better that we go to him," Hydra said. "I'll tell him everything that's happened, but he'll want to stay in Itza and get his people ready. Not that I'm in any hurry to leave my *own* people, but I'll escort you to Itza, then pop back here as I need."

Tor looked doubtful, but he nodded. "We'll get Florus to add his floreia to our cause. Gather our armies and confront Anathrasa—all within her timeline of a month."

His eyes went to Ash. She noted how he'd said *get Florus to add his floreia to our cause* and not *get Florus to give his floreia to Ash.*

This scared him. It scared her, too.

Madoc nodded. "And I'll get aereia and bioseia in that time, too."

"We can aim to meet you in Crixion," Tor continued, his warrior side taking over. "You can—transfer over the energeias. Then Ash can—" He swallowed, his jaw tensing. "We can defeat Anathrasa."

Ash's lungs clenched tighter, tighter, driven by Tor's unease, by Madoc's odd confidence. She had never heard him sound so sure of himself, and it was about stealing energeias from gods *for her.*

"But—how will we know you're all right?" she asked Madoc, her voice small in her own ears. "When you're in Crixion, how will we know if something happens?"

Hydra waggled her fingers. Standing before them, her body changed from her solid human form into a translucent, rippling sculpture of water. "Goddess, remember?" A blink, and she was herself again. "I can pop in on him from time to time. And you have Ignitus's and Geoxus's powers too, so it's likely you can do the same—communicate and travel through fire and stone. I'll teach you. Are we decided, then? Good. I'll get a ship ready."

She spun away. Tor chased after her, arguing some other point Ash couldn't make herself care about. Taro and Spark, still lingering, were smart enough to give Ash and Madoc space.

They had barely had any time together. Running for their lives in Crixion, two weeks on a crowded ship, one stolen night in a storage tent. It wasn't enough, and as Ash turned into Madoc's arms, she felt a familiar sensation wriggle up her chest and heat her body with shame: loneliness.

She didn't want Madoc to go. She had Tor, Taro, and Spark, but none of them was the person she wanted to hold her when she was afraid or the one she trusted to always take her side. She had spent so much of her life secluded from other people out of fear of them discovering her disloyalty to Ignitus that she wasn't ready to let go of this. To let go of Madoc.

Ash shoved herself up onto her toes, locking her lips with his. She needed to feel his mouth on hers, his hands on the small of her back, arching her against his chest. She needed to remember this sensation in the coming days when war loomed and fear crept in and she woke up without him.

Because of course she would let him go. That was what this war demanded of her, and she would always do what was right, even if it killed her.

Freeing Kula had cost Ash her mother. It had cost Ash her god. It had chased her from her home and made her a target, and now it asked her to let go of Madoc, too.

A selfish burn singed her gut. How much else would this war take from her?

When would she get to start taking things back?

Ash pressed her forehead to Madoc's, their breaths mingling.

"You know Anathrasa won't hurt me," he said, "not if she thinks there's any hope that I'll get the gods' powers and give them to her."

"Like you're doing for me." Ash laughed brittlely. "Is this any better than her plan?"

"Yes." Madoc's response was instant and firm. "Let me do this. When I come back, we can be together. We—" He stopped, swallowed hard. "We won't have to worry anymore."

Ash's fingers curled into the short hairs at the back of his neck and she planted her other hand on his chest, over his heart, savoring the feel of it thudding against her palm.

They would both be fine. Anathrasa wouldn't hurt Madoc.

Because if she did, she would have to contend with the wrath of a goddess.

FIVE

MADOC

WITH ASH'S KISS seared into his memory and the freedom of the world on his shoulders, Madoc sailed home to Deimos to face his mother.

Propelled by a strong current created by a small crew of Water Divine sailors, the ship cut through the waves as it raced through the nights, pressing on too quickly for Madoc to succumb to his previous seasickness. Where the trip to the Apuit Islands had taken two weeks, the return voyage took only three days. Soon he found himself facing a fleet of Deiman ships bearing black sails, a hailstorm of gravel suspended over the hull of his boat, ready to sink him into the sea.

Furiously, he waved a white flag over the side of the deck, his eyes bouncing from the sky peppered with stones to the fleet five hundred paces away. As many times as he'd practiced this in his mind, nothing could prepare him for the horrific awe of this moment, and the gripping fear of what might happen if he never made it to land.

Barely two weeks ago, he had fled Crixion, half conscious, terrified for his family and with no idea of the effect Anathrasa's war had on the world.

Now he was returning in much the same way.

"Come on," he muttered, sweat streaking down his face, burning the sea salt on his chapped lips. The heat had increased dramatically from the islands, and his tunic—the one shredded on the side from Tor's training—clung to his chest. Hydra's people had offered him new clothes, but he couldn't risk appearing on friendly terms with the water goddess. It was better if he showed up in his Deiman clothes, weathered as they were.

"It's not going to work," he heard a sailor whisper. They'd left Hydra's lands with only three Water Divine sailors and a first mate to captain the vessel. If they were going to make it look as though he'd used anathreia to sway Hydra's people to sail him home, they couldn't afford to have a fully crewed ship. Now they'd been waiting at the edge of Deiman waters for over an hour.

Panic pressed against the edges of his control. Ash was counting on him. He could not fail.

"They haven't attacked us yet," Madoc growled, waving the flag harder. "They're stalling until Anathrasa gives her orders."

We surrender.

He focused on the words, willing them to stretch across the waves. Willing his anathreia to save their necks.

Mother, I'm here.

A cool breeze lifted the hairs on his arms, climbing up his chest to his throat.

Not a breeze—this came from inside him. A healing, the broken parts of his energeia fusing together in pulsing relief.

But there was something different about it. It was like spun sugar that was too sweet—good, but not quite right.

It felt like it had when he'd tried to take Anathrasa's energeia.

He didn't have time to wonder about it. He ignored it and concentrated on the nearest ship. With a focused breath, he reached across the waves, invisible strands of energeia seeking purchase on the souls, pulsing like lantern light on the crowded deck.

We surrender. Tell my mother I've come home.

"Look!" called one of the sailors at the helm. "They're pulling back!"

Madoc glanced up, huffing a sigh as the rocks overhead crumbled in midair, raining a harmless dust that stuck to his damp skin.

Madoc lowered the flag, keeping it hanging in sight over the side of the deck.

"Approach slowly," he called to his crew.

The Water Divine warriors lowered the sails, and as they carved a line through the waves toward the fleet, Madoc's pulse pounded in his ears.

The closer they got to the other ships, the more alive his anathreia became. It buzzed through him with no regard to his tense muscles or his wary thoughts. Despite their progress, a frown pulled at his lips. Even when he couldn't control it, his energeia had always been in sync with the rest of his body. But now it felt strange inside him, as if it wasn't entirely his own.

Like when he'd taken Petros's geoeia and felt it slipping through his veins.

He hadn't tithed on anyone. He hadn't even used his anathreia since four nights ago, when they'd been attacked at the barrier outside the Apuit Islands. He'd been trying to conserve his energy, rebuild his strength, so that when he faced Anathrasa he'd be ready. But something still felt wrong.

Dread mingled with his power as he considered whether this might have something to do with his proximity to the Mother Goddess. When they'd clashed on the water, something had happened. He'd felt gutted, broken—it wasn't the rush he'd experienced every other time he'd used anathreia, but rather the opposite effect. And now he was in Deimos, facing a fleet of her soldiers, and his anathreia was acting up again.

He shook his head. He didn't have time to worry about the unruliness of his energeia now. He had a surrender to fake, and two more gods to somehow siphon enough power from to turn Ash into a gladiator strong enough to defeat Anathrasa.

He felt a lot like the boy who'd stood in those fighting rings in South Gate—a fraud, boasting a power he didn't have. A kid with quick fists who could put on a decent show.

And just like he had then, he would let the crowd believe what they wanted, until he'd taken everything he'd come for.

The Deiman ships cleared a path for their boat, and as they steered toward the Port of Iov, Madoc lifted his chin to the sun, and to the lighthouse he thought he'd never see again.

His heart gave a hard lurch. *Home.*

Was Ilena safe? Had she found Elias? What about Danon and Ava? Without thinking, his gaze turned west, to the fields outside the city where the dead were buried to reunite their geoeia with the earth.

Pain rippled through his chest. Had they laid Cassia to rest in his absence?

The sailors remained silent, their wary gazes bouncing between him and the approaching shoreline, where a legion of soldiers were gathering. So many Deimans, already loyal to his mother. Their silver armor glinted in the sun, and Madoc didn't need to see them up close to know that stones and weapons were ready in each of their hands.

"You have no memory of what's happened since we left the islands," he called to the sailors as they slowed their approach. "If you're questioned, the last thing you remember was me telling you to board this boat."

He'd tried to use soul energeia to muddle their memories about their departure from the Apuit Islands—a precaution in case Anathrasa captured and questioned them. But the closer they'd come to Crixion, the more unruly his power felt, as if it had been damaged in the attack on Anathrasa. He didn't want to risk hurting the sailors by losing control—he'd seen what had happened to Jann in the arena when he'd tried before. He hoped that they could act well enough to deter suspicion.

The sailors nodded in wary acceptance, but he could hear the water churning against the hull beneath them and knew that if it came to a fight, their instincts would steer them toward self-preservation.

He could not let it come to that.

As they passed the narrow peninsula hosting the lighthouse, his anathreia staggered his breath, pushing him onto the balls of his feet, and when he glanced down his hands were spread, as if prepared for attack.

The move had been unconscious, and he fisted his hands at his sides.

Be calm, he told himself. But the power in him said, *be ready.*

When the ship docked, they were boarded by two dozen centurions in full armor, ready with stones spinning above their hands. It felt like a lifetime ago that he'd fought the centurions off in the palace, and any confidence he'd had that he could turn their thoughts if needed evaporated into the dry air.

He pulled Ash into his mind and planted his feet.

"We surrender!" he shouted as they surrounded him and shoved him to his knees. "Please. Take me to Anathrasa. I don't intend any harm!"

He was dragged down the loading plank to the stone dock where the centurions waited in lines, staring at him uncertainly. Word must have spread about his part in Geoxus's defeat. He took some comfort in their fear, hoping it meant they would not be quick to attack.

Silently, the crowd parted, and his mother approached, her clean white gown fluttering in the breeze.

His stomach pitted.

"Madoc," she said, eyes narrowed. "I don't suppose you're here for the festivities."

He didn't know what she meant. His blunt nails dug into the callused heels of his hands. "I come to beg for sanctuary, and your forgiveness."

As she lifted her chin, his anathreia prickled inside him, feeding an anger that caught him by surprise. She stepped closer, and he saw, with some discomfort, that his onetime neighbor—an old woman they'd called Seneca—moved with more ease than he'd ever seen. Her back was straighter. Her skin, tighter, and flushed with a healthy glow. Even her white hair looked golden.

Instead of a woman nearing a century, she looked scarcely older than Ilena.

Tithes. That was the only answer. Anathrasa was feeding on innocent Deimans. Draining the energeia from their bodies, and leaving them as shells, like she had with Cassia and Ash.

He wiped any trace of revulsion from his face. She would not know his heart.

"Forgiveness," she said, even her voice clearer than he'd known when they were neighbors. "Sanctuary? These are powerful words, my son."

His stomach twisted. She may have been his mother by birth, but she had no right to call him *son*.

"The Kulan gladiators are beyond reason," he said as the Water Divine sailors disembarked in shackles. They blinked in confusion, seeming surprised that they'd come to Deimos—part of the plan that Madoc had devised. "I was wrong to trust them. I tried to convince them to turn back after that night at the blockade, but they wouldn't listen. They'll stop at nothing to avenge their god."

Anathrasa paused before him, close enough that he could reach out and wring her slender neck.

"And what of Hydra? What does the goddess of water say about this?"

Madoc shook his head, looking tired, torn. "She sided with them."

"Pity," Anathrasa said, as if she'd expected this. Her lips curled into a patronizing smile. She may have looked younger, but there were still shadows under her eyes and creases around her mouth. "How did you manage to get away?"

Madoc pictured Ash. Remembered the steadiness in her gaze when he'd left on this mission.

"I snuck out while they were summoning Florus. Convinced a few sailors to bring me back. My hold on the sailors' minds prevented Hydra from tracking them across the water."

A glimmer of interest arched Anathrasa's brows, but it was stifled by a hard glare.

"Or she chose not to follow you so you could spy for her." Fear chilled Madoc's blood as she stepped closer. "For all I know, she sent you to turn this legion against me and use the anathreia I gave you to make them do your bidding." She leaned closer, dropping her voice to a whisper. "We both know you'd like that."

He would. And he could do it. Tell the soldiers behind her to grab her arms. Those beside him to ram their spears through her heart.

"It would only delay the inevitable," he said, and it was true. "I want no part of Hydra's pact with the Kulans. Fighting you will just lead to more bloodshed. I've seen enough war."

"Oh, my dear," she clucked. "What you've seen could fill the palm of my hand."

Again, his anathreia pulsed with a strange, sticky-sweet urgency. *Fight*, it whispered. *Feed.*

Feed.

The hunger was returning, with teeth like knives. It rose in him like a wave, forcing his breath out in a huff.

He wanted to end this now.

He wanted to destroy her, so Ash would never have to fight again.

He shook his head, sweat burning his eyes. *No.* Hydra had told him he couldn't use his anathreia against the Mother Goddess, just as her Water Divine couldn't use hydreia against Hydra. That was why attacking Anathrasa on the ship had nearly broken him.

He had to stick to his plan. Join Anathrasa. Find Biotus and Aera. Give their energeias to Ash so that she could harness the power of the six gods and destroy the Mother Goddess.

"Even so," he said. "I pledge myself to you."

Her eyes narrowed. "You've pledged yourself to another, Madoc. A girl your fingers long to touch, even now."

Madoc's jaw clenched. He would not let her get to Ash—not until Ash was ready to kill her.

"She's made her choice," Madoc said, tension lacing between them, thin and brittle as ice.

Anathrasa cackled.

He willed the roar of his blood to settle. He could still make this work. He had sold hundreds of people on his performance as an Earth Divine fighter in the rings of Crixion. He could convince his mother he was on her side.

He dropped his chin. "She doesn't want me. Her only love is Kula. Is . . . *was* . . . Ignitus. I tried to get her to come, but . . ." He shook his head, looking crestfallen. "She would see the world burn, and dance on the embers."

Anathrasa assessed him long enough that he began to fidget.

"Then why didn't you change her mind?" she asked.

The thought of forcing Ash to do anything made him ill.

"Were you not strong enough?" Anathrasa pressed. "Did you not take Ignitus's fire? Geoxus's ability to manipulate the very earth we stand on?"

He could hear the test in her tone. She must have suspected he'd given those powers to Ash and was waiting to catch him in a lie.

If he didn't play this carefully, he'd lose his only shot at getting close to Anathrasa, and to Aera and Biotus. He wouldn't be able to give Ash the power she needed to defeat the Mother Goddess.

His head hung forward. "The gods' energeias were killing me. I couldn't hold them."

"And *Ash* could?" Her teeth pressed together over the name, like she'd bitten into bitter fruit. "How interesting."

Madoc reminded himself that Ash had Hydra and the Water Divine. She had Tor. And Taro and Spark and a crew of Kulan sailors that would rise to her defense if needed—but he still felt sick about siphoning this attention her way.

"She tricked me into giving them to her. I was weak." He swallowed, a blush rising in his cheeks. "She was . . . convincing."

"You expect me to believe your surrender is the result of a broken heart?" Anathrasa shook her head. "You take me for a pitying fool, Madoc."

Madoc went still. Anathrasa wasn't buying his story. With a wave of her hand, she spoke quietly to one of her guards, then turned to go.

He'd faced this moment a dozen times in street fights—the

moment when the act either became real, and his fate relied on his own fists, or the truth came out and everyone saw him for what he was. A liar.

He lifted his chin, clenched his fists, and fought.

"Wait!" he shouted as the guard drew his sword. "It's Hydra. She didn't trust me. She wanted me dead. If Ash hadn't helped me sneak out, I wouldn't be here now."

Anathrasa paused. Turned.

"Why would she want you dead?"

"She knows I am your son," Madoc said in a rush. "She thinks I'm loyal to you."

"And are you?" The sparkle in Anathrasa's eyes drove a stake of fear through him.

If he lied now, he was sure she would see it. But if he didn't, she might kill him before he had the chance to accomplish what he'd come to do.

"Does it matter?" He added a strain to his voice, a hunch to his shoulders. "I have nowhere else to go that she won't find me."

Anathrasa considered this for a long moment. "Now that their god has been brutally murdered, these soldiers belong to Geoxus's creator—me. I could have them cut you to pieces if you're lying."

"It is no lie."

She stepped closer, lifting her hand. Her fingers trailed down his cheek. Show or not, he fought the urge to jerk back; her touch revolted him.

"You should have considered that you might need me before you attacked me on that ship four days ago."

She wheeled back, faster than Madoc expected, and struck him hard across the jaw.

The slap stung his skin, radiating through his teeth and sending white sparks across his vision. His breath ripped through his dry throat.

But it was his mother who cried out.

Before him, Anathrasa's cheek stained pink, a perfect handprint appearing on her tan skin. She gasped in surprise, the sound that came from her lips a mixture of shock and pain. Stumbling back, she bumped into one of her guards, who caught her around the elbow. She shook him off, covering the mark on her face with her hands.

Had her power backfired? How had she injured them both by striking him?

Excitement doused his confusion, overriding his own physical pain. Up until this moment, they hadn't been sure they could hurt her without him draining what remained of her power, but now the proof was before him. Anathrasa could feel pain.

But could she die?

Around him, the other centurions erupted in confused shouts. Those nearest Madoc threw him to the dock. He blinked up at the sky, blinded by the pale circle of the sun for a moment, before a swift kick caught his gut. The wind fled from his lungs. He curled into a ball, but his back was exposed to the whipping spear shafts that rained down.

"Stop!" Anathrasa screamed. Fury and desperation crackled through the air like lightning.

The beating ceased immediately, and when the crowd cleared, Madoc found his mother on her hands and knees before him. Three soldiers tried to pull her up to safety, but she shoved them back. Her breath came out in a wheeze, and one hand was wrapped over her stomach, right where he'd been kicked.

Their gazes met, and a new wave of horror shook him as his stare moved to her still-red cheek.

She could sense his pain, and his own anathreia recoiled in empathy, an echo of the night at the blockade, when his soul had felt like it shattered.

It took another breath to realize there was no separation between her pain and his. They were one and the same—every welt, every gathering bruise.

Somehow, she'd hurt herself by hurting him. He didn't know what that meant, or how it was possible, only that this connection between them was very, very bad.

Ash was coming to kill the Mother Goddess. Would doing so kill him too?

Anathrasa grabbed a centurion's leg, pulling herself up only to lean against his side.

"Bring him to the palace," she snapped, her lips drawn back over her teeth. As he was dragged to his feet, her blue eyes seared with fury. "It appears he'll get a second chance to prove his worth to me after all."

She turned, with some effort, and was assisted off the dock, back toward land and the carriages that awaited.

In two weeks and four days, Madoc's home city had changed completely.

Through the carriage windows, he followed the routes he'd

walked all his life—streets that led to alleys that gave way to Market Square, where the great arena towered over the Temple of Geoxus.

Now the temple was in ruins, demolished in the violence that had ensued after Geoxus's death while Madoc was fleeing the city with Ash and Tor. The golden statue that had once stood three stories high had been knocked on its side and pounded by boulders of all sizes. The walls of the sanctuary were painted with goat's blood—signs saying *the gods are dead*, and *goddess pigstock*. Crude paintings of Geoxus crushed by a boulder, and Ignitus being defiled by a horse.

The market had once been filled with vendors and savory foods but now was empty except for a gathering of people all in white with chalk smeared across their mouths, chanting words Madoc couldn't make out. The carriage had to carve a path around boulders and rocks that had been pulled from the surrounding shops and apartments, half of which were blackened by fire.

I don't suppose you're here for the festivities. Had that been a joke? There were no celebrations here. Riots had destroyed the city.

Madoc moved to the edge of his seat, his heels drumming against the wooden floor. He pressed his palm against his jaw, feeling the edges of a bruise, and forced himself to think of this strange tie to Anathrasa, and not what had become of Ilena, Elias, Danon, and Ava in these harsh streets.

It seemed impossible, but Anathrasa's wounds had mirrored Madoc's, and his pain and hers had braided together into a single cord. He hadn't done this, at least not deliberately. But his anathreia had been acting strangely since returning to Deimos, or maybe since coming closer to her. For all he knew, he'd caused the mark on her face unconsciously.

She definitely hadn't done it to herself.

His mind kept returning to that night on the ocean outside the blockade—the connection he'd felt to her just moments before his world erupted. Had something happened between them then? Whatever tied them didn't seem to take effect until he'd come back to Deimos—until he'd tried to use anathreia again.

He wished he could talk to Ash about it.

But if he did, and Hydra found out, would they pull him out of Crixion? Think him a liability, too close to Anathrasa to do what he'd come to do?

His hands clasped together. Would he still be able to steal Aera's and Biotus's energeias now that he appeared to be linked to Anathrasa?

He'd have to find a way—he hadn't come here to fail. It wasn't just Ash depending on him, it was the entire world. If he didn't get the other energeias to Ash, she could never stop Anathrasa from overtaking the world.

The carriage slowed, tearing him from his thoughts. He looked out through the window again and sucked in a tight breath at the sight of the palace before him. The towers that had reached into the sky had fallen now, but here, at least, the structure had been rebuilt. The rubble in the gardens had been cleared away. The high walls had been widened into graceful, sloping balconies of white marble. No longer did murals of Geoxus tower beside the entrance. Now there were twin likenesses of Anathrasa—an even younger version than he'd seen at the docks—naked, holding her hands in a circle over her head.

He thought of the people in the market with the chalk on their mouths, and of the legion of soldiers that had accompanied her to the docks, and got a very bad feeling.

Madoc had assumed he'd be taken to the jail, a festering block of wooden cells, impenetrable by the many Earth-divine prisoners, on the south side of Crixion. He didn't know what she had in store for him here, and the uncertainty had his knuckles rapping against his thighs.

But when they reached the palace, he wasn't brought to Anathrasa, or to any holding cell. Surrounded by guards, he was led to a wide, new stairway and brought to the eastern wing of the palace—a private courtyard, surrounded by lounging chairs and tables already topped with decadent food. The circular balcony above led to open rooms, and through the doorways, past the fine furniture and art, Madoc could see the hazy skyline of the city.

His stomach growled as he registered the scent of honey bread. For the last three days, he'd eaten little other than salted fish, dried kelp, and seal meat.

"Madoc? Madoc!"

For the second time that day, Madoc felt the wind knocked out of him.

"Ava?"

The five-year-old girl came charging through the courtyard, her dark hair and blue ankle-length gown rippling behind her. Her arms lifted a moment before Madoc fell to his knees, and when she collided into him, he breathed in the scent of lavender water, and dust, and home.

He swallowed the emotion gripping his throat. Four guards still stood around him, though they made no move to stop his younger sister.

"Are you all right?" he asked urgently, suddenly fearing that she'd been brought here against her will, or worse, because Ilena was dead.

"Of course I'm all right," she said. "We've been waiting for you!"

"You've been . . ." He rose to his feet as a woman came running toward him, her black hair tied in a red wrap, her gown fine and expensive. Behind her was a younger boy of twelve, all limbs and awkward smiles.

"Ilena?" He couldn't believe his eyes. "Danon?"

"I told you," his adopted mother said, eyes glistening. "I told you we would meet again." She pulled him into a hug that crushed his shoulder and likely cracked a few ribs, but he didn't care. Tears streaked down his face. His heart felt too big for his chest.

"You did," he managed. Questions began catching up with him—how they'd come here, and why they'd been given such nice things. Ava had said she'd been waiting for him, but Anathrasa hadn't known he'd be coming.

Had she?

"I don't understand," he said. "How did you get . . . Why are you . . . *here?*"

"We're guests of the Mother Goddess," Ilena told him, and he didn't miss the tick of a small muscle in her neck as she said the words.

"Seneca—I mean, Anathrasa, of course—she wanted to thank us for caring for you all those years."

"I certainly emptied my fair share of her chamber pots," Danon added, earning a slap on the arm from his mother.

"She's letting us stay as long as we like," Ilena said. "Isn't that wonderful?"

It was wonderful that his family was alive and safe, at least for now. But Madoc knew Anathrasa, and she wasn't grateful for anyone or anything. The only reason his family had been brought here was because she had some hidden purpose for them, and based on their lack of surprise at his arrival, they had surmised the same. Whatever his birth mother wanted would come at a heavy cost.

His elation was sinking like a stone when the guards stepped back and retreated, and a steady clap of footsteps stopped behind him.

"It's about time you showed up."

Madoc turned and came face-to-face with his brother.

"Elias." The word was barely a breath, sanded down by fear and distance, and an anger he'd forced himself to swallow. The last time he'd seen his brother had been when Elias attacked Ash in the grand arena during the final fight of the war with Kula. He'd been unhinged, a tornado of grief and geoeia, ready to avenge their sister even if it meant losing his own life.

But those memories were overshadowed by others. The night they'd run from the centurions after cheating in a fight against Fentus in South Gate. Early mornings walking to work at the quarry. Late nights in their bunks in the quarter, laughing about something stupid that Danon had said.

The night they'd carried Cassia home from Petros's villa.

Elias stood before him now, older looking, as if years had passed instead of weeks. He was thinner than before, and his dark hair was trimmed like a man's instead of a boy's. The tunic he wore was tied with a belt instead of a spare piece of rope, and there wasn't a streak of mortar anywhere on it. Even his sandals were new, with silver circle buckles across the front of his shins.

He waited for Madoc to do more, looking uncertain, and that was all the apology Madoc needed.

He embraced Elias as he should have the night Cassia died. Maybe if he had, Elias would have known he wasn't alone in his guilt, and things would have been different. They stood there for some time, chest to chest, arms locked around each other's shoulders, while Ilena wept tears of joy, and Danon swung Ava onto his back and galloped around them.

But before Madoc drew back, Elias hooked one hand around the back of his neck and whispered, "Watch yourself, brother. The Mother Goddess sees all."

SIX

ASH

ASH HAULED HERSELF onto the raft, coughing frigid water across the salt-beaten wood. On her hands and knees, she glared across to where Hydra lounged on a wave she had morphed into something like a chaise, her head propped on one hand, her other arm draped over her curved hip.

"You're still trying to use hydreia as you do igneia," Hydra chastised in a singsong voice that Ash was really starting to hate. "But it isn't igneia. It is, in fact, hydreia."

"That doesn't get any more helpful the more times you say it."

Hydra lifted the arm from her hip. A separate wave rose behind her, a rippling sheet of blue and translucent white with an angry foam cap at the head.

Ash flew to her feet, hands out, body racking with an involuntary shudder. "Wait! Wait."

What other way could she deflect the water? Last time Hydra had thrown a wave at her, Ash had tried to divert it with a sharp shove to the left, but the water had simply risen higher and barreled over her. For the sixth time that morning.

Ash shook out her hands by her sides, flicking water on her bare feet, and tried to think of some other hydreia deflection method. But *gods*, she was just tired of being thrown into the sea in the tight sealskin suit Hydra's servants had given her. The material stopped midthigh and at Ash's shoulders, hugging her body so closely that she felt half naked in the icy air.

Despite the cold, she wished she could see Madoc's reaction to her in this outfit. She wished she could sneak into his room again wearing this, and pull him out of a groggy sleep back into the storage hut—

Heat climbed from Ash's stomach, spreading out to each limb and warming her cheeks. She sighed involuntarily, just glad to feel warm for a change, and that warmth pulled up memories she relived more often than was healthy.

That night with Madoc had been tentative. Neither of them had truly known what they were doing—Ash only knew from her own fleeting, private moments where Madoc should touch her and what motions snatched the breath from her lungs; she had found some of his places too, mostly by accident.

Spark had warned it might hurt the first time. She, Char, and Taro had explained a great many things to Ash, but all of it had been to help her avoid getting pregnant so as not to give Ignitus another Nikau Fire Divine gladiator to use in his arenas.

They hadn't told her how *good* it could be. Touches and kisses that Ash lost herself in like a dance. She moved, and Madoc followed; she swayed, and he bowed.

A water whip flicked Ash's nose.

She shuddered and blinked at Hydra.

"You're distracted," Hydra said.

Ash scoffed. "What do I have to be distracted by? My looming fight with the Mother Goddess, the deterioration of the godless countries, our ships preparing to sail to Itza tomorrow, the fact that Madoc is alone in Crixion doing who knows what—"

"I checked on him two days ago! I saw him arrive in Crixion—Anathrasa didn't see me, Madoc didn't see me, he's safe, *everyone's safe*. He's even back with his family. What more do you want?"

"I want—" Ash's voice cut off sharply. *I want to know how I'm supposed to do any of this*, she wanted to say, but she bit her tongue hard, until calmer words formed. "You said I could use Ignitus's or Geoxus's powers to communicate and travel through their energeia like you do with hydreia—I want to learn that so I can communicate with Kula, and with Madoc, and even Tor, who is just on the other side of this island. Not *this*." She waved at the sea around them, the water dripping off her hair.

Since Madoc had left five days ago, this was all Hydra had done. While Tor prepared the Kulans and some of Hydra's people to travel to Itza tomorrow, Hydra would drag Ash out at dawn, get her set up on this raft, and pummel her with waves and water whips and ice shards, all while spouting truly unhelpful advice like *Cold water feels pointy while warm water feels smooth.*

Yes, Ash now could call water into her hands the same way she could call fire and stone. But she'd learned from the first day of Hydra's training that she couldn't *do* much with water once she summoned it.

Just like she couldn't do much with stones, either, but who on this earth could teach her how to be the god of geoeia? That was the only spurt of regret she'd ever felt about stabbing Geoxus—that her best chance of learning how to harness geoeia was dead.

Hydra talked in circles if she let her, never getting to the point, a whirlpool lazily spinning. Ash was cold and tired of trying to get slippery, uncooperative water to listen to her.

"Will I even need to control hydreia to defeat Anathrasa?" Ash pressed. She tried not to scream, but she wanted to—she wanted to *rage*. "Don't I just need to combine all the energeias into one? Does it truly matter whether I can *control* each and every one?"

"And if you have to fight your way to Anathrasa?" The wave behind Hydra edged taller. Ash fought to ignore it and the dread that welled in her stomach. "The plan is to face her in Crixion. What if she has the whole of the city set against you, and our armies are falling, and all you have to fight with is igneia and unpredictable spurts of other energeias? What good will you be then?"

Ash glowered. "Well, none of this training will matter if I don't obtain floreia too. Can't you talk to your brother again? Have him travel here on floreia and just give me a piece of it, then he can go back to preparing Itza for war."

Hydra flopped back into her water-chaise with a dramatic moan. The water enveloped her and she sank down, the wave splashing over her. The movement rocked Ash's raft, and she widened her stance for balance.

A flash of foam, and Hydra materialized on the raft in front of Ash. Her arms were folded, one eyebrow curved, her lips puckered.

"I believe in you," she said, "but that doesn't mean Florus has to. If he's going to give you a piece of his *soul*, the least you can do is travel to meet him on his own land to do it."

Ash closed her eyes. She was being childish, but part of her was nothing but nervous energy, frail and shaking. "I know." She whipped her eyes open. "But if you taught me how to travel through fire, you and I could go to Itza instantly."

She was still pushing the matter, and the look on Hydra's face was indignant.

"Mortals, always in such a rush." Hydra rolled her eyes. "You need to sail there because you'll want your people with you when you meet him. Never underestimate the importance of support. Besides, this delay isn't just for us—Florus is making the same preparations I am, getting armies ready, yes, but also hiding those who can't fight, rationing food, building defenses of Itzan cities. Try to understand, this is the first we've heard of Anathrasa being back—"

"No, it isn't." Ash frowned. An unexpected surge of defensiveness straightened her shoulders. "Ignitus told you that he suspected Anathrasa was back. You ignored him."

Hydra jerked away with an exasperated snort. "Do you have siblings, Ash?"

She knew Ash didn't. She'd already found out everything about their group.

Hydra faced the shore and the rear of her palace stretching up toward the cloudy gray sky. Off to the side, part of the harbor was in view; ships bobbed in it, people bustling around them and on the docks, readying to sail to Itza with the morning tide.

"Anathrasa created Geoxus first," Hydra said to the distance. "Then me. Then Biotus and Ignitus, then Florus, and finally Aera. The dynamic of that—damn, Geoxus loved to taunt us about being oldest and strongest, as if that somehow earned him our loyalty. Biotus doesn't have a single independent thought in his head, so he was always happy to trail where Geoxus led. Ignitus *tried*, I'll give him that. He tried to make his own way, but one whiff of challenge from Geoxus or Biotus, and Ignitus couldn't resist rising to it. Florus only half pays attention to anything going on, so he and I spent many decades watching those three raze each other's countries and hurt each other's mortals."

She looked back at Ash. "So you'll have to forgive me for not acting on Ignitus's plea that I step in, because—and this was his message—*Geoxus is planning something with our mother.* Geoxus was always poking at Ignitus because he knew he could rile him up. And Anathrasa?" She snorted. "It sounded like empty nonsense. We'd sacrificed too much for her not to be dead."

Ash swallowed, rocking with the gentle waves. She could see why Hydra had ignored her brother's cry for help. Ash hadn't taken Ignitus seriously until the end, either.

"What about Aera?" Ash asked. "You didn't say how the air goddess fits into everything."

Something dark passed over Hydra's face, a shadow drifting across the surface of a deep-blue pond. "She's a pest. A mosquito who flits around Geoxus, Biotus, and Ignitus, pitting them against each other, darting away if they swat at her. She's a nuisance, and I should have told Madoc not to just take a piece of her aereia, but to drain her completely."

The rage that had built in Hydra's voice sent Ash teetering back a step. More than that, the sea around them had started to churn as though the water itself were boiling.

Ash eyed it, then turned back to Hydra, who had closed her eyes and dragged in a few slow, deep breaths.

"You know what?" Hydra rubbed a hand over her face. "I think I've been employing the wrong training methods."

Ash had to stop herself from making a sarcastic quip.

Hydra gave her a cruel smile. "You want to learn how to travel through fire? You want to learn how to listen to Kula? Focus on fire. Stretch your mind. Meditate. The sun's going down—maybe the extra cold will motivate you to get off this raft."

With a jolt of panic Ash realized what Hydra meant to do.

"Wait—"

But Hydra vanished, a cascade of water and foam, leaving Ash stranded on the bobbing raft.

"Damn you," Ash grumbled.

Ash spent an hour sitting on the raft, employing Hydra's vague suggestions.

Stretch your mind. Meditate. Focus on fire.

Traveling through fire proved far too difficult—the setting sun and falling temperature had Ash's teeth clacking together, and it was all she could do to pull a flame into her hand to keep herself from turning into an ice cube. It was easier to focus on the palmful of fire she called—something small yet intense.

Maybe Tor was near a fire, and she could talk to him, ask him to get a boat and come save her. Only she didn't need saving—didn't *want* to be saved—but she closed her eyes and hunched over the flame in her hand, giving herself a moment just to breathe in the smoke.

The smoke smelled like Igna. How long had it been since she'd been home? What was happening there now—surely Brand had spread the word about Ignitus's death? Were people mourning or rejoicing? In the palace, was—

She saw fires. Candle flames and lanterns spotted across a city. No—she knew that city.

Igna.

Her body surged into each flame, rebounding from one into another. A candle on a table in a kitchen; a lantern on a street post; a fire in a stove; a torch burning in someone's hand.

Stunned to silence, Ash let the fires pull her, afraid if she reacted too much or not enough this connection would break.

She was in Igna . . . in a way, her eyes and ears now each flame, a soul untethered yet bound to this flickering, feasting burning.

A bonfire drew her most strongly. It burned in the center of the city, a raging spurt of flame controlled by a ring of Kulan Fire Divine. People crowded the area around the fire, some holding hands, others weeping softly.

At the edge of the fire, someone started playing a harp. Lutes followed, and then voices swept in, and Ash's heart kicked with recognition—this was the song of the Great Defeat, the song she had danced to on the sands of Igna's arena so many weeks ago.

It had been Ignitus's favorite song and dance.

This was a memorial for him.

The shock yanked Ash from the fire. Her soul slithered out of the candle flames and torches, gathering back on itself and flooding into her body, where it sat, shivering, on the raft in the middle of the sea.

Gasping, Ash hugged her arms to herself. The people of Igna were mourning their dead god. Their cruel, bloodthirsty god, who had put so many of them in arenas, who had whittled away Kula's resources to the point of starvation, who had gotten Char *killed*—

And who had been willing to try to fix things in Kula. Who had admitted he was wrong and wanted to try again.

Tears fell. They instantly dried on Ash's cheeks and she scrubbed them away.

She wasn't crying for the loss of Ignitus, she told herself. She was crying for the loss of potential, for the memorial that should have been for her mother. For the wrongness of so much about their world's current situation and how she was supposed to fix it even though she couldn't get off this stupid *raft*.

The sun set fully, throwing Ash into darkness, and she wept into her empty palms, embracing the cold.

By the time Ash got back to the island, she was nearly frozen. As she finally collapsed on the frigid, rock-strewn shore, her muscles wailed in relief. She'd given up traveling through igneia and opted to move her raft using hydreia—which hadn't been any easier. But she'd caught an errant current for the last bit of the trip, otherwise she'd still be drifting aimlessly in the bay—she suspected Hydra had gotten tired of watching her painfully slow progress.

But even so, Ash *had* made progress. She'd gotten in a few solid, swift pushes with hydreia once she'd forced herself to sit and analyze why the water wasn't listening to her. Something Hydra had said kept coming back to her—*It isn't igneia. It's hydreia.*

Hydra never moved as Ash did, or as Ignitus had, all harsh jabs and forceful punches. Hydra's moves were subtle—flicks of her wrists, twitches of her fingers.

So Ash had done that. Embraced subtlety and softness. And she had *moved the water.*

She chuckled to herself on the rocky shore, utterly spent. Water and sweat mingled, trickling down her face, wetting the sand in the moon- and starlit darkness.

She needed to find Tor. She needed to tell him she'd been able to see Igna, that they were safe—for now—and she might be able to communicate with Brand and the other leaders there—

She felt a presence beyond her closed eyelids. Hydra.

"If you've come to gloat about how your methods worked," Ash started, smirking, "don't think I'll ever admit that you're the reason I finally got hydreia to listen to me. I don't—"

"I do not gloat."

Ash's eyes flew open and in an instant she was on her feet, the tide lapping at her bare ankles. The voice was thin and high, almost childlike, so she didn't instantly drop to the defense.

The moon shone light on a figure standing just back from her on the sands, a boy of no more than twelve or thirteen, thin but tall, with a soft face, wide green-brown eyes, and a feathery flop of brown hair. Twigs and leaves poked out of his hair and vines wrapped around his limbs—only Ash noted with a jolt that these plants were actually poking out of his skin. Tiny sprouts peppered his arms; one was growing out of his cheek.

"Florus?" Ash wheezed the name.

He tipped his head, an impish smile playing across his lips. "Ash Nikau."

Ash glanced up and down the shore. "You came. Did you talk to Hydra? Where is—"

"I understand you are hoping to meet with me. My sister wants me to give you floreia." His smile held.

There was a long moment of silence as he just stared at her on the empty beach.

"Yes." Ash drew out the response. Still, he was quiet, and she remembered what Hydra had said—if he was going to give her a piece of his soul, she needed to be worthy of it, to treat it with the respect such an act deserved.

She bowed her head at him, not sure if that was the right thing to do or not.

Florus's deep-green eyes didn't stray from her face. He was more youthful than the other gods Ash had seen, but now that she knew to look, there was the same agelessness in his eyes that she had feared so long in Ignitus—that irascible power that could level cities and snap mortal necks.

A prickle of unease started at the base of Ash's neck. "We *are* preparing to go to Itza—why are you here? Does Hydra know—"

"Centuries ago, we trusted Ciela, and she still failed."

"Ciela?"

"The first gladiator who fought Anathrasa. The one before you.

You don't even know your own history—how are you supposed to step into her place?"

Florus's words took up too much space in Ash's chest.

He was right—she hadn't heard the gladiator's name before. It had been easier when that person had been *the gladiator who fought Anathrasa*, some vague and distant mythical character. But she'd had a name, like Ash. She'd had a family. She'd had a *life*.

"I don't know," Ash admitted. "I'm trying. I want to face Anathrasa. I want to be ready to fight her—"

Florus shook his head, lips twisting. "Wrong answer. The correct answer is: it doesn't matter if you will step into her place. We were wrong about Ciela." His voice was worn with centuries of regret. "I don't want to be wrong again."

A splash made Ash turn.

Instinct clawed at her to get out of the way as a thick green vine shot up from the sea. But the vine still caught her, slamming into her chest and knocking her back into one of the tall boulders on the rocky shore. The angry, violent snake of writhing green wriggled and squirmed against her sealskin suit.

The impact sucked the air from her lungs. Too late, she realized she should pray to Hydra; too late, she got a grip on the vine and started to peel it off her chest—

But a flower grew from the top of it, close to her face. Bloodred petals peeled back to show a yellow core surrounded by an obsidian ring.

The flower convulsed and a burst of pollen clouded Ash's face.

"Florus!" Ash coughed. "What—what are you . . ."

The sea rippled. The sky went from black to pink to a swirl of yellow-red, and in that sky, she saw the god of plants, his youthful face set in a glare.

"We won't be wrong again," he told her, and the world fell into darkness.

SEVEN

MADOC

THAT NIGHT, WHEN the palace was quiet, Madoc snuck out.

A tray of food had been delivered earlier—crunchy bread and charred lamb—and though the aroma alone had been enough to make his mouth water and his stomach clench in hunger, he'd barely touched it. His mind was still churning with all that had happened at the dock—and the handprint that had appeared on Anathrasa's face when she'd struck him.

He could have imagined it—a shadow, or a blush in her cheek from the heat. But when he'd been attacked by the guards, she'd doubled over in pain, as if she'd been hurt alongside him.

There was something very strange going on, and he needed to find out what.

Lifting the tray with one hand, he pulled open the door of his quarters—a lavish room, with a bed twice the size of any he'd slept in before. Two guards waited outside, and at the sound, they turned, bracing their weapons before them.

Their tension moved over his skin like the legs of an insect. The need rose inside him to pull on it, to feed, but he held back. These soldiers were loyal to Anathrasa, and if she sensed he'd used soul energeia on them, what would she do to his family? To him?

He needed to be very careful. To only use enough anathreia to sway their thoughts.

"I can't eat this." The guards jumped back as he shoved the tray at them. "It's rotten."

The knife he'd been given with his meal was tucked into his pocket. He didn't want to use it, but knowing it was there made him feel slightly better.

The younger guard, a woman with a scar on her jaw, looked to her gray-bearded partner and grimaced.

"It looks fine to me," she said.

Madoc inhaled the smallest bit of their geoeia, hiding his sigh when it buzzed in his veins.

Just a little. Just enough so that they would let him leave. Breathing in their energeia made it easier to use his own power, a give and take, an ebb and flow. His thoughts shot to the ship, to Tor telling him to reach inside himself and use his own soul for fuel, but he couldn't focus on training exercises now. He had to figure out what was going on between himself and the Mother Goddess. And he needed to find Aera and Biotus so he could siphon off enough of their power to give to Ash.

"Look at it." He stepped closer, finding the man's thoughts

guarded by a hard layer of skepticism. The woman was easier to reach—her curiosity made her vulnerable, and he pressed an image into her mind.

"Maggots!" She jolted back, cupping her hand to her nose. "They're all over the meat!"

"A trick." The man examined the plate as Madoc's hand slid subtly over the knife. If this guard attacked him, he would have to defend himself. "Anathrasa said he might try something. I don't see any—"

"Look closer." Madoc pushed through the guard's uncertainty to the senses beneath. His own anathreia swelled, soothing and hungry for more. The man blinked, then grimaced.

"We'll take this back to the kitchen," the guard said. "Apologies, dominus. Our mistake."

Madoc nodded. He felt more in control than he had at the dock, when his anathreia had swirled inside him like a tempest. Maybe he'd been wrong to think he could tithe on his own soul to use his power. Maybe this was the way it had to be.

He pushed the thought from his head as the two guards walked away.

Keeping his steps quiet, he hurried down the breezeway in the opposite direction, staying close to the stone wall beneath the flickering sconces. The railing on his other side blocked a three-story fall to the courtyard below, where he'd been reunited earlier with his family. He hadn't seen where they'd been taken, but he had a good guess it was to the rooms on the second floor, where two other guards now stood watch.

He considered convincing them to abandon their post so he could have a word with Elias and Ilena, but he didn't want to draw unneeded attention their way.

Heart pounding, he made his way toward the stairs, jogging down the steps, then hiding in a shadow at the bottom as another guard walked by on his nightly rounds.

Anathrasa was keeping them well contained in this wing of the palace. Still, she would have known what Madoc was capable of. He couldn't help wondering if the ease of his escape was something she'd anticipated, even counted on.

Maybe this was a test Anathrasa had set up to see if he'd run—to see if she could trust him. For all he knew, she could sense that he'd left just as she'd felt that slap across her cheek.

He needed to find her and learn exactly what this connection between them entailed, but setting an intentional meeting would give her an opportunity to lie. If he could spy on her without alerting her to his presence, he might be able to gain valuable information for Ash and Hydra.

Geoxus's chambers had been in the northern wing of the palace, a tower that had fallen when he and Ignitus had fought. None of the rooms in this wing were grand enough for a goddess, and he didn't see any servants, so she had to be in one of the chambers above the throne room.

But as he set a course in that direction, he felt pulled another way, as if an invisible hook had caught his spine and was dragging him outside. Giving in to the strange sensation, he crept down a corridor lined with marble statues, remembering, with a chill, the way Geoxus had traveled through them. Now that Ash had his abilities, could she peer through stones the way he had? Could she come here, to Deimos, through the earth?

The thought of seeing her now, even for a moment, made his burden of fear feel lighter.

The hall opened to a marble staircase that descended into the palace gardens. From behind him came the scuffle of sandals—another guard, most likely—and Madoc rushed down the steps, ducking behind the stone railing. The pull was stronger now, unwieldy. His anathreia was responding to another call—coming to life without his bidding.

He was certain it meant the Mother Goddess was close.

When all was quiet, he continued on.

The gardens were as peaceful as they were haunting. Crickets chirped in flower beds, while carriage-sized boulders that had fallen from the towers during the battle lay half embedded in the scorched earth. He stepped through a vine-laced trellis, through trees toppled, their roots ripped from the ground and now reaching toward the half-moon. Everywhere he looked was a reminder of the power that had been, and the power that had destroyed it.

"Come closer, dear."

He froze at the woman's voice, hair prickling on the back of his neck. Ahead, he could see two figures. He recognized Anathrasa immediately, dressed in a fine white gown, standing beside a white marble fountain. She was motioning to a servant, a girl no more than fifteen, who complied with her goddess's will and knelt at her feet.

Realizing with some relief that he hadn't been seen, Madoc

ducked behind a boulder, flattening himself against the cold, jagged stone. Dread sank into his chest, the only anchor to his anathreia, which continued to whirl inside in a strange, unsettling way—like a power he'd taken from someone else and was holding in his body.

Anathrasa threw her head back, face turned toward the sky. She hadn't looked his way. For all Madoc knew, she didn't see him, but he could feel something happening. The quickening of blood in his veins. The rise of strength in his muscles.

Soul energeia.

She was tithing, and he could feel it.

He knew what would come next. The girl's power would be sucked out of her body. She would die, like Cassia had died. Like so many others must have for Anathrasa to look as youthful and strong as she did now.

Horror raked through him. He felt the urge to call out a warning, to tell her to run. But if he did, Anathrasa would know he wasn't loyal. The Metaxas might be punished. He wouldn't be able to get close to Aera or Biotus.

Anathrasa wasn't the woman Madoc had lived below in the stone-mason's quarter. She was already stronger, which meant she was a threat to Ash, even with the gods' energeias.

Every moment, his mother was growing more dangerous.

In a new wave of panic, a cold sweat dripped between his shoulder blades. If he could feel Anathrasa tithing on a Deiman woman, she would very likely feel him taking the power from a god.

He couldn't think of that now. He only knew he had to stop this.

Think.

He needed to create a distraction. To turn the girl's mind or alert a guard to interrupt. But his anathreia was still rising, whipping through him, and he couldn't direct it anywhere.

He couldn't stop her.

But he might be able to hurt her.

Silently, he slid the knife free from his belt and sliced a clean line across the palm of his hand. The sudden rush of pain had him gritting his teeth. Had his power roaring in his veins.

A shrill cry filled the night. As Madoc watched, Anathrasa stumbled into the edge of the fountain. She gripped her hand against her chest, a blossom of red staining the front of her gown.

It had worked.

Somehow, he and Anathrasa *were* connected. She'd bled when he cut himself. He'd found a way to hurt her.

Had he found a way to kill her?

The girl leaped up, forcing the dark thought from his mind. Sliding the knife back into his belt, Madoc locked his bleeding fist against his thigh. His heartbeat pounded in his temples. He hadn't thought of what would happen after he'd distracted Anathrasa, only that stopping her might save the girl.

But her fate had been sealed as soon as she'd stepped into this courtyard. To Anathrasa, mortals were only fuel. All he'd done was delay the inevitable.

"Goddess, are you all right?" The girl was terrified—more so than before. Her hands were clasped before her.

Anathrasa didn't respond. She rushed toward the palace, the girl on her heels begging for forgiveness.

Madoc jumped as a hand closed around his shoulder. He spun to find Elias crouched behind him, one finger pressed to his lips in an order to be silent.

Madoc's muscles tensed. What was Elias doing here? It wasn't safe. The Mother Goddess might try to tithe on him next.

Elias motioned toward the palace, and Madoc followed him in silence. He thought Elias meant to go back inside, but he skirted around the outside of the building, running to the back of the stables, where Madoc had once taken Ash after the ball so that they could sneak away.

They'd never made it past the gates.

Elias stopped and, breathing hard, leaned against the back of the barn, sinking into the shadows on the ground.

"What are you doing?" Madoc asked when his heart finally settled.

"Following you," Elias said. "You're not the only one who can sneak around this place."

Madoc didn't like this. It was one thing for him to risk Anathrasa's wrath. Another for Elias, who hadn't signed up for any of this.

"I made a hole in the floor of our room," Elias continued. "Now. You want to tell me what that was all about?"

He didn't know if Elias was referring to his spying or to the cut on his hand. It occurred to him that Elias didn't even know what Anathrasa had been attempting to do.

"She's tithing," Madoc said. "Feeding on energeia. It's making her stronger."

"I noticed. The old bat pulled me out of prison and said you were coming. That if we so much as tried to run you would suffer. She looked . . . *healthy.*" He said the word like a curse. "I wasn't talking about that part," he added.

Anger spilled through Madoc's veins, mingling with the realization of what Elias meant.

He unfurled his palm, showing the already-scabbed line where he'd cut himself.

"Somehow, we're connected," he said. "When I get hurt, she gets hurt."

Elias's eyes widened. "What happens if *she* gets hurt?"

Madoc shrugged. He supposed the same principle worked in reverse, and it worried him to think that at any moment he might start bleeding as a result of her own experimentation.

"And if you die?" Elias pressed, his voice raw.

Madoc grasped his hands tightly. He didn't know the answer. If he could end the world's suffering with his own sacrifice—if he could save Ash's life by trading his—he had no choice but to do it. But he didn't know for certain that their connection went that deep. Anathrasa was still a goddess, after all, and had lived thousands of years. If he died and she survived, he would be of no help to Ash or their cause.

"I'm still trying to figure out how it works," he said.

"That's why you're here? To figure this out?" Elias didn't sound pleased with this plan.

"No. The connection—that's new," Madoc said. "I'm here because we found a way to beat her. I just need to get Aera's and Biotus's energeias first. Have you seen them?"

"They're here for the newest round of bloodshed," Elias said. "Aera eats men like us for breakfast. And good luck with Biotus. His arms are as thick as your chest."

Madoc scowled. He'd seen the god of animals from afar during wars between Deimos and Cenhelm and recalled thinking he was formidable. If there was a way to draw the energeia from him without a physical confrontation, that would be ideal.

"You're serious," Elias said, as if he'd been waiting for the punch line of a joke. "I heard rumors in prison about what had happened at the palace. I thought they were just stories."

Quickly, Madoc explained everything that had happened since they'd parted. The battle with Geoxus and Ignitus, how Ash had killed a god. The run through the city and the fight outside the ice blockade at the Apuit Islands. Their plan to make Ash strong enough to defeat Anathrasa.

"She can hold the powers of the gods within her." He pictured her standing in Hydra's throne room, water pouring from her hands. "She's going to use them to beat Anathrasa."

Elias considered this for a long minute, the crickets chirping in the grass around them.

"So . . ." Elias pulled a long piece of grass from the ground and wound it around his finger. "You came all the way back here for a girl?"

Madoc jabbed him in the ribs. "I came back to save the world, you idiot."

"Well," said Elias. "You're in deep."

Madoc was quiet, remembering the feel of Ash's skin, and the hitch of her sigh. The taste of sellenroot that had wound into their kiss.

The way he'd failed her on the ship with Anathrasa. The way he'd accidentally bound himself to his mother, making him unsure if he could even help Ash now without Anathrasa knowing.

Doubt weighed on him, slick and heavy.

He shook it off, changing the subject.

"Where's Cassia?" Her name brought a tension to his chest, and a heaviness between them.

"Anathrasa let me take her to the fields outside the city," Elias said. "Near an orange tree."

She'd always liked oranges.

"I put a stone on her grave for you. A big, ugly one, because it reminded me of you."

Madoc gave a watery chuckle. "Thanks for that."

Elias sighed, then rested his forehead on Madoc's shoulder. "I missed you, brother."

Madoc only nodded, because a knot in his throat made it impossible to speak.

Elias lifted his head, then pushed off the ground. He extended a hand toward Madoc and helped him up.

"Anathrasa's not taking any more of my family," he said, like a man twice his age. "If draining two more gods is how we take her down, you can count on my help."

Madoc stood, his lungs too big within his ribs.

But as they headed back toward the palace, he couldn't help thinking of his strange connection with the Mother Goddess and the unscratchable itch on his soul that told him that Anathrasa had not survived hundreds of years on tithes alone without considering just how she would exact her revenge.

They had to be ready for anything.

🔥 🔥 🔥

Madoc woke to a breeze blowing across his skin. It carried a soft, clean scent, like freshly laundered clothes, and behind his closed eyes, he saw the rocky western outlet of the Nien River, where everyone in the quarter went to wash their dusty tunics and robes. He sighed, thinking of how he had once carried the heavy, waterlogged basket home for Ilena, and how, after she'd hung the pieces to dry on the line, he and Elias would fling stones at them for target practice.

A high giggle made his eyes pop open.

There was a woman sitting on his bed.

Startled, he scrambled to the head of the mattress, dragging the covers over his naked chest.

"Good morning, sleepyhead," she said with a smile. "You had sweet dreams, I trust?"

She was as small as Ilena, with delicate curves and long hair like spun sunshine. Her dress—if that was what it was called—was pale blue, a single braid of fabric over her left shoulder that spread to a thin sheath over her breasts and ended just below the crux of her thighs.

His eyes widened involuntarily, and then his brain caught up with him.

The woman before him wasn't a woman at all, but a goddess whose likeness he had seen in a painting during the last war Deimos had had with Lakhu.

Aera.

Instantly, the power in him swelled, all gnashing teeth and sharp hunger—a response to the raw, god energeia surrounding her. His anathreia was reckless and primal, everything Tor had tried to teach him to control, and stole Madoc's breath. His gaze flicked to the three guards behind her, in the same small, wispy skirts. They were whispering to each other and ogling him in a way that made him very uncomfortable.

"So you're him," she said, her voice breathy and high, her pink lips parting around the words. His eyes lowered, but there was nowhere to look that he couldn't see skin. Bare shoulders, and wrists, and fingers, and legs. "The mortal son I've heard so much about."

He thought of Ash's legs, wrapped around his. Her hands splaying on his chest.

"Madoc," he said, his voice still rough with sleep. "Can I help you with something, goddess?"

"I can think of one or two things," said one of her guards with a quirk of her brow.

Madoc cleared his throat.

Aera leaned closer, her hand brushing Madoc's bare shoulder, teasing the swell of muscle. He had the distinct impression that he was being measured in some way. Evaluated.

"Anathrasa thinks you can help us," Aera said. "I hope, for your sake, she isn't wrong."

He nearly choked. Anathrasa didn't trust him. He'd been met on the docks by half the legion. His room was guarded, however lightly. His own family was being held prisoner.

But the glimmer in her eyes was filled with promise.

If he betrayed them, she would kill him.

His mind reeled. He could take some of Aera's power—if he was subtle, she might not even notice. He could hold it inside him until he took Biotus's energeia, then he'd find the Apuitian sailors and speed back to the islands.

This was what he'd come to do. This was what they needed to defeat Anathrasa.

But he thought of the cut on his hand and the blood that had risen on hers. Even if Aera couldn't sense what he was doing, would Anathrasa know? Would she feel it?

His family would be held accountable for his treason. Drained like Cassia. Killed.

But if he couldn't take Aera's and Biotus's power and give it to Ash, what good was he?

Panic pressed his teeth together as Aera slid closer on the mattress. The breeze that he'd felt before had come with her, a movement of the still air, threatening to calm his ragged senses.

"I came to wake you," she said, glancing out the window, to the gray sky now growing bright with dawn. "We're leaving soon."

"Where are we going?" he asked.

She rose and strode toward the door, her bare feet making no sound against the floor.

"To the arena," she called. "The gladiator games are about to begin."

She disappeared out the door, leaving him gaping in her wake.

Half an hour later, a carriage took him from the palace into the heart of the city, where people were already gathering on street corners and heading toward the arena. With a lurch, he remembered how fans had painted his name on their bodies when the gladiators had rolled through town. How girls had offered to meet him after a match. It was a game to them, just as it was a game to the gods.

Anathrasa's words echoed through his head: *I don't suppose you're here for the festivities.* Had she been talking about this? Elias had said the gods were here for *the newest round of bloodshed*, but Madoc had thought he'd meant the attack from Hydra and Florus, not gladiator fights.

He was almost glad his family had been left behind at the palace. Still, he didn't like being separated from them. The fact that they hadn't been invited today made him worry what was happening to them in his absence.

Sick with anticipation, Madoc leaned toward the window, breathing in a city that still reeked of smoke. It was better than inhaling whatever intoxicating scent floated around Aera.

He stole a glance at her, laughing at something one of the guards on her right had said. They fit together like woven strands. Two women on her left, another on her right. Geoxus's guards had always been solemn and cold, but these warriors clung close to their goddess, as if to make a shield with their bodies.

Madoc couldn't pick her energeia out from the rest if he tried.

"Who will be participating in these games? Hydra and Florus haven't sent anyone to fight, have they?" He tried to keep his voice steady, but nerves were cresting inside him.

Was Ash here? He wasn't ready. He'd been in Crixion for a night.

He wasn't even sure that Aera hadn't drawn him away from the palace to murder him.

"Don't you think you'd notice if Hydra and Florus had arrived?"

she said, laughing at something another guard whispered. They all looked at Madoc in a way that made him feel very awkward, as if he were wearing a lot less than the fine white toga that had been delivered to his room just after Aera's departure this morning. It reminded him of Anathrasa's gown last night, and he hoped that had been a deliberate choice the Mother Goddess had made. Whether she knew he'd been responsible for the cut on her hand or not, he hoped she still wanted him close.

The carriage slowed, then turned onto a narrow path that led to the gladiator entrance beneath the stands. Madoc had once ridden with Lucius and Elias here before he'd fought Jann, and before that, when he'd first met Ash face-to-face. That all seemed a lifetime ago now.

"Then which gladiators are fighting?" he asked, frustrated by her vague answers. "Earth Divine? Your Air Divine?"

His gut twisted at the thought that he might be made to fight. Was that what she'd meant when she'd said that Anathrasa had thought he could help them?

In that moment, he wished he'd never come home.

Aera registered his tone and met his gaze, her sky-blue eyes bright with amusement.

"Deimos. Lakhu. Cenhelm. We'll hardly stand a chance against Hydra's fleet next month with the city in shambles and half its people moping around, crying for their beloved god of earth." She walked her fingers over the bare knee of one of her guards as the carriage pulled under the archway, into the dusty belly of the massive stone structure. "We needed to raise an army. And what better way to determine the best fighters than by a trial on the sands of my brother's grand arena? Imagine it! No more elite gladiators—any Divine citizen can join the games, man, woman, child. We'll let them all fight, won't that be wonderful? And with a force made of the strongest mortals to subdue the rest, the world will be ours."

Horror rippled through him as the carriage pulled to a stop. Anathrasa was sending Deimans into the arena—children included— to determine the strongest fighters for her army in the coming war against Hydra and Florus. These weren't gladiators, they were common citizens. They would die, and if he tried to stop it, Anathrasa would punish him, and he wouldn't be able to do what he needed to in order to help Ash defeat her.

As he got out, the thunder of footsteps echoed from the seats above them, scratching Madoc's raw nerves. He could already hear the familiar cheers from the audience within.

He stuffed down his revulsion. He had to keep to the plan.

Aera. Biotus. *Ash.*

He needed to make Ash powerful enough to destroy the Mother Goddess, and to do that he needed to get close to the gods Anathrasa had sided with.

Bile rose in his throat as he and Aera were met by a team of centurions and led down a hallway. They traveled up a long, narrow flight of stairs lit by the phosphorescent green stones Geoxus had once installed instead of torches, to keep Ignitus's gladiators from accessing igneia. At the top, they crossed a wide corridor and came to a brightly lit box, already brimming with people.

Madoc stumbled as he crossed the threshold. The last time he'd been here had been with his gladiator trainer, Lucius, when he'd wanted to beg Geoxus for Cassia's freedom, and had instead been blocked by Petros.

He'd failed that day with Geoxus, but he was no longer a trembling boy who believed his god could save him. Mortals had no choice but to save themselves.

He spotted her, sitting on a white marble throne in the center of the box, surrounded by servants and fawning nobles. Her gown was white, like last night, and fastened around one shoulder by a silver circle.

If she noticed his arrival, she didn't show it. She took a drink of wine from a goblet and continued her conversation. But he could feel the strange pull of power in his veins and wondered if she, too, could sense him drawing near.

He was making his way over to a lavish table of food, from which he could watch the action in the box unfold from a safe distance, when a giant stepped before him, his shadow blocking the light.

"Have you met Madoc yet, brother?" Aera asked, sliding her arm around Madoc's.

The god of animals was a beast beside delicate Aera, his chest broad and bare, crossed by pelt straps, and his ship-mast thighs covered by a swatch of fur. Auburn braids of hair stretched to his muscular neck and shoulders, which flexed as he narrowed his black eyes on Madoc.

Madoc swallowed, feeling his bravery wither.

"Biotus." He bowed his head.

"Madoc." Biotus growled his name. "The one who drained my

brothers dry. You must be proud. It's not every day a mortal takes down a god."

He stared at Madoc in the way a predator eyes his prey.

Madoc's mouth was parched. He couldn't think of what to say.

"Leave him alone, Biotus." Aera slapped his shoulder playfully. "Madoc's on our side. Isn't that right?"

She smiled at him.

He nodded quickly. "I am, goddess."

With a hard look, Biotus shoved past Madoc, nearly knocking him over on his way to the box's exit. Madoc could feel the anger pulsing off him, the taste of copper on the back of his tongue that he knew was animal energeia. His heart begged to try it, even as his mind cautioned him to hold back.

His eyes flicked to Anathrasa, still talking with her servants.

"Don't mind him. He's just angry because his best soldiers haven't yet arrived from Cenhelm. Their ships are quite slow."

Her words reminded him of the way Crixion's ships had flown over the waves, aided by Air Divine sailors, when they'd attacked with Anathrasa at the blockade before the Apuit Islands. The tension behind his neck increased.

"Where is he going?" he asked, worried about his family, back at the palace, and Ash, even though she was over the sea. And anyone who might cross paths with the god of animals.

"To track the rest of his fleet, I'd guess," she said, her voice like a tinkling bell as she twisted a finger around a lock of her golden hair. It didn't ease his mind—he'd rather Biotus stay within sight, and the possibility of an entire Cenhelmian fleet's arrival in Crixion was daunting—but he couldn't follow him and not raise Aera's suspicion.

"This all must be very exciting for you," she said. "Have you ever seen an Air Divine warrior fight an Animal Divine *and* an Earth Divine at once?"

Three people in the arena together? In past wars, it had been only one champion against another.

"How many rounds are there?" he asked.

"Just one." She linked her arm with his and dragged him through the crowd of gossiping Deimans and Laks to the railing, where they could overlook the sparkling sand. Pots of flowers had been brought alongside it, and the sweet scent of jasmine and rose filled his nostrils.

His heart locked in his throat.

He could see the spot where he'd fought Jann below. Where he'd stood when Geoxus had chosen him for the Honored Eight. Where Ash had fallen when Elias had thrown all his geoeia at her.

The seats below and around them were filled to capacity. The spectators' voices rose like thunder, their excitement thick in the morning air.

"Anathrasa!" called an announcer positioned near the base of the arena, his voice magnified on the wind. "We honor you with this first of three tribute games—a battle of strength between our fearless Earth Divine, the Air Divine from Lakhu, and the mighty Animal Divine of Cenhelm! The best among them will receive the ultimate honor—to serve in your army." He paused, and the crowd roared their approval, but Madoc's heart sank.

"Now," the announcer continued. "Bring out the champions!"

EIGHT

ASH

THE WORLD BECAME a forest.

Thick brown trees shot up to support a fluffy emerald canopy that let shafts of golden light peek through. Ash stood on a bed of dew-laden undergrowth, watching leaves drift on a breeze in lazy spirals. The air smelled of moss and decay but also of life.

Everything was peaceful here.

Ash turned, watching the sunlight play in the canopy. The effect spun colors across the leaves—bright red and slants of butter yellow. It made her dizzy.

She was so dizzy.

She wanted to sleep.

"Ash, you have to wake up."

Ash turned, her arms drifting through the velvety warm air, and then she was dancing, a luxurious spiral from a lifetime ago. As she danced, she saw Char standing nearby, watching.

"Mama?" Ash giggled. "Mama!"

She stopped. Pulses of red and yellow and black throbbed around her. The decay smell was stronger now and Ash grabbed her head. She was so dizzy. Why was she so dizzy?

"You have to fight through it, Ash," Char said. "You know this isn't right. Wake up!"

Ash shuddered, not cold, not feeling much of anything.

"Wake up!" Char begged again, and Ash twitched, rubbing her eyes hard.

When she blinked them open, Char was gone; the forest, gone. Around her towered scarlet flowers with hypnotic yellow centers and black smeared across their insides, all of them swaying in a breeze.

Ash swayed too. She tipped over, crying out, and when her hands and knees dropped to the undergrowth, she felt only thorns. They stabbed her hands and blood fell, staining the leaves and rising up her arms—

Ash screamed, flailing, but the blood rose and rose into her mouth, salty and metallic.

She was still screaming when her eyes opened, and the flowers were gone. No forest, no Char, no thorns or blood.

She was curled in the corner of a bare room. Six hexagonal walls wrapped around her with a solid floor and ceiling—no doors, no windows. The only light came from gently pulsing spots on each wall—they flickered in and out, a yellow-green hue much like Geoxus's phosphorescent stones or Hydra's algae.

Ash held still for one full breath. Her head throbbed, an ache in the veins at her temples, and her tongue tasted like she'd licked sand. Where was she? She had the foggiest memory of Florus showing up on the shore. And thorns? No, a vine—

A vine with a red flower.

The bastard had poisoned her.

Ash rose, slowly finding her footing on the rough floor.

Florus had poisoned and captured her.

Her stomach roiled, and she forced herself not to vomit. She wouldn't think through the implications of this yet.

She would *get out*.

Gritting her teeth, she pulled blue flames into each hand and launched fire at the far wall. She pushed it hotter, as hot as she could handle; and even then, she gave it more. The floor and walls rippled in a scalding red glow as her heat sank into them, and still she pushed more, sweat breaking across her face and back, exertion tugging at the edges of her vision.

The entire room tipped upside down. Ash flipped, slamming against the far wall, the ceiling, the floor again. Embers from her escape attempt peppered the air around her as she spun, each toss ricocheting pain up her shoulder, her thigh, her skull.

"Florus!" Ash screamed. "Florus—*stop!*"

The room came to a halt, righted again—or maybe upside down now—but Ash crouched on the floor, shaking, her hair wild around her and the taste of blood in her mouth.

The god of plants materialized in the middle of the room, bringing with him the smell of earth, rich and heavy with life and fresh oxygen. It contrasted with how stale this room smelled, like a thousand years of neglect and rot.

Ash glared up at Florus. Should she attack him outright? Could she murder a god without Madoc first draining him?

The thought of his name broke her.

"Where is Madoc?" Ash gasped to the floor. "Did you side with Anathrasa? If you so much as—"

"Madoc? There's no one by that name here," Florus responded. "And I am *not* allied with Anathrasa."

Ash watched his face for any sign of a lie, but his eyes were wide and innocent, his lips soft in a half smile. Only a crease on his forehead showed he was at all distressed.

Ash bolted to her feet and lunged at him.

Instantly, a dozen vines shot out of the floor, knotted around her, and yanked her back. Her shoulder blades crashed into the rough wall and the vines held her against it, more of them squirming up to hold each limb in a locked, solid embrace.

"What are you doing?" Ash screamed. "Stop this!"

Florus shook his head. "No."

"I can break out of this," Ash threatened. Her skin started to burn, a blue flame on her hands and feet that crackled the vines. "I'll incinerate this whole prison."

That earned a thoughtful smile. "This prison was made for one such as you. You cannot escape." He stomped on the floor. "Petrified wood. It isn't alive, so no water to use; it isn't a stone, so no earth to use. It cannot be burned. It can only be manipulated by Plant Divine. And I will not give you floreia, Ash Nikau. You are not strong enough to save us."

She let her fire fall, let the vines keep her against the wall. Her chest beat in and out, and with rasping breaths she wanted to scream again, but she managed, "What do you want?"

Florus stepped closer. "I told you. We won't fail against Anathrasa again. I won't let us."

"You won't let us." Ash's heart sank into her stomach. "Where's Hydra?"

Had Hydra betrayed her? And where were Tor, Taro, Spark?

Ash felt her body heat spike again, but Florus shook his head. "Hydra will be quite upset when she finds out what I did. But she will get over it. We always do."

Florus flicked his wrist and a fan of razor-sharp leaves grew out of the floor, each as long as Ash's arm. Florus plucked one, testing its edge as one might a blade.

Ash bucked against the vines. "Florus." But her throat constricted. She couldn't breathe.

"Last time, our best efforts to kill Anathrasa failed," Florus started, still looking at the sharp leaf. "We only made it so she can't sustain her own anathreia. She can't retain the souls she draws into herself. She can't manipulate the emotions and thoughts of others—yet. But we tried with everything we had to accomplish more—we tried to defeat her, and we couldn't."

His eyes flicked to Ash.

"If she gets you, she'll have my brothers' energeias. She'll be at her full power again. And what will we be able to do to stop her then? We *can't* defeat her. We can only keep her in this weakened state."

"I'm going to stop her, Florus." Ash knew she sounded frantic, but she *was*. Her head still throbbed and each nerve tingled with desperate fear. "Ciela—that was her name?—I'm not Ciela. When I obtain all six energeias and become Soul Divine like Anathrasa, I'm going to kill her."

"Anathrasa survived Ciela."

"She won't survive me. I know Anathrasa's tricks. I know not to stop fighting until I'm *sure* she's dead."

"No." Florus pointed the leaf at her. "It won't matter. I won't risk the possibility of Anathrasa getting my brothers' powers from you. I'm ending this."

He leaned forward, his eyes scrambling over her face, her matted hair, a gash on her chin dripping blood onto her collarbone.

"Ignitus? Geoxus? Are you in there?" Florus whispered. "Can you hear me, brothers? I'm going to kill these last pieces of you. I've prepared for this moment—Hydra always thought you'd leave us alone forever, but I knew you'd eventually come and ruin everything. So I made you this prison. It will contain your igneia, Ignitus. And your geoeia, Geoxus. So don't try to fight me."

Ash gasped, a bitter sob. "Florus, Ignitus and Geoxus aren't here—it's just me. I'm—"

Florus put the tip of the leaf against Ash's lips. It sliced her skin and she tasted more blood, but she couldn't pull away, her head bound to the wall.

Florus met her eyes again, and Ash saw the insanity in him. She lost herself in it; even when Ignitus had been at his most unhinged, he had never been calm like this, and Florus's youthful face made it all the more horrifying.

"I'm going to kill this mortal shell," Florus told her. Told Ignitus and Geoxus within her.

Ash heaved against the vines. "Wait, wait—"

"It's the only way," he said, and he almost looked sad. "When the shell dies, my brothers' energeias will dissipate into the ether. They will be gone, and Anathrasa will never again be able to resume her full strength. This will all be over."

"No, Florus!" Ash fought, but more vines held her; she burned, but when one vine snapped away, another was there to take its place. "That won't stop Anathrasa! She'll still be here, terrorizing the world—I have to kill her, Florus! *Let me fight her!*"

"Shh," Florus cooed as though she was some tantruming child. "This will all be over soon."

He lowered the spiked leaf.

"Florus!" Ash screamed. "Florus, *don't*—"

He reared his arm back, shifted his weight, and drove the point of the leaf into her gut.

Ash choked. Before she could feel any pain, he stabbed her with another pointed leaf, and another, and another, until that was what held her body to the wall, not the vines.

Satisfied, Florus stepped back and folded his arms over his chest.

He was just going to stand there and watch her die.

Blood surged up Ash's throat and spilled down her chin, until all she felt was an iron tang of blood everywhere, consuming her senses.

She couldn't be dying. She couldn't *die* at all—Madoc needed her. Tor needed her.

A tear streaked down her cheek. She sputtered, gasping, and the act wrenched her body against the leaves, sending a spark of pain up her side. That pain lit others until her mouth cracked open, but she couldn't even scream; this pain was unbearable, unfathomable, an ache she couldn't put a name to because it was so beyond what a body should experience.

With one last effort, Ash pushed fire at the leaves that held her. They burned to the wall and she dropped, freed, only to collapse on the floor in a puddle of blood and broken vines.

"Really, Ignitus?" Florus chastised. "Die with honor."

"I . . . am not . . . Ignitus," Ash gasped, each word agony. She pushed herself onto her hands and glowered up at Florus. "I am not . . . Geoxus. I am . . ."

Pain seized her. She doubled over, wailing, her insides constricting in a spasm that shot stars across her eyes.

She rolled to the side, hands around her middle—

Her wounds.

Her wounds were healing.

The ones on her stomach. The gaping hole in her shoulder.

She writhed on the floor, half taken by the throbbing sensation of healing and half terrified as the holes made by Florus's leaves mended themselves.

Ash came to her knees, trembling, covered in blood and sweat and righteous fury. She looked up at Florus again, and his eyes were wide with realization.

"You have Ignitus's and Geoxus's energeias," he said, "and you have their immortality too, it seems."

Ash's chest heaved. She used the wall to pull herself to her feet. Her focus sharpened to a single point, something dark rising from the pit of her soul and hunching her shoulders, curling her fingers into fists, peeling back her lips in a snarl.

"I am more god than you," she growled.

"No," Florus told her. But his voice was clipped. She had rattled him; she had rattled herself. "Anathrasa will never find you. She will never resume her full power. It is still over."

When Ash lunged at Florus this time, she didn't want to burn him; no, she wanted to rip his head off and let him bathe in his own blood.

But before she'd crossed the room, Florus was gone.

Ash slammed into the opposite wall in his wake. She whirled, searching for him, but she saw only the vines, now withering away; the razor leaves covered in her blood; the stain on the floor of all the blood she had lost; and she knew she must look like death itself.

Ash beat her fists on the walls. Bruises formed, but she felt them tingle and heal. It was happening fast. She was a god. She couldn't be killed. She couldn't—

"Florus!" she screamed. "Florus! HYDRA!"

Ash reared back, gasping.

Hydra had briefly tried to teach Ash to travel like the gods. *Focus. Meditate.*

Ash knotted her fingers in her hair and turned in a circle, eyes shut, pulse hammering.

Hydra, she willed herself. *Get to Hydra.*

Madoc. Get to Madoc.

Madoc. If he took Aera's aereia or Biotus's bioseia without Ash there to receive it, the energeia would eventually kill him.

Ash sobbed. Her knees cracked to the floor, and she heaved, crying so hard she thought she might be sick.

Florus had tried to kill her. And that still might be her fate if she didn't get out of this prison.

If she didn't, no one would ever know what had happened to her. Tor, Taro, Spark—she would never see them again. Madoc—she would never touch him again, never feel the way he held her.

Her mind spiraled, thoughts and intentions too slippery to hold. All she could do was kneel there, weeping, half a god, half a girl, entirely defeated.

NINE

MADOC

THE GATES ON the south side of the arena, where Madoc himself had once entered, opened, and a line of Deimans stepped onto
the golden sand. These weren't the trained fighters Geoxus had trea-
sured—most weren't thick enough to fill out the gladiator armor
they'd borrowed. Some weren't even strong enough to lift their own
weapons, dragging their swords on the ground behind them, or hoist-
ing wobbling spears with both hands.

"They're all fighting at once?" Madoc asked. He'd assumed Aera
had meant one champion of each country, but now it looked as if this
was going to include everyone.

"Yes, isn't it exciting?" The goddess of air clapped her hands. "I
heard Deimans were lined up in the streets all last week for a chance to
appear in the arena. Everyone wants to be a hero and avenge Geoxus!"

A sheen of sweat coated Madoc's skin. In the box beside him, he
heard an audible grunt of disgust, and when he turned, he saw Lucius,
the gladiator trainer he'd once served. The man met Madoc's gaze, his

eyes filled with anger, then looked away.

Madoc's mouth went dry. The last time he'd seen Lucius, he'd been training to fight as an Earth Divine champion. Surely by now the sponsor knew that had been a lie. Was he disgusted now at the very sight of Madoc? Did he know Anathrasa was Madoc's mother? He had to be wondering why Madoc was here, among some of the most powerful people in the world.

Regardless what the sponsor thought, Madoc felt his surprise settle into a tentative relief. There was at least one other Deiman displeased with Anathrasa's rule—even if Lucius's disgust was reserved for him.

Forty Deimans were on the sand now, but Madoc's gaze locked on the smallest among them—a boy with dark curls and a small wooden knife. He glanced again to Lucius. The sponsor never would have put a child on the sand, or any of these fighters for that matter. He'd taken only the best. The strongest.

Or at least those who'd appeared to be the strongest.

He had a sudden, desperate desire to talk to Ash, to tell her what was happening here. Did she know? Did Hydra look through the water to learn of the horrors about to take place?

Had Ash learned how to do the same?

No. She would have tried to contact him if she could. Still, too much time had passed since he'd left the islands. Was she all right? Had something happened? He wished there was a way that he could reach her, but how? He wasn't a god. They didn't even share the same energeia.

He was overcome by a wave of insignificance. This was the kind of thing they were fighting to stop. These people were risking their lives for the pleasures of the gods. And yet he was forced to stand by and do nothing.

Not nothing.

He was close to Aera. If he could figure out how to drain some of her power, they would be one step closer to ending these events forever.

"There they are!" The goddess of air squealed as the northern gate was pulled back to reveal another group—men and women with fair hair and skin, who carried thin golden shields and small handheld weapons. They moved over the ground like their goddess did—light on their feet, their gazes constantly in motion.

A moment later, seven warriors in fur skins stomped out of the far exit. They were braced for a fight, and even from the box, Madoc could feel the charge of their bioseia. As soon as the gate behind them had closed, the sand began to shift. At first, Madoc thought this was the work of geoeia, but as he watched, a trapdoor opened in the ground and a giant white mountain cat lunged up a hidden ramp. Two more followed, lithe beasts the size of horses, with paws as big as a man's head and claws like knives. When the last cat tried to pounce at the nearest Animal Divine fighter, it was caught around the neck by a metal collar and crashed to its side with a shriek.

The crowd went wild.

Madoc's gaze darted back to the Deiman boy, who clearly had no idea what he'd gotten himself into. This wasn't the gladiator fights of the old wars; this was a free-for-all—Earth Divine against Air Divine against Animal Divine. Like last night in the garden, the urge rose in him to stop this, but before he could say or do anything, the announcer raised his hands.

"Let the games begin!"

The audience screamed as the three divinities in the arena clashed in a torrent of wind and dust and clanging metal. Despite the unprepared look of the Deimans, they hurled themselves toward the Air and Animal Divine with a reckless bravery, and soon, a hundred energeias were heaving across the sand.

Madoc gripped the railing, sick to his core. He searched for the boy and found him near the outskirts of the fight, flinging balls of gravel into the fray before sprinting to a new position. As he neared the back of the arena, he came close to one of the jungle cats, and Madoc found himself yelling for the boy to move as the animal swiped at him with its monstrous paw.

The boy ducked just in time, but as the animal crouched to attack again, it twisted, its head ducked low in pain, and stumbled to its side. Behind it, an Animal Divine warrior lowered his hands from where he'd reached and drawn out the beast's life force, and he roared, bioseia flooding his veins.

Before he could attack, he was swept into the air by a Lak fighter and flung into the stands.

"Oh my," Aera giggled.

Madoc could feel the tingle of her victory dancing over his skin, and beyond it, the pulse of her energeia—a cool, invisible fog. It was different than this morning in the carriage. This was unchecked and unprotected, and as the moments passed, he became more aware of it, until his vision had fallen out of focus and he'd lost track of the boy in the crowd.

He eased closer to Aera, a dark hunger licking his soul. Everyone was distracted now. If the goddess of air didn't notice Madoc sipping the smallest bit of her energeia, would anyone else? Would Anathrasa?

Now might be his best chance to test how much, if any, he could take without her noticing.

Inhaling, he felt Aera's consciousness, light as a cloud. When he grasped for it with his anathreia, it slipped away. Drawing back, he steadied himself, then tried again.

Just a little, he thought.

He kept his eyes on the battle, vaguely acknowledging the four Earth Divine fighters who'd made a clay wall to block the attacks of the other two divinities. The Air Divine were picking off Biotus's warriors one by one, and soon had turned on the Deimans.

Madoc pressed against the threshold of Aera's energeia, invisible strands of his anathreia reaching for the goddess's soul. The sweet taste of spun sugar filled his mouth, then was gone a second later.

Aera flinched. She looked behind her, as if someone had tapped her on the shoulder.

"Wine?"

Madoc turned sharply to find Anathrasa standing beside him. She'd taken two goblets off a tray and was extending one toward Madoc.

He accepted it with a shaking hand but didn't drink. Had she known what he was trying to do? Was that why she'd interrupted him?

He tried to read her emotions, but his anathreia was unsteady from trying to tithe on Aera, so he searched her face for confirmation, only to find her staring at her reflection in the silver goblet with a frown.

"I've given you the finest bed in the palace in hopes that your good sleep will get rid of these bags under my eyes." She pulled gently at the corner of one eye, flattening the wrinkles. "I don't think it's helped, do you?"

The fight before him faded. Aera, who'd moved away to watch with her guards, slipped from his mind.

"So we are connected." He knew this—he'd seen it—and yet her confirmation made his chest feel as though it was filled with stones.

Anathrasa lowered the goblet, meeting his gaze with an unamused stare. "There are no accounts of mortals and gods who have been linked in this way before." Her chin lifted. "Then again, there are no accounts of mortals living after an attack on their god, either."

A shiver worked its way down Madoc's chest. So she did think what he'd done to her on the ship had caused this. He wasn't sure if that made him feel proud, or incredibly stupid.

She opened her hand, eyeing the scar across her palm. It had healed quickly—perhaps she was like Madoc in that way—but it still sent a new wave of fear through him.

She knew, or at least suspected, what he'd done last night.

"How does it work, I wonder?" she mused, her voice quiet amid the screams around them. "You didn't feel anything strange last night after you cut your hand, did you? Anything on your shoulder?" He flinched as she pushed open the collar of his robe, examining his right shoulder the way Aera had done this morning.

Wariness scrunched his brows. "Should I have, Mother Goddess?"

She moved the strap of her dress to the side, showing a red scab.

Had she cut herself as he had, to see if he'd bleed?

He was just starting to grasp what this might mean—that he could hurt her without being hurt in return—when she leaned down to a rosebush beside her and wrapped her fist around the thorned stem beneath a white blossom.

A pinch of pain ricocheted up his right hand, and when he looked down, he saw four points of blood beading on his palm.

"Interesting," she said, wiping her bloody palm on a servant girl standing behind them. "So why didn't it work last night? What were you doing?"

He'd been with Elias after the garden. Was it merely a matter of proximity, or had her attempt to hurt him not worked because of something else?

All he and Elias had been doing was talking. It didn't make sense.

"Nothing," he said. "I was in my room."

"No doubt plotting my demise," she said with a grim smile. "First a cut on the hand, then a knife to the heart, hmm?"

Again, a dark question penetrated his thoughts. If he died, would she die also? If he ceased to exist, this war could be over in moments. His family would be free. Ash wouldn't have to fight.

But he had to be certain it would work.

Frantically, he replayed last night's events. He and Elias had gone to the barn. They'd talked about Anathrasa. About Ash. It had been a welcome relief from the tension he'd felt since arriving back in Crixion.

Why hadn't her experiment worked, as his had? What had been different?

He'd been content with Elias. He'd felt *safe.*

Was that it? Was the difference as simple as the comfort of his brother's presence?

Straightening, Anathrasa turned to him, the sun glinting off her light hair. "Believe me, son, it will take more than your death to kill me. I've tithed enough souls to keep us alive a long, long time. Trying to end your life will only inconvenience us both."

He was equally relieved and disappointed.

"What do we do about this?" he asked carefully.

Her eyes met his, and a strange look crossed her face—something like hope, but more desperate. Though he was reluctant to believe it, part of him wondered if Anathrasa wanted his help.

He could use that to his advantage.

"We make ourselves strong," she said. "So that I can fix what has been broken."

"You mean so that you can rule the six countries." His tone had gone hard.

She inhaled slowly, locking her gaze on his. Even in this younger body, his old neighbor was still visible, looking at him as if she could see every unconscious desire that lurked within.

He bit the inside of his cheek, trying to remain steady. Trying not to think of Cassia.

"I was wrong to split my soul for these gods," she said quietly enough that no one, gods included, could hear. "When I made them, I thought they would love their children as I loved them, but they became worse than mortals. Fighting for power. Fighting for land. Turning on me, the one who made them." She made a sound of disgust that had his jaw clenching. "They're bent on destroying everything."

Aera and Biotus had turned on her in the past, as well, yet now they were preparing to stand beside her in war. Aera had even seemed to pity Anathrasa and her trusting nature. Perhaps she didn't know the Mother Goddess was speaking this way about her behind her back.

Or perhaps this speech was a lie, meant to lure Madoc in.

"So you'll destroy them instead?" he asked, wondering again where Biotus had gone when he'd left the grand arena. Was he truly investigating the delayed arrival of his people, or was he doing something for Anathrasa?

"Your mother's son, through and through." She inhaled slowly. "Yes. Help me, and you'll be free to do what you will."

"And the Metaxas?"

She smiled tightly. "We'll see how loyal you truly prove to be."

He froze, the shouts of the crowd drowned out by the buzzing in his ears. "What would you have me do?"

She faced him, leaning her hip against the railing. "Return the six gods' powers to me so that I can reunite the mortal world under one reigning goddess."

He scoffed. "You want me to take the energeias from Aera and Biotus?"

Anathrasa smiled, a look filled with dangerous promise. "Why do you think I called them here?"

He remembered the conversation with Aera earlier and was now certain she didn't know Anathrasa's true intent: to drain two gods, just as he'd come here to do.

"Biotus is very strong, and Aera, though she doesn't look it, is cunning. She'll be hard to pin down. You'll need my help." Anathrasa turned back to the fighting. "Which leaves the energeias you gave to the Kulan girl."

Ash. At the mention, Madoc's chest seized.

"We'll have to get them back when she arrives. It won't be easy. Not many are trained for the arena as thoroughly as your little gladiator friend," Anathrasa continued, motioning toward the fight below. "Clearly."

Madoc forced his eyes back to the fight so that he didn't give away his anger. His gaze found the boy just as he was hit in the shoulder by an arrow and thrown backward with a stunted cry.

Madoc felt as if the wind had been knocked out of him.

"Stop this," he said. "I'll help you, but please. These people aren't fighters."

"Neither were you," said Anathrasa, almost sounding proud. "The time has come for us all to be champions."

Below him, a Deiman woman sprinted toward the boy, her shoulders gleaming with ill-fitting silver armor, her hair shaved up one side and braided down the other. She grabbed the boy under the arms and dragged him aside, then sent a quake of sand toward two approaching Air Divine warriors, knocking them to the ground.

Half the fighters were strewn across the sand, bleeding and moaning, or fighting to stand. The cats were all down. One tossed its head in obvious pain. The others were drained, their lush white coats now clinging to their bones as if they'd been starved to death.

Only three fighters remained standing. Two Lak men, and the Deiman woman with the braid in her hair who'd helped the boy. They approached each other cautiously from three points of a triangle, their bodies heavy with fatigue but their hands raised and deadly.

"Please." Anger seared beneath Madoc's skin; it took all his control to keep his expression even. "If you truly want to win the heart of Deimos, you'll need more than just its finest fighters."

He couldn't watch this. He didn't know what he intended to do, but he couldn't stay here with her. He couldn't pretend this was all right.

Her chin lifted. "There is little room for mercy in times like these, Madoc."

He bit back a scoff. "There is no better time for mercy," he argued, aware now that he'd caught the eye of some of the others in the box, who were watching and whispering. "Tomorrow these champions will be forgotten, and the people who watched them fight will return to their broken lives—a life I knew well before I stepped into the arena." When she flinched, he stepped closer, but it wasn't her face he saw. It was Ilena, calling him *son* when his own father wouldn't. Cassia, who'd taken Madoc's hand and led him to what he would learn to call home. Elias, his brother in all the ways that mattered. Madoc knew he should be placating Anathrasa, earning her favor, but trust was earned with truth, and he was done standing by while gods used mortals as tools.

"Give them blood and they're yours for a day," he told her. "Show them mercy, and they're yours for a lifetime."

Without another word, he left the box.

It was a short walk to the Temple of Geoxus—not the sanctuary, where the fallen statue lay, but the sheltered area behind it, still enclosed by a singed wall. A guard at the arena, flushed with stress, had told Madoc that this was where the injured would be brought after the fight. The city hospital was already overrun with survivors from the riots, and the healers could not afford to leave those they were already caring for.

Madoc climbed the stone steps, blinking at the metal slot on the tall door where offerings were collected. He'd delivered his street fight winnings here, and once, long before, gotten his arm caught trying to steal coin to buy food.

He knocked twice, and when no answer came, he pushed the door inward. The courtyard was crowded with injured fighters—some propped against the walls or each other, others strewn out over the ground. Centurions and priests in white robes ran between them. Groans of pain filled the air, accented by crying and calls for help.

"No more room," a centurion snapped at him. "If there's anyone else, they're on their own."

"I'm here to help," Madoc said, chest tight.

The guard only shook his head and jogged toward the well, where a dozen people were fighting over a pail of water.

Memories clogged Madoc's throat. Inside these walls, he'd slept on bunks with dozens of other children—orphans, runaways, those who'd been shut out of their homes like he had. He'd been given food and water, and taught the proper ways to pray to Geoxus, with one hand on a stone and gratitude in his heart.

As he stepped into the dusty courtyard, a centurion shoved the wooden door closed behind him. The scent of blood and bile had him fighting the urge to gag. Pain was so thick in the air, he coughed breathing it in.

He shouldn't have come. He couldn't help these people. He'd healed Ash once, but that had been an accident. Maybe he could help clean wounds or bandage injuries—he'd worked as a stonemason long enough to know how to patch someone up after a stone broke or slid free from its mooring—but he didn't know where to start.

Biting back a surge of helplessness, he caught the arm of a passing priest—a young man whose lips were white with the chalk that had been smeared across his mouth.

"What can I do?" he asked.

The priest looked him over, brows scrunching in confusion at Madoc's fine cloak. They both knew this was not a place for privilege.

"Water," the priest said a moment later. "Make them comfortable. It's the least we can do before the circle is complete."

Madoc didn't know what this meant, but the priest was already gone.

Rolling up his sleeves, Madoc raced to the well. He filled a bucket with water and grabbed a ladle, then moved to a man with a mangled foot, offering a sip. Two girls, no more than seventeen, followed, blinking at the sky and prodding weeping cuts on their heads. He knelt beside a man in a dusty white robe who was crouched over a child with a puncture wound in his shoulder. Madoc recognized the boy from the arena—he'd been the one saved by the Deiman woman with the braid in her hair. His brow was pale and sweaty now, and he fought for air with quick, raspy breaths.

"I have water," Madoc said.

"He needs more than water."

Madoc's chin jerked up at the familiar rasp of the man's voice. "Tyber?"

The priest touched his jaw as Madoc's gaze lowered to the smear of white chalk over his mouth that had been mostly wiped away by sweat. Though his brows scrunched, he did not seem surprised at Madoc's presence.

"Much has changed since you were last here," Tyber said.

"You included," Madoc answered. It wasn't a question, but Tyber nodded anyway.

"The circle is loyal to Anathrasa's cause. We spread her message to the people."

"What circle?" Madoc asked tightly, his gaze falling again to the boy. "What are you talking about?"

"All priests of the Father God are recommitted to Anathrasa now," Tyber said. "We are part of her circle. The circle of energeia. Of life. The Mother Goddess is the bringing back together of all things, and we serve her to avenge Geoxus. Her return signifies a rebirth for the world. In the ashes of Geoxus's death, the Mother Goddess has returned to bring peace."

A bitter taste filled Madoc's mouth. "Forgive me, Tyber, but this doesn't look like peace."

"Peace is earned in sweat and blood," Tyber answered simply. "You of all people should know that, Madoc."

Madoc cringed, thinking of the ribs he'd been able to count when he'd lived here. Of the home he'd found with the Metaxas after Cassia had found him on the temple steps.

"This boy fought bravely to serve the Mother Goddess," Tyber said. "His wound is beyond the work of our priests. If his lung collapses, there's nothing more we can do."

Anger mingled with pity, turning Madoc's muscles to lead. This boy didn't deserve to die—not for Anathrasa, or any god. He was only a child.

Madoc's mind shot to Ash, who had watched her mother battle in the arena for as long as she could remember . She'd always known Char's fate would be to kill or die. He wondered if Ash had been told the same thing—that she'd have to fight bravely to honor Ignitus.

How easily he'd once believed Geoxus deserved such glory.

"Dying honors no one," Madoc said bitterly. Anathreia pulsed inside him, angry. Hungry. He could feel the tempest of emotions all around him, and the growing demand inside him to draw from their souls and soothe his own fury.

Shame rose in his throat.

The boy gave a rattling gasp, drawing Madoc's focus to a point. He dropped the water bucket beside him, the contents sloshing out onto the dusty ground. He couldn't look away from the boy's face, twisted in pain, and his trembling blue lips. The pain and fear rose in ragged waves, and Madoc longed to take it to comfort him.

To drain him.

No. He didn't want that. He wanted to save the boy the way he'd saved Ash.

Ash.

He'd healed her once, in the arena after Elias had attacked her. He remembered, with a twist of his gut, how Hydra had said Ash had been dead before that.

He shook the thought from his head. If he was strong enough, he could save this boy. But when he'd healed Ash, he'd used too much energeia and nearly died from the exertion. He couldn't risk depleting his strength and failing his task with Aera and Biotus just to save one person—one *stranger*—even if he wanted to.

If he could tithe on someone the way Anathrasa had once told him, he could be strong enough to heal this boy with soul energy. If Madoc could tithe on the boy's pain, maybe he could make himself powerful enough to heal him.

Shaking, Madoc swallowed and focused on the beads of sweat across the boy's pale brow. He reached toward him with his consciousness, the air shivering between them like the sky over hot sand. The boy's pain was a beacon, as bright as any emotion he'd ever sensed.

I won't hurt you, he willed the child to know, but the boy only squeezed his eyes shut and held his breath.

"Madoc?" Tyber asked, worry thinning his voice. "What are you doing?"

Carefully, Madoc inhaled, pulling that bright spot of pain away from the boy, into himself, until he could taste the sour bite of it in the back of his jaw.

His anathreia sighed in pleasure. It didn't care what part of the soul he fed on as long as it was sated, and Madoc gasped, feeling as though he hadn't truly breathed in weeks.

He exhaled and sent a warm wave of soul energy over the boy. It blanketed him, soaking into his pores like rain into parched earth.

The boy shivered.

Tyber gave a surprised grunt. "Madoc, what is this?"

Madoc blinked, finding the arrow wound in the boy's shoulder now gone. The boy took a steady breath. He sat up, and when he rolled his arm in a slow circle, he smiled.

Then he launched himself into Madoc's arms.

Whispers rose around them, excited murmurs and heated spikes of energeia, but Madoc didn't care. He'd done it. He'd healed someone without hurting them and was somehow stronger than before. When he looked up, he saw his own shock mirrored on Tyber's face.

"How did you do that?" Tyber asked as the boy ran off, telling everyone he passed what Madoc had done.

"By tithing."

Madoc's stomach dropped at the sound of Anathrasa's voice. He stood at once, finding the Mother Goddess making her way through the courtyard, flanked by centurions.

"That is what you came here to do, isn't it? Save these poor people?" As she approached Madoc, a circle formed around them. Centurions and circle priests, but others too. The injured began moving toward them—limping, dragging themselves closer. The Earth Divine seemed eager to do whatever she might ask, but he also saw Air Divine and Animal Divine, battered from the fight, who clung to the back of the group with wary looks on their faces.

Madoc was staggered by the sudden fear of what Anathrasa might do. He tried to tell himself to be calm, that even after all he'd said to her, he could not risk severing her trust. But if she intended to harm these people further, he would not stand by.

"At your wishes, Mother Goddess," he said carefully. "I know you didn't want anyone to suffer needlessly in these games."

A muscle in her neck twitched, and he braced for her wrath. Instead, she smiled.

"Tithing?" Tyber was standing now, too, and looked to Madoc, confused.

"Children of Deimos, Lakhu, and Cenhelm," Anathrasa interrupted, raising her arms. "The Earth Divine's beloved Geoxus may have been rendered mortal by Ignitus and murdered by the God Killer, but all is not lost."

At the mention of Ash—the "God Killer," as Anathrasa had named her—Madoc's knees threatened to buckle. He could still hear Anathrasa screaming about what Ash had done as the Kulans dragged him out of the crumbling palace, the raging power of both gods inside him.

Rendered mortal by Ignitus. He didn't realize Anathrasa was spreading that lie, but it made sense. Better to have the people think only a god could tear down another god, rather than a mortal like them.

"My son has been returned to me."

Madoc's teeth pressed together. He couldn't believe she'd just claimed him as her son. His gaze spun around the courtyard, wariness rising in him as he gauged the wide-eyed responses of those who listened. He couldn't help thinking of when Petros had done the same in front of Geoxus, and the gladiators he'd been training with at Lucius's villa had suddenly wanted him dead.

Anathrasa walked a slow circle around him. "Geoxus made my son a champion to show the people of Deimos how he would fight for your honor regardless of lineage. The god of earth protected Madoc, as he protected me, in the hope that one day Madoc would be embraced by his father's people." Anathrasa paused, giving Madoc a strange look of fondness that made him want to crawl out of his skin. "When the God Killer and Ignitus's gladiators stole my son from us, I thought him lost. But he persevered, just as he did in the great arena. He returned to fight for Deimos."

The relief Madoc felt at healing the boy was replaced by a bolt of panic. For all he knew, these people thought he was an Earth Divine gladiator—that was what Geoxus had said when he'd chosen Madoc for the Honored Eight to fight for Deimos in the war against Kula. But now they knew he wasn't what he'd claimed.

Whispers rose, prickling a defensive shield over Madoc's skin. He felt as if he were balancing on the edge of a knife, torn between running and holding his ground. But the people were nodding now, looking at him with wonder in their eyes, and when Anathrasa touched his shoulder fondly, they didn't flee.

He couldn't tell if that was because they bought her story, or because of the centurions now blocking every exit of the courtyard.

"I've sent Madoc here to continue his fight on the streets of Crixion," Anathrasa continued. "With the people he was raised to defend."

Madoc shuddered at her acknowledgment of his street fights with Elias. Anathrasa may have accepted his claim that he'd come here at her bidding, but it hardly relieved him. What was she playing at? One word, and her centurions could slaughter everyone in this courtyard. There was a reason she was going along with his claim, and he doubted it had anything to do with mercy.

Tyber hastened a woman to the front of the circle. She leaned heavily against another fighter, unable to walk, and based on the limp swing of her ankle, it looked as if her leg had been broken below the knee. Her tight grimace of pain tugged at Madoc's wariness.

"Will you help her, Madoc?" Tyber asked.

"I . . ." Madoc stumbled back a step. He glanced to Anathrasa, who smiled.

"I've heard this is the perfect time for mercy," she said quietly.

It was a trick, but he didn't know what else to do. His palms were sweating.

"Energeia is an unending cycle of give-and-take. I created Geoxus, and Geoxus created this woman. These people are all part of anathreia, and all part of you. This is the unending circle."

He glanced to Tyber, to the smear of chalk over his mouth. *Her return signifies a rebirth for the world. In the ashes of Geoxus's death, the Mother Goddess has returned to bring peace.*

"Pretty sentiment," Madoc said. "But why did you create something just to abuse it? Is that all we are to you—pigstock to feed off of?"

Again, Madoc could feel that hunger rearing inside him, gnawing at his control.

His gaze dropped to the woman, to the fear and hope in her eyes. He could help her. Even if Anathrasa was telling him to do it, it wasn't wrong. It had been his idea first. That boy was alive because of him.

"You'll tithe on her, just as you tithed on that child. Just as you tithed on Petros," Anathrasa said quietly, coming close. "Just as you tithed on the gladiator Jann in the arena when you pulled out his self-control. You took Ash's pain that day, Madoc. Her broken parts. You fed on them and left her changed. *Better.* Everything you think you've done has begun with extraction."

Madoc's gaze shot to Anathrasa. He'd felt this with the boy—the pull and push of energeia, like completing a circle.

"If you can't take from the willing, how will you do what you must with those who refuse? With those who now know what you're capable of?"

The threat whispered over his skin like the promising touch of a blade. She could pretend as much as she liked that he was her beloved son, but they both knew the truth. He was only as valuable as his ability to drain Aera and Biotus.

"The circle is unending," Tyber said, and other priests behind him took up the chant in an eerie, low tone. "The circle is unending."

Madoc reset his mind to the task she'd ordered. He looked at the woman, knowing his mind had already been made up. He would help her, and if Anathrasa wanted Deimos to think it was her idea, that was fine. Maybe it would prove his loyalty to her.

She would never suspect that the air and animal energeia he'd promised her would go to Ash.

He closed his eyes, and tithed on the woman's pain, finding it easier to take the second time. Healing her was easier too, and when it was done, he felt the thrum of power in his veins.

"You're a gift." Tyber clasped his hands together. "A gift from the Mother Goddess!" He bowed at Madoc's feet, the same man who'd once freed him from an offering box and smacked him upside the head for trying to steal. He and the other priests started herding the injured into lines to be healed.

This was good, Madoc told himself, even though something about it didn't feel right. He accepted the woman's thanks, and when she kissed his hand, he didn't object.

Beside him, Anathrasa smiled.

"The circle is complete," she said.

TEN

ASH

"ASH!"

Ash jolted awake, fingers splayed and body awash with cold sweat before she even knew where she was. Pinpricks of blue fire lit on her palms, ready to throw, ready to fight—

The speckled beige of the petrified wood walls came into focus. The floor was clean now; all traces of Ash's blood were gone, the broken vines and razor leaves removed. Florus must have come in while Ash was unconscious. At least he wasn't forcing her to stay trapped with her own carnage.

At that thought, Ash turned and vomited against the wall.

"Ash! Are you in there?"

She blinked, dazed, wiping one hand across her lips and swallowing, throat dry and sour.

That voice—it wasn't Florus. Was she drugged again? Part of her soul squeezed with the longing to be hallucinating. She had seen Char. She needed her mother right now, or Tor, or—

A fist pounded on the outside of the box. "Ash! ASH!"

Something heavier crashed against it, but the walls didn't so much as rattle.

Ash flew to the corner where she'd heard the voice. "Tor?"

How had he found her? She didn't even know where she was—

A pause, then the crash came again. "I'm getting you out of here."

His calm, collected voice dragged a sob from the pit of her lungs, forcing her to shove her fist against her mouth, quelling her need to scream.

"You're here," she managed, and a tear fled down her cheek.

Of course he'd found her. Of course he'd save her.

Another crash came, followed by the sounds of something shattering outside. "Damn it—what is this made out of? My igneia's doing nothing, and I can't break it."

"Fossilized wood," Ash said. "Fire won't burn it."

"Damn it," Tor cursed again. The noises of his efforts stilled. "What do you see in there? Can you—can you do anything with igneia?"

He meant Ignitus's igneia, but he didn't say it.

"I tried, but it didn't make any difference."

Tor was silent a beat. "You have Ignitus's powers," he said. "Maybe you can move like a god too? Can you travel through igneia?"

Another sob built, but Ash willed it down. Oh, she was a god, more than even Tor knew. She touched the spots on her tattered seal-skin suit where Florus's razor leaves had speared her.

"All right," she said. "I'll try. Where are we? What's out there?"

"We're in Itza," he said. "In Florus's palace."

Panic turned her cold. "Is he here?"

"Don't worry about him right now. We're alone."

Alone? Florus didn't have her under guard?

Or had Tor killed everyone to get to her?

It didn't matter—what mattered was that she would *not* lose her chance.

Ash braced herself on her hands and knees. The tart smell of vomit was choking her, but she willed her mind to focus on the gritty petrified wood, on the weight of her own body.

How did the gods travel through the very ether using their energeias? Was it just a thought? When she'd managed to hear through fire and see Igna, it had been almost an unconscious will, just a focus and a wish—

Ash's fingers curled against the wood and she willed herself to dissolve into flames. She thought of Tor, standing just outside this box. If they were in Itza, in Florus's palace, did that mean the room was made of the same kinds of vines that Florus had dragged everywhere? Ash should have asked before she risked burning a hole through the floor. Hopefully they were on solid earth—

That word echoed through her mind. *Earth.*

The floor rose under Ash's palm.

She rocked back, gaping at the wood. It stayed in a slightly curved position before melting back to become flush with the floor.

Eyes wide, Ash waited, expecting Florus to appear. He had to have done that.

"Ash?" Tor's voice was pinched. "Are you all right? What's happening?"

"I—I think I moved the wood." Ash stared at the spot. "But it isn't *wood*, not really. How—is this a trick? Where is Florus?"

"He's not here, Ash. So whatever happened was *you*. What was it?"

"The floor. I think I made it move."

Tor was silent, and Ash knew what look was on his face—calculating, thoughtful, focused.

"It's fossilized wood," he said, "so no hydreia, no igneia. But . . . it has geoeia."

"No." But Ash hesitated. "Florus told me I couldn't manipulate it because it was only plant, that he'd taken all other energeias out of it to fossilize it."

"Touch it again. Try whatever you did before. Maybe there's more to this petrified wood than what Florus said."

Her breath held, Ash leaned forward and spread her palm flat on the wood again. She focused on the rough petrified wood, the long, thin fragments forever frozen together. It was mostly floreia, plant life suspended in time; she felt that and could do nothing about it.

But there was more to it. Tiny particles clinging to the once-wood that made her gasp.

This fossil wasn't quite anything—because it was pieces of *everything*.

It was air. She breathed, but aereia wasn't hers yet.

It had once been fire, heat and pressure bearing down on these trees to transform them. But the fire was long gone.

And, most important, it was stone.

Yes, this petrified wood was mostly plant—but Ash could feel grains of stone buried in the petrified wood. They didn't rage strongly like igneia did, but the geoeia was there all the same, quiet and steady and strong.

"Geoeia!" She kept her eyes closed, her voice tight with relief. "Tor—it's geoeia!"

"Open this box," he told her. "You have Geoxus's power now? Use it. Remember how he moved—thunderous but intentional, heavy and grounded."

Ash's brow furrowed and sweat popped up along her hairline.

She couldn't treat geoeia like igneia, just as she hadn't been able to treat hydreia like igneia either. Geoeia was in no hurry. It was content to wait and watch, so much of what Ash was not.

On a deep inhale, Ash called out to the stone particles around her. Some responded, tingling to life at the pull of her geoeia. One type of rock was strongest, shards of it all around her, humming at her awareness.

"Quartz," she said, half to herself, half to Tor.

"Ah—Geoxus loved quartz. Remember? He'd drape himself in it. Rose and white and gray and black. Make it listen to you. You are its god now."

Ash seized that thought. *I am your god now.*

Quartz was like a long-beloved pet of the earth god, and it reacted to Ash, thousands of slivers of it vibrating in every strand of petrified wood.

Ash contracted her fingers, each one curling slowly, steadily. She was in no rush.

Then she *pushed.*

The floor of the petrified wood prison trembled, bucking Ash backward.

"Good, Ash!" Tor called.

She held her grip on the quartz, forcing every particle of it to expand outward, dragging the plant and air particles with it—

The room quivered, and cracked, and exploded apart.

Ash tucked into a ball as pieces of the petrified wood prison erupted around her. When the last one stilled, she yanked her hands down and blinked through the dust and debris.

Tor was upon her in an instant, scooping her to her feet and sweeping her into a bear hug. She clung to him, arms knotted around his neck, hanging off the ground with the force of his grip around her waist.

He set her down abruptly and looked her over from head to toe, noting the smears of dried blood on her body, her tattered clothing. "Are you all right? Where are you hurt?"

Ash scrubbed the heel of her hand across her eyes, clearing her tears. "I'm fine," she lied, because physically, she was. Everything else about her, though—her mind, her heart, her soul—teetered on the brink of collapse. But she couldn't break down yet.

The space they were in was a kind of holding cell. A low ceiling and wide floor were covered in velvety moss of the softest, calmest shade of hunter green, and steps at the edge of the room led to an open iron door.

"What's happening?" Ash looked back up at Tor. He was outfitted for battle, no surprise, and his eyes were bloodshot, likely from lack of sleep.

"How long have I been missing?" she amended, though she wasn't sure she wanted to know the answer.

Tor's face was grim. "Over a week."

Ash rocked backward. A *week*? Gods, what had happened in that time—to Hydra, to their building army, to Anathrasa's own growing power, but mostly, to *Madoc*?

In response to the questions on Ash's face, Tor's lips thinned. "Hydra has been here, looking for you. I followed just behind with a Water Divine crew. Hydra sensed this box by means of the water in these plants, but she had me come for you—she and Florus are in his throne room." Darkness raced across Tor's face. "Biotus is here."

Ash blinked, stunned. "What? Why?"

"He's demanding they surrender to Anathrasa and come with him to Crixion."

"Anathrasa said we had a month before she'd make a move!" But the plea sounded childlike in Ash's ears. Of course Anathrasa hadn't waited; likely she'd said that after the battle in the Apuit Islands just so she could get away.

A low growl rumbled in her throat. *Stupid.* How could she not have foreseen this? Believing in Anathrasa's promise of a timeline had made Ash soft, made her *weak*—

Tor touched her shoulders. "We all believed her, Ash." His face softened. "We're going back to the Apuit Islands," he said, and took a step away.

But Ash stayed in place.

"And leave Hydra to face Biotus?" Ash shook her head. "She's earned my help."

"She's a *goddess*, Ash. She can handle this."

"We need Hydra to prepare for our own attack. And I need floreia."

That made Ash's chest swell. With all she had endured at the plant god's hands, she was *not* leaving Itza without his energeia.

And with Biotus here, she would make him give her bioseia too. She would get it all.

Ash pushed around Tor. "Take me to them or go back to the Apuit Islands yourself."

"Ash." Tor said her name, a warning. "We're leaving. You need to rest."

Instinct screamed for Ash to listen to him. The gods were distracted now—she could get back on the boat Tor had used and flee to the Apuit Islands. She could get as far away from Florus—and Biotus—as possible.

Her insides clenched with a desperate wail that she managed to choke down. She wanted to get away. She was tired and hungry and sore, and she was terrified still—so terrified that she was shaking before she could stop herself.

Fury overcame her, pushed down for the past hours—days?— beneath her terror. But it leaped at her call now, raging and ready to obey and destroy.

"I need," she said, running a tongue over her lips, "*floreia.*"

The world dissolved in orange and gilded blue, and before Ash could stop herself, she was an inferno. The moss-covered room faded around her.

Hydra. Go to Hydra.

The next thing she knew, Hydra was shrieking.

"What the—*Ash*?" Her voice was sharp with shock and fear, but Ash barely had the sense to focus on that.

She'd done it. She'd traveled through fire. She glanced down at her body. Alongside the melted divots she'd made in Hydra's ice platform, her sealskin suit was entirely burned up, leaving only her fireproof Kulan underthings.

And she was in Florus's throne room.

A towering ceiling arched over a long, narrow floor. Like that storage room, every surface was covered in moss, but peppered with trees and branches and vines—Ash expected to hear the chirping of birds or the buzzing of insects, but the silence around her was thick. Not the peaceful silence of a still forest; the tense silence of a held breath.

Hydra stood next to her, tears in her eyes, hands to her mouth. Her watery eyes shot from Ash to the two gods beside her, and she looked like she was only barely restraining herself from grabbing Ash in a hug.

But Florus was here, too, sitting on a throne made of one solid piece of tree trunk, formed and curved to his body. He stared at her, his expression blank; Ash appearing here was probably the last thing he'd expected.

Right now, Florus was the least of Ash's concerns.

The god of bioseia towered next to Florus, clearly someone who was used to his size being intimidating enough to make everyone cower. Pelts of various furs were bundled over one shoulder, not for warmth, but more like trophies of kills, and he wore only worn fur wrappings around his muscular thighs. His pale chest was cut with swollen muscles, veins bulged up his rippling neck, and his dark eyes were filled with intensity beneath thick braids of red-brown hair.

He looked as though he'd been in the middle of yelling. His dark eyes locked on Ash, like an animal sensing prey.

His intensity took on a seductive air and he made a show of slowly analyzing her. "Well, well. Anathrasa mentioned I might run into you—Ash Nikau, is it? The mortal who thinks she can defeat gods."

Ash returned his look with a grim smile. "I *have* defeated gods."

His facade tightened. "I didn't come here to waste breath on a mortal girl," he spat. He looked back at Florus. "I'm done playing games. I'm taking all of you to Crixion. You'd be smart to come quietly, or I'll have fun laying waste to your islands with my creatures."

Ash noted then that the room was empty except for the four of them. There were surely mortals living in Florus's palace—had they gotten to safety? She had to hope so.

"That's all this is—you playing Anathrasa's servant?" Hydra stepped closer, hands on her hips. "Does she make you fetch her robe for her, too?"

Biotus growled. "Careful. I've broken you once, I can break you again."

Hydra's nostrils flared, her cheeks reddening. Ash didn't know what Biotus had meant by that, but she was ready to fight if Hydra moved.

The water goddess needed no one's help, though. Hydra surged toward Biotus, rising high on a small wave of water that shot out of the plants at their feet. She was level with his soulless eyes. "We both know you did nothing but obey Aera's orders just as you're obeying Anathrasa now. You are a chained dog, Biotus, and I will drown you."

She reared a fist back, but vines shot up from the floor and twisted around her wrist.

Hydra whipped a glare at Florus, who was now standing.

"We'll go with you, Biotus," Florus said. "Willingly."

Biotus swung on him with a manic grin.

Ash watched the plant god, who was looking straight at her, and wavered, the healed wounds from his attack aching.

"If," Florus added, "you can defeat my champion."

Biotus's grin tightened. "Your champion? Ha! I'll rip any Plant Divine to—"

But Florus pointed at Ash. "Not Plant Divine. Her."

ELEVEN

MADOC

"I DON'T UNDERSTAND why everything must be white," Ilena muttered as a tight-lipped servant fastened a silver circle brooch to the front of her pristine white gown. She and Elias had been sent to Madoc's room to prepare for tonight's ball, a celebration Anathrasa had announced after Madoc's visit to the temple, ten days ago.

"It will be stained before they even bring out the feast," she continued, worrying her bottom lip between her teeth. "Someone's going to bump into me and spill their wine and this beautiful gown will be ruined."

Elias passed Madoc a knowing look as he adjusted the belt over his own white tunic. Ilena had been making subtle jabs about the ball all week. At first she'd been careful not to say anything in front of the palace staff, but as the days grew closer, she'd become bolder with her complaints.

It wasn't hard to figure out why. After Anathrasa's announcement in the temple, word had spread of her mortal son—a human with the healing power of anathreia. Hundreds of Deimos's most influential citizens would gather to celebrate his return tonight, and Ilena, who had loved Madoc as her own since he was six years old, was not taking the news well.

She wasn't alone, either. It was one thing for Anathrasa to announce their connection to a courtyard of injured fighters, but entirely another to stand before the most powerful people in Deimos and admit that Madoc had not been the Earth Divine gladiator they'd once called champion. He shuddered to think what the gladiators he used to train with would say about that. Given Lucius's bitter expression at the arena ten days prior, he doubted the old sponsor would be too happy about it.

He paced toward Ilena, the servant backing away wordlessly to give him room. There was little they could say without being overheard, so he simply hugged her close, calmed by the steel grip of her wiry arms.

"You look lovely, Mother." It didn't matter who claimed him, or why. Ilena would always be his true mother.

When he pulled back, her lip trembled.

"I don't like this, Madoc," she said. "I don't like being this close to her. Not after what she did."

Memory punched into Madoc's chest. Every moment around Ilena brought thoughts of Cassia, and usually he managed to focus on other things to avoid the pain. But this moment, Ilena's closeness brought memories of Cassia raging up through his mind and heart, the ache of missing her like a scar on his soul.

"I know," he whispered.

"If she touches another one of my children, I . . ." Her hands fisted in his tunic.

Madoc squeezed her shoulders.

"I know," he said again.

Elias cleared his throat, gaze tilting to the servant who entered the room with a box of hairpins for Ilena. It was safe to assume Anathrasa's staff was listening to everything.

"We've hardly seen you this week," he said, changing the subject as he sat on the edge of Madoc's bed. "Where have you been?"

"Everywhere," Madoc answered, aware of the guards just outside the door, and the woman now trying to twist up Ilena's unruly hair. "We went to the poorhouses in South Gate. Then the stonemason's quarter. The shelters along the Nien River. I've been ti—" He swallowed the word, not wanting to worry his family. "Healing people."

After Anathrasa had seen the way the people responded to his work in the sanctuary, she'd prepared a tour around Crixion to earn the people's loyalty. It was a chance for Madoc not only to gain her approval—something he'd need if she was going to be aware of him taking Aera's and Biotus's energeias—but also for him to continue to test their connection in small, subtle ways.

When her focus was elsewhere, as it had been when she'd been trying to tithe in the garden, he could harm her. A small pinch to his arm or rib had her absently rubbing the afflicted area.

When she was agitated, as she frequently became at her guards and servants, he could prick her heel by stepping on a small rock.

When she was pleased with his healing, and with the gratitude of the people, nothing he did got to her.

It had to be a matter of distraction. Tor had talked about being strong, protecting the people and things that mattered with the power he'd been given. Anathrasa had tried to wound him after he'd interrupted her tithing—a cut to her shoulder that he'd never felt. He'd been with Elias then at the palace barn. He'd felt like he had before all this began—when it was just the two of them, taking on the brutes of the city in a street fight.

He'd felt safe, because Elias had his back.

At the gladiator games, the thorns on the rose Anathrasa had grasped had cut his hand. He'd been anxious about the fighting. When she'd been angry at him on the docks, she'd attacked him and felt the slap.

Every time they hurt each other they'd been upset.

If that vulnerability made them weak, then he needed to guard himself against it. Keep calm. Keep his temper in check. If not, she could injure him.

Maybe even do more. Apart from tithing on the servant girl in the garden, Anathrasa hadn't shown an ability to fully use anathreia yet, but she might not need it. If she didn't trust him, she could keep him in line through pain.

"Healing people." Ilena's huff softened the lines that had formed between his brows, pulling him back to the room with his family. "Is it working? Are you . . ." She motioned toward him.

He forced a smile, pushing his experiment with Anathrasa to the back of his mind. "Yeah. I'm pretty good at it, actually."

"Of course you are." Her lips curved, but her eyes stayed wary.

"And the people? They're pleased to see you?" Elias's pointed look said he meant Anathrasa, not Madoc.

"Of course," Madoc said. It wasn't like he could object when centurions shoved a man who'd called him a traitor into a carriage or removed a group of sick women who'd declined his healing from a hospital in South Gate. He had to stay quiet and look the part of the loyal son to gain Anathrasa's trust. If the Mother Goddess seemed healthier with each healing, he noted it in silence and kept his mouth shut. He could no sooner risk her sensing his true intent than he could deny the people of Deimos—people Geoxus had ignored—the help they needed.

And it wasn't like he was hurting anyone. Quite the opposite—for the first time in his life, he was doing something that mattered. Not just winning a few coins in some street fight to donate to the temple, but making real change in people's lives. Taking the cough from a baby. Watching a woman stand straight after removing the arthritis from her spine. Fixing a man's hands that had been burned in the riots.

He wanted to tell Ash about it. All of it—the smiles and relief. The rush of anathreia in his veins. The limitlessness of the power he was finally learning to control. Anathrasa wasn't the only one getting stronger; he was too. But Ash hadn't made contact with him since his arrival almost two weeks ago—Hydra hadn't either—and that worried him. He knew she was busy learning her new powers and preparing for war, but he couldn't help feeling as though something bad was happening. Something he could have helped her with.

He told himself he was being lovesick and foolish. That this was the price of loving a goddess. When they did talk, he'd tell her about all of it—all except his link with Anathrasa. Ash would be too concerned, and with good reason. If she told Hydra, she might see him as a liability. Pull him away before he could do what he'd come to do.

He couldn't let that happen.

He'd promised to help her. He'd vowed to be worthy enough to stand beside her.

He couldn't do any of that if he was deemed dangerous to their cause.

"Well, I hope you're still being careful," Ilena cautioned. "The city is not safe."

Like Elias, she was talking about Anathrasa. He nodded.

"You need to get dressed, dominus." A man in white robes carried Madoc's evening attire into the room—a black silk toga and silver-strapped sandals. It was almost exactly what he'd seen Geoxus wear at events during the war with Kula, and he was sure that wasn't a coincidence. Anathrasa wanted the people of Deimos to know that her son was still one of them, and that their beloved fallen god was not forgotten.

"Of course you get to wear black," Ilena said under her breath.

He reached for the clothing in the man's arms, taking the thin silver crown with a small sphere in the center off the top. An unending circle. People in the city were always talking about that when he helped them.

As he traced the circle under his fingers, warmth tingled under his collarbone. There was something soothing about that circle. The shape of it. The meaning behind it. It was like his anathreia, ebbing and flowing. He hadn't truly understood the nature of energeia before now.

Before Anathrasa had taught him at the temple.

"Madoc," Elias said, tearing his focus from the crown. His brother and mother were staring at him, grim expressions on their faces. He looked down again at the circle, but the metal was now cold in his hands.

What was he doing? Anathrasa wasn't helping him do anything to get closer to the other gods. This crown was a leash tethering him to her, nothing more. He had the sudden urge to snap it in half.

Gritting his teeth, he placed it on his head. Another time, another place, Elias would have laughed at him, but tonight he only looked away. Grabbing the black toga, Madoc stepped behind a screen, removed his tunic, and slid into the fine black silk. It slipped over his shoulders, cascading down his back. It was difficult to close—the knot in the sash at his waist wouldn't stay tied. He had the sudden fear that it would loosen while he was at the party, and when the toga fell open everyone would see him naked.

Ash would find that very funny, he imagined. The thought of her laughter settled him. He would have given anything to hear it now.

"Dominus? The ball is about to begin." The man who'd brought his clothes shifted nervously beside the door.

With a sigh, Madoc stepped out. Elias gave a huff at the sight of his silk toga, but Ilena shot him a withering look as she approached and fastened the sash into a tight knot.

"Keep your eyes open tonight," she said quietly.

He wanted to tell her this ball didn't mean anything. Anathrasa would never be his mother. But too many ears were listening.

He smiled. "You do the same."

She kissed his cheek and strode to the door, where four palace guards escorted them down the corridor and stairs toward the heart of the palace. He sensed their consciousness as they walked—it was as easy as breathing, after all the pain he'd tithed. A charged fog of worry wrapped around each of them, hidden behind their stoic demeanors. He hadn't felt this in any of the guards before—they'd been pleased to serve the Mother Goddess, as eager as any of the palace staff. But now, he couldn't help wondering if the guards, like Lucius, were wary of him.

Madoc's brows pinched together. He didn't like the idea of people being frightened of him. He wasn't like Anathrasa—he didn't want war, or for people to be needlessly hurt. But how could anyone see that? All week he'd been telling the people his aid was her idea.

He wanted to explain to them that he was different, that he was here to help them, but he couldn't do that without betraying Anathrasa.

Unless she didn't have to know.

He could rid these guards of their fear the way he had freed the people in the city of their pain. They didn't have to talk about it. He could tithe before they'd even noticed. What was the harm in that? If nothing else, it was good practice for when he would take Aera's and Biotus's powers.

Stepping closer to the front two guards, he inhaled, reaching for the tight tendrils of fear around their chests. Then he simply sliced the bands around them and set them free.

The guard on his right, a lanky boy with a ghost of a beard, stumbled, then straightened. His steps were lighter, his shoulders drawn back. The guard to his left blew out a slow breath, his stocky arms relaxing at his sides.

Elias gave Madoc a strange look, but Madoc only smiled.

Music reached his ears, a flutter of strings and a warbling flute. The beat of a drum put a bounce in his step, and as he entered the courtyard, the buzz of emotion was as constant as the voices from the crowd. Respected Deiman men and women were in attendance, along with Aera's entourage—a flock of beautiful, fierce people in barely there wisps of gauze and lace—and Biotus's leather-clad warriors, who seemed content to feast and ogle the Air Divine in the absence of their leader, who still had yet to return after leaving the arena during the fight.

But beneath the pulse of mingling energeias, Madoc felt the steady, familiar consciousness of the Undivine. Not just servants, but also attendees. Merchants in the harshly woven tunics of the working class. Esteemed tradeswomen in dresses no finer than Ilena's had been when they'd lived in the quarter.

He was certain Geoxus had never held a party that mixed Divine and Undivine guests, and as his gaze landed on Anathrasa, seated on a white marble throne beneath the starry sky, something bent in his soul straightened.

He felt himself smile at her.

She smiled back.

Guilt ate at him. But this was what he'd always wanted, wasn't it? Divine and Undivine on equal footing.

And Anathrasa had brought it about.

He didn't want to be grateful for anything she offered. He knew it was wrong. And yet . . . he was glad.

Perhaps she wasn't as completely rotten as he'd thought.

When she rose, the courtyard fell silent, as if everyone had been waiting for her to speak.

"Our guest of honor has arrived," she announced, raising her hands in his direction. A gap opened in the crowd, and he made his way toward her, returning the smiles of those he passed. Each one made his tense shoulders ease a little more.

"You all know Madoc Aurelius," she called as he took his place beside her. As every eye moved over him, he felt the heat creep up his spine. "Champion of Deimos. Beloved by our great Geoxus before his untimely death. He is a hero in every sense of the word, and I have spent the week proudly watching him attend to the sick and injured of our city as he would a beloved member of his own family."

Madoc scanned the crowd, finding Ilena and Elias still where he'd left them, on the far end of the courtyard. He could see that, despite her earlier complaints about possible stains on her white dress, Ilena held a goblet of wine in her hand, one she was making quick work of finishing.

"It is with great honor that I present the pride of Deimos, and my heart—my beloved, too-long-estranged son, Madoc."

Madoc had expected to feel rage. Disgust. To force a smile to cover the scowl he was sure would twist his lips. But as the crowd erupted in cheers, he felt none of it. That strange tingling that he'd felt when he'd relieved the guards' wariness on the walk over had returned beneath his breastbone, and he was almost . . . relieved.

These people weren't afraid of him, as he'd thought the guards had been. They were pleased.

He wasn't sure what to make of that. Were they happy with how Anathrasa had shaped their world?

Was he?

A centurion was waiting nearby, and as Anathrasa excused herself to speak to him, the crowd overran Madoc. Some simply wanted to make his acquaintance or say they'd cheered for him in the arena during the last war with Kula. Others wanted to thank him for healing their sister, or their father. It was overwhelming—all the gratitude and emotion pooling around him.

But it was also . . . nice.

Living with Petros as a child, he'd watched these parties from the back rooms, hidden because of his Undivine status. He'd been cursed at, and beaten, and had fully embraced his future as pigstock when Cassia had brought him home to live with the Metaxas. But even when he'd fought alongside Elias, he'd known he was a fraud—using Elias's geoeia to trick the crowds.

Now people knew who he was. They knew who his mother was. And they weren't afraid or disgusted.

A buzz filled his brain, headier than any wine could provide. He wished Ash were here. She belonged in a place like this—

A cool hand grasped his. Madoc looked up into a Deiman woman's face, her dark eyes lined with kohl and her lips curved in a sultry smile.

"Does our champion dance?" she asked, but it was more of a command—before Madoc could reply, she'd dragged him out onto the floor.

The woman entwined her arms around his neck, her body flush with his. Madoc went rigid, but music thrummed from instruments in the far corner, and as other bodies joined the dance alongside them, his tension again dissipated.

Madoc's hands settled on the woman's hips and she swayed against him, pulling him along to the music.

Everyone around him was smiling. Enjoying themselves.

Happy.

Anathrasa had made them happy.

Maybe he should talk to her. Maybe she wasn't fully set on the cruelty he'd thought—

"Madoc. You're needed."

He turned to see Elias standing too close to him. The woman looked at him with a frown that turned into a quick smile.

"You could join us," she purred.

Madoc expected Elias to grin back at her. She was his type— pretty, flirty.

But Elias grabbed Madoc's forearm. "Not likely."

And he dragged Madoc off the dance floor.

"What is wrong with you?" Madoc stumbled after him until they were both standing beside one of the stout white columns, where tables held suckling pigs and baked fish.

"What is wrong with *you*?" Elias shot back. "What do you think you're doing out there?"

Madoc swallowed a knot of guilt, realizing he hadn't looked for Elias and Ilena since the announcement had been made.

"Jealous?" he asked, trying to lighten the mood.

"Hardly," Elias muttered. "I think Ash might feel differently if she'd seen you dancing like that, though."

Madoc blinked, his mind clearing. Ash.

He shook his head. He'd danced with that woman—and hadn't thought at all about whether or not he *should*.

"Half the guests are props, you know," Elias continued. "Anathrasa probably told that woman to dance with you. Centurions pulled most of the people here out of their homes to put on a show tonight. Threatened to throw them in jail if they didn't display the proper respect. Look at that man over there dancing. Have you ever seen someone less happy in your life?"

Madoc followed Elias's gaze to a man dancing alone beside the musicians. He didn't look like he was in dancing shape—sweat dripped from his ruddy face, and he favored his left side—but his smile was as broad as the half-moon overhead.

So broad, it appeared forced.

But as Madoc focused on him, he felt only gratitude.

"If he was unhappy, I would sense it," he said, a frown pulling at his brows. People were talking all around, masking their private conversation, but he couldn't be too careful.

"Because nothing gets past you, is that it?"

Madoc hesitated. He wasn't claiming to know everything. But he had power—one that magnified the emotions of other people and was getting stronger by the day. He'd know if people were pretending for his benefit.

He could tell for a fact that Elias felt no such pressure.

Madoc looked for Anathrasa, but she must have gone somewhere with the centurion he'd seen her with earlier. Slowly, he took a plate and piled on food. "How do you know these people were taken out of their homes?"

"I heard some centurions talking about it yesterday." Elias reached for a goblet of wine a server carried by on a tray. "Said they were to arrest anyone who put up a fight."

Madoc remembered the way Anathrasa's guards in the city had ushered away anyone who wasn't happy with their presence. Had they been jailed as well, or were they at this party, forced to make amends by playing a part? His stomach was starting to churn.

"She's dangerous, Madoc. I've been thinking about what we discussed. About your . . . shared abilities."

Madoc hushed him, his teeth pressed together. The last thing he needed was Elias getting arrested with the others.

"What happens to *you* if Ash really can destroy her?" his brother whispered.

Madoc tried to swallow, but a knot had formed in his throat. "Anathrasa says I can't kill her if I die because she's too strong. I think the same is true in reverse."

"You think?" Elias scoffed, and Madoc felt his uncertainty, as thin and sharp as his own. "Well, that's encouraging."

Doubt slivered through the lightness left over from his tithes on the palace guards. "It's fine. We're only connected to a point. She can tithe, but she still can't use anathreia."

"I don't know," Elias said. "You seem like you're having a good time."

Madoc stiffened. "What's that supposed to mean?"

Elias pulled him by the silky sleeve of his toga behind a pillar. "It just seems a little odd that I can tell this party's one step above prison torture and you can't."

Madoc flinched, glaring into the rainbow of colorful gowns sweeping across the courtyard. Lines cut between his brows as he measured the shadows beneath his brother's eyes and wondered what he'd been through before Anathrasa had pulled him from prison.

His gaze broke from Elias's and shot around the courtyard, bouncing from one smiling face to the next as the laughter turned harsh in his ears. They appreciated him, he could feel it. But Anathrasa wanted him to drain the energeias from Aera and Biotus. To do that, she didn't just need Madoc strong, she needed him willing. She needed him to believe in her cause.

She needed him to trust her as much as he needed her to trust him. Otherwise he'd never do as she asked.

"Boys." Ilena strode toward them, the lines around her eyes strained, her white gown a sharp contrast to the sun-kissed tan of her skin. She was holding a new goblet of wine in her hand. "Having fun?"

"How could we not?" Elias said, turning away. He didn't mention Madoc's connection to Anathrasa, and Madoc knew he never would. It was in their code as brothers to carry the burdens of each other's secrets. "Madoc and I were just talking about how generous the Mother Goddess has been to the people of Deimos."

"Good," Ilena said tightly, and her hard glare put Madoc in his place. "Because I'd hate to think what would happen if you weren't enjoying yourselves."

It was one thing for Elias to point out something he'd been

missing. It was entirely another for Ilena to do it. Her words cut him with the jagged edge of reality, and on his next breath, he tasted it— the sour bite of anxiety lacing through the air. It wafted off every person here, young and old, rich and poor, Divine and Undivine.

He looked again at the man Elias had pointed out, dancing faster now, sweat leaking down his face, a pure stream of terror radiating off him. The woman who'd dragged Madoc to the dance floor was tangled up now with an Undivine man, but need pulsed off her, to dance, and keep dancing, to have *fun*. Near the corridor to their right, one of the guards Madoc had followed earlier was picking a fight with an Animal Divine warrior twice his size without a single ounce of self-preservation.

Without the fear Madoc had taken from him.

His pulse beat faster.

How had he missed it?

"It is a lovely celebration," Ilena said, then gave a small smile. "I'm tired. I think I'll go check on Ava and Danon."

With a strained look that punctured Madoc's heart, she turned and strode back toward the corridor they'd come from. Before Elias could follow, Madoc snagged his arm.

"She's doing this to me," he said, anxiety thinning his words. "Anathrasa. She's making me see what she wants me to see."

Elias met his gaze, worried but steady, and Madoc knew what he was thinking.

If Anathrasa was clouding Madoc's mind, her anathreia was coming back. Once she could use it, she would be harder to kill. She could turn not just Geoxus's centurions against Ash, but anyone she wished.

Even him.

He had to get the other gods' energeias before Anathrasa's power grew. If she sensed what he'd done, he'd say he'd done it for her. He'd just have to get the powers to Ash before the Mother Goddess took them.

"Aera," he said. "She's here somewhere. Help me get her alone."

Elias glanced over Madoc's shoulder, to the far side of the courtyard. "I saw her go that way not too long ago."

Madoc set off that direction, a grim smile pulling his lips thin. Tonight, he would take Aera's energeia—enough of it to transfer to Ash.

Tonight, Anathrasa's hold on his mind ended.

TWELVE

ASH

SHE WAS FLORUS'S champion?

Ash's pulse beat in her temples, rocking her vision, making her dizzy. "I'm not yours, Florus," she spat, and she felt flames lick up her back, giving her wings of fire. "You just tried to kill me and held me prisoner for a week. I will *not* fight for you."

Biotus eyed her, her blue flames reflected in his dark eyes, and beamed as though she hadn't spoken at all. "It's an interesting challenge. I accept. If I defeat this mortal, you will come with me willingly to Crixion."

"You can't sacrifice her, Florus!" Hydra shouted. "He'll kill her!"

"No." Florus flicked a speck of something off his green tunic. "She can't die. The fight will be to the surrender."

That made Biotus flinch and eye Ash again, the fire on her back, the way she'd appeared like a god.

"*Florus.*" Hydra said his name like a gasp of pain. She was realizing how he knew that Ash couldn't die—because he had tested the theory himself.

Ash couldn't look at Hydra. Couldn't fall apart any more than she already had. "I am not yours, Florus," she said again, her jaw clenched.

"No, you're the *world's*, aren't you?" Florus's eyes were narrowed on her. "Prove it. Defeat the mighty god of bioseia. Save us, Ash Nikau."

"Yes, Ash Nikau," Biotus purred. He laughed, the sound like a roar. Ash inadvertently tensed, her fire wavering. *"Save us."*

He swung at her, a fist to the gut; she danced aside on instinct only. She dodged two more blows the same way before one connected—but it wasn't a punch. Biotus grabbed her, wrapping his beefy arms around her, and hauled her bodily from the throne room.

"Biotus!" Hydra shouted. *"STOP—"*

Ash screamed, but wordlessly; she was horror embodied, every raw ache from the beating she'd taken at Florus's hands coming back on her tenfold. Her whole body lit up like a sunset, but Biotus held tight, running, running, until he leaped into the air—and out a window.

Briefly, Ash was aware of the palace giving way to the sky and a small bay jutting out from the land. Where the palace ended and the shore began, she couldn't tell; this entire island was moss and vines and growing things. But out in the water, the liquid-blue sky and bay created a bowl.

A bowl that looked very much like an arena.

Biotus laughed again, the sound grating against Ash's flaming back, and released her.

She dropped, plummeting through the air. She hadn't realized how high he'd taken her until she flipped upside down and saw Biotus, above her, now in the form of a massive golden eagle.

Then she flipped again, and the bay waters were coming up fast, too fast—

A spurt of water shot up from the bay and gulped Ash into it. She flailed, fighting for the surface as the water lowered her to the bay's surface and solidified into an ice platform.

Ash doubled over, coughing on the ice, shivering, as Hydra materialized into her human self.

She dived at Ash, ripping her to her feet and throwing her arms around her. "I'm sorry—Florus had no right. I tried to find you as soon as I could, but he's lost his *mind*, and now this—"

Ash almost came apart. She clung to Hydra, and she could have rested there too long—but they were floating in the middle of the bay, easy targets for the massive eagle above them, banking in the sky.

Other birds joined him. Falcons and hawks and wicked, hook-beaked things with sharp talons and hungry eyes.

Ash stiffened in Hydra's arms, and Hydra looked up.

"Travel again," Hydra told her. "Get back to my islands. I'll handle him."

Ash sucked in a shaking breath, and with it came a surge of will. She pushed onto her feet, but the ice rocked, and she squatted low.

"I'm here to fight," Ash told Hydra.

Hydra appeared exhausted, suddenly, with rings of bruises around her eyes and hollow cheeks. She might not have been able to die, but she looked close.

"*No*—you've been through enough."

"So have you!" Ash screamed. She was shaking so hard she could barely see Hydra before her. "So has *everyone*! This is why I am what I am, right? To *fight*. So let's fight."

Ash looked up at the birds. The giant eagle at their center hovered above Ash, beating his wings to stay steady.

She flared fire up both arms.

The birds, as one, swiveled to face her. Biotus as an eagle angled his body and speared through the air toward them.

Ash knotted the fire into a ball, ready to throw, but Hydra didn't move, didn't raise her arms or flinch. She stared at Biotus, letting him and his vicious birds come closer, closer—

The moment he was close enough to touch, Hydra thrust her arms up, and a wicked gush of water wrapped around them all—Biotus, his birds, Ash, and Hydra. It dragged them all into the frigid depths.

The water hit Ash like a rock to the chest, knocking the breath from her lungs. She twisted in a curtain of bubbles and foam, angling for the surface, but hydreia grabbed all of them and yanked down, keeping the fight in Hydra's realm. Panic crested as Ash's mouth popped open in an involuntary scream.

The noise should have been muted, but it rang clear in her ears, which jolted her enough that she inhaled before she could think not to.

Water gushed into her lungs. Her body seized, fighting the invasion—

But she wasn't drowning.

Again, her lungs clawed for breath, and she relented, pulling water in, pushing bubbles out.

She could breathe underwater. And *hear* underwater.

All those times Hydra had thrown her into the sea during their awful training, Ash had never once *inhaled*. Now that she thought about it, it made perfect sense—being Fire Divine made her impervious to burning, so being Water Divine would make her impervious to drowning.

The wonder of this new discovery was short-lived.

Biotus was not as confident in the water—his large frame thrashed and, much less fluidly than he'd changed from falcon to man, his body elongated, darkened, writhed and rippled—

Until he was a shark.

He whipped around, tail flinging bubbles through the water.

The birds splashed feebly to the surface, useless here; Ash reveled in that for only a breath before she saw all manner of other sea creatures gathering behind him. Sharks and stingrays, grotesque-looking eels with electricity flicking off their skin—they rallied to his cry, pulled by bioseia, helpless not to obey the animal god.

Hydra was gone. Or maybe she was everywhere, the water personified—Ash couldn't see the goddess, but she could *feel* her, a charged rage that sizzled on her skin with each brush of the tide.

Biotus in his shark form flipped and writhed, fighting something unseen. Hydra had to have been holding him trapped with hydreia.

But the rest of his sea creatures stayed focused on Ash. They were weapons at the ready.

Ash treaded water, her hair wild and free in the shifting current. Her head roared with a hundred past fights, the call of a ghost crowd demanding bloodshed and death.

The sea creatures, poor beasts at Biotus's whims, charged her.

Ash flailed, trying to get away, but everything was liquid and she couldn't get traction. Dread pushed her into action and she moved, either by hydreia or her own force, bubbles brushing her face like gentle, comforting fingers.

She needed to fight. But how?

She couldn't control animals. She couldn't fight off dozens at once.

The first of the sea creatures reached her, its rounded nose driving into her side. Pain flared as the force launched her back. She spun and spun and crashed into a jagged rock.

The long, angular fish that had thrown her fell back, swiping around to regroup. There was almost a formation with the creatures, organization roughly given from Biotus as he battled nearby.

Ash thought she saw a face in the water, a giant, liquid version of Hydra, but she blinked, and it was gone.

The sea creatures were heading for her again, all of them hissing and heaving, while Ash remained pinned against the rock. One of the creatures made a croaking bark, filled with frustration and anger, as though it was trying to resist attacking her but was helpless not to.

Ash felt that frustration to her toes.

This life had been brutal and unfair, but she would be damned if she let it defeat her.

She would fight because Char would have done so. Because Madoc needed her to. Because she wanted more than just one stolen night with him—she wanted a lifetime, and she would *not* let Anathrasa, or Biotus, or anyone take that from her.

She would show them just how godlike she could be. She was *more* than a god. She couldn't be killed and she could command three of the six energeias—and Biotus and Florus both would rue the day they had stood against her.

Holding the image of Madoc in her head, Ash moved.

She flung her hands outward, trying to call fire, but of course it wouldn't come. Not down here. All she got was boiling water, and she growled in frustration.

Even if she could use igneia, something about that sort of aggressive attack felt wrong. Time slowed as she looked back up at the creatures. They were *alive*, trapped as she was, but controlled by Biotus. Ash didn't want to—couldn't—kill them.

Hydreia. She'd have to use hydreia.

Ash widened her hands, kicking her legs to push off the rock.

Stop, she willed, fingers splayed, arms braced. She wasn't sure whether she spoke to the water or the animals or the world at large. *Stop.*

The fastest creature, a barracuda, reared back as though it had struck a wall. It blinked at her, glassy eyes startled, and Ash almost laughed with feeling the same. Had she done it? Had she managed to harden the water around her enough to—

Hydra materialized next to her. With a shove of her arm, the sea creatures tumbled away, sucked into the abyss of the sea by a twisting water cyclone.

"Learn faster," Hydra snapped, and shot away, her body zooming through the water, back for the main attack.

Ash glared after her. Biotus in his shark form was fighting twisting funnels of water, tearing at shards of ice with glinting, pearly teeth.

Purely by instinct, Ash lunged, and on a whisper of intention, she appeared on top of Biotus, her body a lit iron even underwater. The shark reared at the flames and Ash watched blisters pop across its gray skin. She clung to Biotus's back, willing her igneia to flare, every piece of her scalding as the water around her boiled and fumed.

Through the chaos, Ash saw a surge of greenery, a knotted tangle of plants rising off the ocean floor—

Florus appeared, vines stretching from him toward the surface, holding his body buoyant under the water. His eyes met hers with vicious determination.

She couldn't bring herself to read anything in that stare.

Beneath her, Ash felt a shift, a tug—and Biotus was himself again. The change stunned her enough that when he spun, she released him, and he landed a punch to her gut with such force, even underwater, that Ash saw stars. Agony ricocheted up her chest and had her coughing for breath—or water, here, whatever appeased her lungs—but Biotus didn't attack her again.

He whirled for Florus.

Hydra formed, launching herself at Biotus, but his lower half shifted into that of a shark once more. His top half remained human, and as he charged through the water, he slammed into Florus, keeping hold of him as he angled for the surface.

"No!" Hydra appeared next to Ash, gasping, her long black hair like tentacles in the water.

"We have to get up there—" Ash started, but Hydra beat her to it, carrying her forward on a wash of hydreia.

The sea capped around Biotus and he hit the invisible wall of hydreia with a gruff roar.

"Hydra!" he shouted. "I will have him, and I will have the both of you! You cannot win this war!"

"Biotus will keep fighting," Hydra said absently, to herself or to Ash.

He would. And Hydra would keep fighting just as hard, and Ash too, and maybe even Florus, and these four gods would be clashing until the world caved in on itself, for none of them would tire and none of them would die.

Ash touched Hydra's arm. "I'm with you," she said.

Hydra looked at her, exhaustion in her deep eyes. She gave a weak smile. "Then we—"

Biotus cut her off with a bellow.

Ash and Hydra whipped around.

He had his powerful arms knotted around Florus's body, leaving only the plant god's head free. But vines spewed from Florus's open mouth, an endless stream of tendrils scurrying out into the water. Half of them pummeled Biotus, burrowing into his eye sockets, yanking at his limbs—

And half shot toward Ash.

She flailed away, but the vines grabbed her, and she screamed, everything in her panicking. *Not again—*

But then a vine traced her ear. "Ash Nikau."

The voice came from the plant. Florus?

"Time is against us," the voice said. "Ironic for immortals, isn't it?"

Biotus yanked off the worst of the vines. He retightened his grip on Florus while Hydra sent funnel after funnel of churning water, but Biotus was calling the sea creatures to him, and more from beyond, a growing army of animals to attack them.

Ash gagged, unable to move in Florus's vines.

"I may have misjudged you," Florus told her. His voice was impossibly sad, worn with pressure. "We were wrong last time with Ciela. Don't let us be wrong again."

One of the thicker vines wound against Ash's chest, and the world blossomed into spring.

There was no endless sea. There was only a forest, silent and sleepy, gleaming with dew and golden light. Thick brown trunks shot up to support a fluffy emerald canopy with leaves drifting down in lazy spirals. All was still, and peaceful, and it smelled of moss and decay but also of life.

It made the terror she had endured in Itza less shattering.

That haven retreated into Ash's body. It was inside her now: floreia. A piece of the life that sprouted from earth, the life that bloomed in ashes, the life that fed on water.

The connections were forming. Ash could feel the tapestry weaving together in her chest, floreia sighing to be together with igneia, geoeia, hydreia. Two spaces remained, and their absence throbbed, echoing with loneliness.

Aereia. Bioseia. Her soul stretched to reach for them.

She was coming together. Shattered pieces reforming into a nearly complete whole.

Florus's vines retreated. Across the water, she saw him in Biotus's arms.

He nodded at her, and she knew what he intended to do. Why he had given her a piece of floreia now—because he knew Biotus would take him to Crixion. He had been wrong to think Ash could defeat Biotus, or maybe he'd just wanted them to fight as a distraction; whatever his intentions earlier, he was going to surrender now.

"Hydra!" Ash reached for the water goddess, who was still throwing water and calling shards of ice. "Hydra—Florus gave me floreia."

Hydra spun, hair whipping in the water. Her face went slack with shock, then tensed with rage, and she spun back to glare at Biotus and Florus. "No, you idiot! We can stop him!"

Florus shook his head. He gave a helpless smile.

"We'll save him, Hydra," Ash told her. Part of her wanted the plant god to suffer a little, but he had given her floreia. Even after everything he'd put her through.

But only because Biotus had forced him to act.

Hydra screamed. It was a lifetime of pain and agony.

The only sign that she had lifted her hydreia's grasp on Biotus was his triumphant laugh.

"Good girl, sister," he barked at her. "I'll be back for you."

And he was gone, launching up toward the surface. The moment he broke out of the water with Florus, he transformed back into the eagle, his claws holding the plant god as he swept into the sky.

"This is *war*," Hydra growled. Ash wasn't sure whether the roiling water around them was from her anger or Ash's own.

"It is," Ash told her. She took Hydra's hand. "We're going to get Florus back, and we're going to stop Anathrasa."

Hydra blinked, a calculating glint in her eyes. "You can travel through igneia," she stated. Gone was the lighthearted woman who had pestered Ash during training; this goddess was a general, readying for battle. "Go warn your lover that Anathrasa is accelerating her plan, if he doesn't already know. Find out why Biotus took Florus. Be *discreet*. I have to deal with my people in Itza, and with Florus's own mortals."

"Yes," Ash said. She had no idea how to fully control her igneia travels, but Madoc needed to know that Anathrasa had abducted Florus and would no doubt send Biotus back to get Hydra. "Tor's still in the palace—"

"I'll get him back to the islands," Hydra said. "Meet us there."

Ash nodded. She would get to see Madoc now.

If she could figure out how to appear in Crixion without revealing herself to Anathrasa.

Madoc, she willed herself, her heart fluttering.

Go to Madoc.

THIRTEEN

MADOC

MADOC CUT THROUGH the party in search of Aera, smiling and shaking hands with those who stopped to praise him. Over the heads of the others, he watched Elias skirting the edge of the courtyard behind the musicians. It was impossible now not to feel the fear of those in attendance. Even the Air and Animal Divine who'd fought in the games watched him with barely veiled hostility.

By the time he arrived at the corridor, Elias was waiting. The Deiman guards who blocked their path were easy enough to distract—Madoc had only to suggest they weren't there, and the guards looked straight through them, as if they were invisible.

Soon they reached the double doors of the library, which were cracked open to reveal flickering torchlight within. Low voices came from inside, and as Madoc leaned closer, a chill swept over his skin.

"She's grown soft," a deep, male voice growled, bringing the iron taste of bloody meat to Madoc's tongue, and a rise in his anathreia. "Now that we have Florus, we need to move on Hydra. Take her before she has time to gather her army."

Madoc glanced at Elias, both Biotus's return and the mention of the god of plants taking him by surprise. Who had Florus? He was supposed to be with Hydra. If he'd betrayed the goddess of water, that was less protection for Ash.

Wariness chilled Madoc's blood.

"And sacrifice our chosen battlefield?" Aera responded, her voice light. "You've been back two minutes and you're already prepared to attack?"

"I don't know about your soldiers, but mine can fight anywhere, anytime."

Madoc's breath quickened. He had to find a way to warn Ash. Was this the errand the Mother Goddess had ordered? If Florus had joined Biotus and Aera, and they were conspiring to attack the Apuit Islands, Hydra needed to be ready.

Aera giggled. "How very versatile of them . . ." Her words were cut off by a sharp gasp.

"I grow tired of your mocking tongue, baby sister."

Madoc didn't pretend to understand the dynamics at play between the two gods but couldn't deny the toxic wave of power that pushed through the door. He glanced at Elias, whose eyes went wide as a crash sounded from inside. Aera's cry cut through his resolve.

"Distract them," Madoc whispered.

Elias pressed his hands to the outside wall of the library and closed his eyes. A moment later, the wall began to rumble, and from inside came the groan of wood, and the clattering of books tumbling to the marble floor.

Madoc placed a hand on Elias's shoulder blade, and the small quake stopped.

"You see?" Biotus roared. "She can't even get Geoxus's architects to properly fix this palace!"

Madoc and Elias jumped aside, hiding behind a statue on the opposite side of the wall just before Biotus tore out of the room. He was fuming, a bull driven to fury, draped in the furs of the animals he mastered and smelling strangely of salt water. When he stormed down the corridor toward the party, Madoc gave a quick nod to Elias.

"Make sure he doesn't come back this way," he whispered.

"Right," Elias said, then, "Watch yourself."

He hurried down the hall, keeping quiet.

The inside of the library was now still, and before Madoc entered, he straightened the dark silk of his toga and lifted his chin. This would have to be quick. Subtle. Like tithing pain from a mortal and leaving the rest intact.

Aera had so much energeia that surely she wouldn't notice if he took a little—that was all Ash needed.

He stepped into the library. For a moment, he thought he'd missed his chance. He didn't see Aera, only a dusty pile of scrolls on the floor to his right that had fallen in Elias's quake, and the rows of full shelves that remained. The room glowed with the pale-green light from a dozen phosphorescent stones embedded in the walls and scattered across the ceiling like stars, and he squinted through the dim light for any sign of the goddess or her guards.

It was the breeze that reached him first. It ruffled the ends of his toga and brushed softly over his skin, carrying the scent of old parchment and ink. It reminded him of the orders he used to carry from the foreman at the quarry to the masons who churned mortar. The feel of the thin paper in his hand. A simpler time when he was pigstock, and Elias had never been to prison, and his biggest concern was if Cassia would trade her chores for his.

"A goddess doesn't need a mortal boy coming to her rescue."

Aera's voice seemed to come from all around him, tracing over his skin, ruffling his hair. Had she seen him and Elias outside? He hoped she didn't suspect that he'd been trying to get her alone.

She appeared from one of the shelves to his left, the pale-blue cloth of her short gown glowing in the stones' light. Her golden hair was tied up in a dozen knots, the ends brushing her bare shoulders, and a small pout tilted her lips.

"I'm sorry, Goddess," he said. He bowed his head. "I heard raised voices. I didn't mean to intrude."

She moved closer, so silent he couldn't hear her footsteps. As she neared, he could make out the translucence of her gown—the curve of her breasts beneath the lace, and lower, the small swell of her belly.

He looked to the ground. Then up. His gaze finally landed on her arm, which was marked by a bruise the size of a gripping hand.

Biotus had hurt her.

It brought a sudden surge of anger—and regret for what he was here to do.

"What else did you hear?" she asked.

"Nothing," he said. "I only felt the anger and worry."

She passed him, the breeze rising, then falling around her. For a panicked moment, he thought she meant to leave, but her hand paused on the door handles, and she pulled them closed.

He was alone with Aera.

"My brother thinks he can push everyone around just because he's strong enough to do it," she said. "He learned that from Geoxus."

Madoc's teeth clenched at the mention of the god of earth, who had used him in the arena, and would have made him a weapon to take over the world.

Not for the first time, Madoc wondered why Aera, and even Biotus, had sided with Anathrasa when the Mother Goddess was just as power-hungry as Geoxus had been. Surely they knew the danger of getting close to her, so why did they risk it? Why wouldn't they try to eliminate Anathrasa, like Hydra and Florus?

"Biotus was soft in the beginning. Geoxus always picked on him because of it. It didn't take long for Biotus to realize that nobody bullies the bully."

"You pity him." Madoc could feel it, the soft weight of her sympathy. He tried to reach for it, the way he had the pain of those he'd tithed on this week, but she slipped out of his grasp.

"If I did, you wouldn't tell him, would you?" She turned to face him, leaning against the door. There was amusement in the curl of her lips, but Madoc could feel the apprehension behind it.

"I wouldn't tell him," he said.

"Then we have a secret," she said. "Should we trade another?"

Her smile widened, and when she walked toward him, her hips swaying softly, he got a very bad feeling. He crossed his arms over his chest.

"What do you have in mind?" he asked.

"I want to know why you're here, Madoc."

He swallowed. Forced a smile. "And if I tell you, what will I get in return?" He was stalling, but she seemed to like the game.

"Maybe I'll give you another one of my secrets."

"Why *you're* here?" he asked.

She laughed at this. Her fingers curled around one lock of her hair. "So what really brought you back to Crixion after taking my brothers' energeias?"

He went still, feeling the weight of her threat.

Whatever she tried, he needed to be ready. Ash could not beat Anathrasa without aereia.

"Maybe I wanted to see the gladiator games."

Aera's grin was deadly. "Just because I'm beautiful doesn't mean I'm stupid. I saw your face during the fight. You find the games crude." She came closer, reaching for his wrist and tugging it gently toward her, until his fingers were spread over her hip. A sense of wrongness shot through him as the soft fabric of her dress bunched under his damp palm. He knew gods took mortal lovers, but he had no intention of being one.

He belonged to someone else.

"No," she whispered. "The Soul Divine champion, a mortal so untouchable he can steal the power from a god, does not surrender to anyone without a reason." Her fingers trailed over the back of his hand, making his stomach clench.

He inhaled. Exhaled. He had to give Aera enough truth to keep her from sensing his lies, but not so much that she'd kill him now, or run to the Mother Goddess with stories of treason.

"I am loyal to Anathrasa," he said. "I had information about Hydra for her."

His mouth went dry as Aera's gaze narrowed.

"And what did you learn about my dear sister?"

"That's two secrets," he said. "And I still haven't heard yours."

They both knew she could have ended him right then for his insolence—there was no such thing as a bargain between a mortal and a god. But Madoc could feel her intrigue, and he needed that if she was going to remain unsuspecting of what he planned to do.

"Very well," she said with an amused smile. "You want to know why I'm here? It's because only a fool challenges the Mother Goddess. I played this game before. I sided against her with my brothers and sister, and look where that got us." She huffed. "There will be those who stand beside Anathrasa, and those who die, and I don't plan on ending a long life the way Geoxus and Ignitus did. I want much more, and I'll have it, even if it means pledging my allegiance to that hornet in a white dress and pretending to like my big brother."

He shifted and slowly withdrew his hand from her hip. He was certain now that Aera didn't know Anathrasa's plan to drain her power—she was siding with the Mother Goddess because she thought they'd win. What the "much more" was that Aera had mentioned, Madoc didn't know, but it was enough to keep her holding Biotus back when he would have rushed into an attack on the Apuit Islands.

"What's the matter?" she asked, her voice amused and high. "Going to run to your mother and tell her I called her a name?"

He shook his head.

"You look frightened." She smoothed a hand over her hip, right where his had just been. "Does a woman's form not please you?"

He swallowed thickly, training his gaze on her bare feet as she stopped before him.

"That's more questions," he said.

She laughed. "What's wrong, Madoc?" At the use of his name, his eyes lifted to hers, finding them round and painfully curious. "Deiman women don't honor their bodies the way my Lak women do. We're proud of our shapes. Our lines." Her hand slid down her waist to her hip, and then across her stomach. "Our valleys." She gave a quiet laugh. "We invite others to honor them. We enjoy being worshipped."

He cleared his throat.

Focus, he told himself. *Take her energeia. Give it to Ash.*

He reached toward her with his consciousness, but she moved quickly to his other side, as evasive as the current of air that carried her floral scent.

"Have you ever been with a woman, Madoc?"

An undeniable flush crept up his chest, up his throat, heating his jaw. The question was so direct he felt pinned to the spot. The fact that she was asking at all felt like a betrayal to Ash—this conversation was something he certainly did not want Ash to hear.

"I . . ."

He swallowed. Laughed awkwardly.

Aera smirked.

He couldn't chance pushing her away. He needed to steal her power for Ash, and to do that, he needed Aera to think she had his full attention.

It was just an act. A role, like the one he'd played in the street fights when he and Elias had tricked crowds of people into believing he was Earth Divine. Even if this was a goddess and not some brute with geoeia, he could still pretend.

He had to, or she'd see him for the traitor he was.

A slow smile turned his lips.

"What will you tell me if I answer?"

Aera's hand flattened on his chest, and he hated the heat that rose to his skin, and the way his heart pounded in response—half in panic, half in awe. She was a goddess, after all, and . . .

He shoved the thought from his mind. Ash touched him there—only Ash. But she was across the ocean, training, preparing to destroy the Mother Goddess.

Counting on him to do this one small thing.

Once again he reached for Aera's energeia, but it slipped out of his grasp. She was cunning, as Anathrasa had said, though he doubted Aera guessed his intent. She was like the wind, ever moving, impossible to pin down.

He needed her to be still. To relax.

To trust him.

"Did you love her?" Aera asked. Her fingers climbed up to his shoulder, sliding beneath the silk. Her hand was warm, and when he inhaled, he felt dizzy, as if there wasn't enough air in the room.

"Yes," he whispered, hating that the first time he confessed his true feelings, it was to another woman. For a moment, he closed his eyes and let Aera's touch be Ash's. Her hand on his shoulder. Her body, pressing against his side. It was weak, and wrong. He hated himself for it.

He missed Ash so much he could barely breathe.

He could *barely breathe*. But it wasn't because of Ash.

"Do you love her still?" Aera asked, as his breaths became shallower.

Always.

He wanted to push Aera's hands away. Leave this room. Find Ash and forget all of it. But he couldn't. His hands were starting to tingle with numbness. His head was growing fuzzy. He breathed in the perfume of her skin and was intoxicated.

"What happened to the energeias you stole from my brothers?" she whispered, the change in topic catching Madoc off guard. "What did you learn from Hydra that sent you running home to Mother?"

Panic dripped through his blood. He reached out again, but Aera's energeia was too difficult to hold. She was using her power on him, he was sure of that now. He needed to do something to change the tides. Now, before she overwhelmed him.

There was no way to win without playing her game, however much he detested the idea.

"Those are things you should talk to Anathrasa about," he said, and Aera quirked an eyebrow.

Before she could speak again, steal any more of the air in the room, he kissed her.

He wasn't gentle—he could feel her desire, full of selfish expectations, and gave in to what she wanted. Her lips were cold against his, and when he took her cheeks between his hands, she gasped in delight, snatching his breath. Black rims formed around his vision, and his knees buckled. Her laughter rang in his ears as they fell to the marble floor, and soon she was on top of him, straddling his hips, her hands spread over his chest. She bit his lower lip, her teeth like ice, and his anathreia surged in panic.

He fought for control of his body and mind, focusing on the pulse of her whipping energeia. He reached for it with the last threads of his focus, sealing his lips to hers in a kiss so wrong it turned his stomach. She laughed into his mouth, clouding his brain, and he flipped them over, pressing her to the floor with his body, sickened by the high purr of her moan in his ear.

But he had her. And as he kissed her again, he could feel the edges of her control soften and give way just enough to sip on the cool rush of her aereia.

FOURTEEN

ASH

ASH FADED INTO flames, leaving the bay outside of Florus's palace behind.

Madoc. Go to Madoc.

But at the last moment, she redirected her thoughts. She couldn't very well appear in an inferno randomly in Geoxus's palace. She didn't know where Madoc was—and what if he was with Anathrasa? She had to be discreet.

She let her intention pull her toward the palace. There were a number of small rooms off each hall, storage and servants' closets. She picked one she remembered from her last time there and appeared in a wash of blue and orange fire.

Flames still on her arms, she waited should anyone be there, ready to attack. But the closet was empty, a storeroom with barrels of dried goods, crates of linens, and unmarked boxes.

Ash exhaled in relief and crept to the door.

The hall beyond was quiet, but somewhere nearby swelled with music and the conversation of a party. Her frustration grew—a party meant lots of people, which meant Ash would have a harder time finding Madoc.

She cracked the door to the hall open and called on igneia again.

With Ignitus dead, more flames were alive in Crixion now. A few burned in the party—a fire crackled with fresh-roasted pork; a flame warmed a few different bowls of food.

Ash gasped as wonder filled her, warm and effervescent. She could see the terrace as if she were standing there, the flames as good as eyes, just as she'd looked in on Igna.

People danced in bright, jewel-toned gowns, laughter pealing. The laughter was forced, though, and the smiles rigid. This party was for show only.

And at the head of the room sat Anathrasa, a goblet in one hand, a chiseled smile on her face.

Rage churned in Ash's gut, as hot as the fire she watched through, but she forced herself to stay back. Madoc wasn't at the party, and she couldn't very well confront Anathrasa now.

Ash broadened her awareness. A few lanterns burned in the stable yard; a fire smoldered in the kitchens; a candle was lit in the library—

There.

Ash felt Madoc's presence more than saw him. She gasped, sucking back into herself, and scrambled through the closet until she found a box of new servants' uniforms, simple gray tunics with leather belts. She pulled one on and eased out into the hall, using a towel to rub at the soot and blood on her face. She didn't want anyone to see her and shout about an attack.

Self-consciously, she didn't want Madoc to see her like this, either.

The thought twisted her stomach sharply. He had seen her look far worse than this, but something about this reunion felt important. Ash missed him in ways she hadn't let herself realize, and she wanted to run into the library and throw her arms around him and forget everything that had happened for one precious minute.

She reached the library doors and tamped down her enthusiasm. Hand on the knob, she slowly opened one door.

There were voices speaking. Madoc wasn't alone. What had she seen through the candle flame? Just the shape of him, the feel of him—

The voices changed. They weren't voices at all, but a laugh here, a rustle there. The smack of something falling to the stone floor.

Ash rushed inside, igneia waiting in her chest, ready. But she restrained herself; she had to be cautious, patient like the stones around her, steady like geoeia.

The small library was circular, bookshelves looping around it in spiraling rows. Ash crept up an aisle, keeping to the shadows, following the noises to the middle of the library.

The aisle between the bookshelves ended, the shelves creating a perfect circle around the marble floor.

On that floor, just beneath a massive unlit chandelier, was Madoc—on top of a woman.

Ash's first thought was that he was fighting her, and she lurched forward.

The movement yanked Madoc's attention up to her, pulling his lips off the woman's mouth.

Ash's mind seized.

Had . . . had he been kissing her?

Ash shrank back into the shadows as the woman followed Madoc's gaze.

"Madoc?" The woman's voice was drunk. "Madoc—you—"

She shrieked and shoved her hands against his chest, and a funnel of air kicked up and launched Madoc off her, blowing him against the far bookcase. He almost didn't seem to care; he was still watching the spot where Ash had been, his eyes wide, horror written in the planes of his face.

The woman regained her composure with a laugh. "Were you trying to use your powers on me?" Her voice was thin, trying to force lightness, but she was clearly shaken.

"Is . . . is that another question, goddess?" His voice wavered, but he held his ground, jaw clenched.

Goddess . . . so that was Aera?

Ash stumbled back again, her spine hitting the bookshelf behind her, and she lifted a hand to her mouth, pushing her lips together, fighting a scream.

Madoc and the goddess of air?

Aera glared at Madoc. Her lips spread in a slow smile. "Don't toy with me, mortal."

"No," came Madoc's instant reply. His eyes shot to the bookshelves, then back to Aera, barely containing his nerves. "I wasn't trying to use my powers on you, goddess. I would never dare to be so bold."

Aera gave a stifled laugh. "No. You wouldn't dare, because if you did, I'd suffocate you."

She hurled another funnel of air at him. Madoc ducked and the force hit the books over his shoulder, parchment and scrolls bursting into the air.

Ash blinked, and Aera was gone, nothing but a twisting spiral of dust left in her wake.

"Wait!" Madoc got to his feet and stumbled into the center of the room. His black tunic was hanging half open, held together only by his own hands as he tripped on the hem.

Breath finally entered Ash's lungs, though she knew she couldn't blame it on Aera.

No reason came into her mind. Nothing but that image of Madoc on top of the air goddess. His tunic open. His mouth on hers, lips swollen.

"Ash?" Madoc's voice was tentative. His eyes swam over the dark bookshelves. The candle Ash had originally spied through was on a table off to the side, the only light in here, the flame still burning even with Aera's mad wind. "Ash—are you here?"

Half of Ash wanted to vanish in fire again. Go back to the Apuit Islands and wash her mind of what she had seen.

But she had just spent a week in Florus's prison, hanging on to the image of seeing Madoc again, of getting to be with him, of having more than one night together.

So she stepped out of the darkness and into the ring of light. A snap of her fingers, and the chandelier over them burst to life, igneia raging strong and hard at her command.

Madoc jolted at the sight of her, or maybe at the swell of igneia— either way, he clumsily tied the belt across his tunic and took two lurching steps toward her.

She put up her hand, palm flat, staying him.

He stopped.

"What are you doing here?" The question cut up at the end, and his face convulsed. He ran a hand through his hair, looked around the empty library, and focused back on her with something that was almost a glare. "I—I almost had it. What are you *doing* here?"

He was *mad* at her?

A dry laugh burst out of Ash's chest. "That's what you have to say to me?"

She wanted her words to sound hard. She wanted to make him tremble for the crack he had put in her heart just now.

"No." Madoc ran a hand over his face. "No. I—I'm glad to see you. I am."

"Yes, you sound overjoyed."

"Ash—"

"Don't. Don't talk." But she couldn't fill her own silence.

She realized, standing in this library, barefoot in a Deiman servant's uniform, that maybe she had misunderstood Madoc's attention to her. Maybe she was the only one who had dreamed of something more after this war, of a life together.

"I came to tell you"—her voice was thick, gasping—maybe Aera was back, because Ash was suffocating—"that Biotus took Florus. He's probably here in Crixion. Anathrasa's accelerating her plans. Hydra thought you should know."

She should tell him that Florus had given her floreia, too, but could she trust him with that information? Even that question ached.

Madoc moved closer. He reached out for her. "Ash—"

She started shaking, and she couldn't stop. She wanted to drop to her knees; she managed to stay upright, but she had to turn away from Madoc, arms around her chest, falling apart.

Falling apart from Florus's abduction.

Falling apart from the fight with Biotus.

Everything in her was finally unraveling.

"Don't touch me."

Madoc stormed in front of her. "I was trying to get aereia. That was all."

"Is that how you were planning to get Biotus's energeia too?"

"Stop."

"You managed to get igneia and geoeia without bedding Ignitus and Geoxus."

"Ash—I was doing this for *you!*"

His words were fists to her gut. "So this is my fault?"

"No! That's not—I don't know what I'm doing! This was the first time I managed to get Aera with her guard down. You think I wanted this? You think I haven't spent every night we've been apart thinking of you? And then you show up *now*, and—" He choked, and when Ash looked at him, she almost believed the sorrow on his face. "I've missed you. So much. I didn't mean for that to happen; Aera means *nothing* to me. Tell me what I can do. Please, Ash."

Ash wanted to believe him.

She wanted to leave. She wanted—

She couldn't breathe. She saw stars; she saw darkness and fire, stone and water, and she just wanted to *sleep*.

She buckled, and Madoc caught her, strong hands on her arms keeping her upright.

Tears streamed down her cheeks. She didn't know when she had started crying; maybe she had been since she arrived. Everything was a dream—one long, unending, horrific dream.

"I want to leave." The plea burst out of her, a heaving sob. "Madoc—we should leave. I can keep us safe. We can go somewhere Anathrasa would never find us and we can take your family, and mine, and we can just—we can—"

Ash bowed forward, head to Madoc's chest, and wept. All the tears she had suppressed to survive in Itza; all the pain and fear she had ignored just to get by. She let it out here, now, in his arms, though she hated him and what he had done.

But he was still a soft place to fall, so fall she did.

When she was spent, they sat on the floor, her in his lap, Madoc with his arms around her and his head buried in her neck, her hair.

She leaned back, putting space between them, but Madoc's grip on her tightened, not letting her get up.

His eyes were downcast. "What did he do to you? Florus. You said his name."

Ash's hands went limp on Madoc's forearm. She was turned to the side, her legs draped over his, and she used that position to avoid having to look at him. "He gave me floreia," she said. "After he killed me. Or failed to."

Madoc stiffened. She felt his eyes on the side of her face. He didn't say anything for a long moment. And then, "You're immortal?"

She shrugged.

"You want to run," he said, his voice low. "I'll run. I'll go wherever you want to go."

Tears stung her eyes again. She closed them, but Madoc took her chin and pulled her face to his.

"Ash." He said her name like a prayer, like a promise. "Look at me." She obeyed.

"I love you." His eyes were all brown darkness in the library; her igneia in the chandelier was burning low now. "I love you, and I'll go wherever you want to go. Just say the word, and we'll leave."

There it was. All she had to do was ask him again, and they could leave this war behind.

A breath quivered in her lungs. She was trembling, the aftershocks of her sorrow racking through her like a quake.

The words waited on her tongue. *Let's leave. Let's take our families and hide.*

She closed the space between them and kissed him. It wasn't the gentle kiss she had dreamed of; it was bruising and punishing, a mix of her own heartache and how much she'd missed him and how grotesquely she hated this.

He met her force with a throaty groan, and his hands spasmed against the small of her back, dragging her closer. She rode the motion to straddle him, and she nipped at his lips, all satin tongue and gnashing teeth, her fingers clenching into a fist in his hair, which she used to wrench his head backward and suck along the tendon of his neck. He tasted of sweat and earthy dust, and a deeper sweetness, something like wine or perfume—

A woman's perfume.

The thought kicked through her delirium and Ash stilled, her mouth against his bare collarbone, her heart thundering against her ribs.

"This war will break us," she whispered into his skin.

Madoc was the one trembling now. She felt him shake his head, and when she pulled up to look at him, his eyes were bloodshot and rimmed with tears.

"I won't let it," he told her. "I promise you. We will survive this. We might have to—" He swallowed, wincing. "We might become people we don't recognize, but we'll bring each other back. And I promise I won't touch Aera again. It's just you, Ash. It will always be just you."

She silenced him by pressing her forehead to his. They breathed the same air, her legs twined around his waist, his arms enclosing her hips, and she could feel the charging of their pulses in time.

"I love you too," she whispered, warm and soft and full of more life than any energeia she possessed.

Ash couldn't stay.

Anathrasa's party was still going; Aera was still raging somewhere, hurt by Madoc's attempt at taking her aereia. Heart breaking even more, Ash left him in the library with another kiss, another promise.

They would bring each other back. No matter what this war turned them into. No matter what they had to do.

They would find each other at the end of this, and they would survive.

Ash let Ignitus's fire overtake her and she vanished into the ether, focusing on her room in Hydra's palace. There she landed, the room soaked in midnight, the doors to the balcony shut tight and a fire not yet made in the hearth.

No sooner had she gotten back than the room sloshed with water, and Hydra stood next to her, her eyes narrow and soft.

"Tor was worried you wouldn't come back," Hydra said, her voice level.

"He sent you to make sure I did?"

"He thought you'd see Madoc again and the two of you would run off."

Ash sent a thought at the hearth and it raged with a fresh flame. "I almost did."

"Can't say I'd blame you." Hydra dropped to sit in a chair by the fireplace, head in one hand. She still wore her battle clothes, still had the sunken grayness around her tired eyes and a few recently healed wounds on her body.

"It is kind of what you did, isn't it?" Ash folded her arms over her chest. "Made this alliance with Florus. Blocked everyone else out."

Hydra gave a dry laugh. "Not that. I meant—" Her eyes went to Ash, wide, and flicked away. "It's not important. I'll go let Tor know you're here and ready to—"

"What did you mean?" Ash watched the water goddess, hesitant, but she needed to know. She'd felt this wall go up from Hydra before.

Silence fell. The hairs on Ash's arms rose the longer it stretched.

Hydra let her head drop against the back of the chair. "Her name was Ciela."

Ash blinked. "The first gladiator? Florus told me about her."

"I suspected as much." Hydra's eyes were closed, but her lips curved in a sad smile. "You're too much like her for your own good."

Ash's crossed arms unraveled. "How so?"

"Honorable. So damn honorable."

Something in Hydra's tone pulled Ash forward a step. "You knew her well," she said, a question.

Hydra rubbed her closed eyes and nodded.

"Was she Water Divine?"

"She was born Air Divine."

The mention of air divinity pierced Ash with the image of Aera lying beneath Madoc, and she had to forcefully shut her mind to it.

"There's something you're not telling me about her," Ash guessed. "I felt it with Florus and Biotus, too. They know something about her. Something about *you*."

Hydra mock gasped and finally opened her eyes again. "You mean I haven't divulged all my secrets in the handful of days we've known each other? How rude of me. I have centuries of gossip and woe-is-me stories to tell you, so we'd best get started—"

"Hydra." Ash's brows furrowed. "The more I know about Ciela, the better prepared I can be to not make her mistakes."

The water goddess looked exhausted, and she had lost the only sibling that mattered to her just hours before. But Ash was exhausted too, and she didn't have the strength to relent.

The water goddess finally shrugged, helpless. "I fell in love with her."

Ash's eyebrows rose. "With a mortal?"

Hydra gave a sardonic look. "It does happen."

"Not *love*."

"What do you want me to say?" Hydra shot to her feet. "That I used her like my siblings do with mortals? That I was able to resist her kindness and loyalty, her selflessness, her *strength*? If I said anything like that, it would be a lie. Ciela was fearless. We killed her with no guarantee that we could bring her back or that our plan to defeat Anathrasa would work, and she went along with it, because she had that stupid look in her eyes"—Hydra pointed at Ash's own eyes, tears wetting the goddess's cheeks—"like it would never have occurred to her to refuse, because the world needed her. I had never seen such honor in a mortal or a god."

Ash couldn't breathe. Afraid to set Hydra off. Afraid to make her stop talking.

"What happened to Ciela?" she whispered.

Hydra punched her thigh, grief raw on her face. "After it was all done and we thought Anathrasa was gone, my siblings started to fear Ciela. Didn't like the idea of her turning on them. I tried to protect her, but—she was still mortal. Unlike you, she'd only gotten small pieces of all the gods' energeias, not any god's whole energeia and all their powers. And Aera—" She wilted. "Aera didn't fear Ciela so much as she just didn't want anyone else to have something that had belonged to her, Ciela being originally Air Divine and all. So . . ." Hydra drew in a breath, and Ash wondered suddenly if this was the first time she had ever told this story out loud. "Aera lured me away, pretending to want to negotiate for Ciela's return to Lakhu, while she had secretly coerced Biotus into killing Ciela in my absence."

I've broken you once, Biotus had said as he took Florus.

A wash of regret nearly sent Ash to her knees. Biotus abducting

Florus had been significant for Hydra in more than just losing her brother. And all the help Hydra had given Ash, the training and trust—all of it had been weighed down by this tragedy, but still, Hydra had welcomed her.

Hydra panted, chin to her chest, and Ash knew her suspicions about this being Hydra's first telling of her most secret grief were correct.

"It's terrifying," Ash started, "to love someone who can be hurt."

"Which is everyone. Even gods now." Hydra blew out a breath and peeked up at Ash. "That mortal boy of yours. Madoc? I have half a mind to let the two of you just run away from all this. I would have, if I could go back. I'd take Ciela and just leave."

"No, you wouldn't." Ash's throat was thick. "Just like I wouldn't."

Hydra laughed, head thrown back, but it was pained.

She wasn't just some perfect divine creature, like Ash had once thought of all the gods. She was flawed, just as Ash was flawed, and that, Ash knew how to deal with.

She hooked her arm through Hydra's, trying to take as much of the goddess's weight as she could. "Where's your room? You need rest."

Hydra looked at her askance. "Rest. Sure. That'll solve everything."

"No, it won't. But it'll end this endless day."

That earned a half-hearted chuckle. Hydra relented, leaning into Ash, even dropping her head to Ash's shoulder.

Though they both could travel through energeia, they walked out of Ash's room and took the long, twisting halls to Hydra's chambers, silent and solemn together.

FIFTEEN

MADOC

WITH ASH GONE, Madoc refocused on Aera.

He returned to the party, ready to make amends, to beg for her forgiveness if he had to. He needed to stop her before she went to Biotus and told him what she suspected Madoc had been doing. She and her brother had parted on bad terms in the library, but that didn't mean she wouldn't try to warn him.

The last thing Madoc needed was the god of animals attacking before he could draw the energeia from him.

But Aera was not at the party. And neither were Biotus nor Anathrasa.

He searched the throne room. Then the gardens. By the time he'd made it back to the celebration, he was frantic. The gods had to be together—it was too much of a coincidence that they'd all leave separately, after what had happened between him and Aera. He was heading toward a palace guard to ask if he'd seen anything when someone grabbed his arm.

"I've been looking everywhere for you!" Elias's eyes were wide. Anxiety rolled off him in waves, heightening Madoc's fear.

"I couldn't do it," Madoc said quickly. "Aera ran. I can't find her, or Biotus or Anathrasa."

"Forget the gods," Elias said. "Mother's missing."

Cold sweat dripped down Madoc's brow.

"What do you—"

Elias stepped closer, lowering his voice. "After Biotus left the party with Anathrasa, I went back to the room to check on her. She wasn't there. Danon and Ava said they hadn't seen her. I've looked all over. No one knows where she is."

Madoc's stomach twisted. He'd had a confrontation with Aera. Now the gods were missing, and Ilena as well.

Anathrasa had to have taken her. That's why the Metaxas were here, after all. To keep Madoc in line.

But he'd been doing what Anathrasa had asked—taking the power from Aera.

Urgency whipped through his veins. He needed to find the Mother Goddess. To explain what had happened.

"Go back to your room," he told Elias. "Stay with Danon and Ava. I'll find Ilena."

"But—" Elias began, but Madoc was already shoving his way through the crowd. Once he was in the empty hall, he reached out with his energeia, but he couldn't distinguish Ilena's consciousness from those of the hundreds of other people in the palace. He sensed no gods nearby, no spikes of power. Nothing to lead him in the right direction.

Fearing Ilena had tried to leave the grounds, he ran to the stables, but only a few guards were posted. He went to the baths beneath the garden but found them empty. He even tried the servant quarters, but there was no trace of them.

His panic was wrenching tighter by the minute.

"Anathrasa?" Madoc burst through the door of the kitchen, eliciting a shout of surprise from a cook. Behind him, a dozen servants gaped at Madoc, then immediately bowed their heads.

"Ilena?" he shouted, but his mother did not respond. "You!" Madoc motioned to the cook, a man with a broad chest and dark berry stains on his apron. "Have you seen the gods?" When the man shook his head, Madoc's teeth clenched. "I'm looking for a woman, Ilena Metaxa. She's a guest of the palace. Dark hair, about this tall." He held out a hand to indicate her height, using the other to swipe the sweat out of his eyes.

The cook's brows scrunched together. "I'm sorry, dominus, I don't . . ."

Madoc pressed an image of Ilena into the man's head with his energeia. He reached for any hint of recognition in the cook's memory, but it was like kneading one of the piles of dough on the marble slab beside them. The man's thoughts were soft, his emotions shapeless and dull.

"I don't know this woman," the cook said. He blinked, his eyes unfocused.

Madoc wanted to shake him.

Only someone with soul energeia could manipulate another's thoughts, and since it hadn't been him, it had to be Anathrasa.

She'd made him see what she'd wanted him to at the party, and now she was turning the minds of her servants. How could he not have seen how powerful she'd become?

She must have hidden that from him, too.

"Aera," Madoc said, raising his voice to the rest of the staff. "Biotus. Where are they?"

The cook blinked. The servants behind him seemed confused.

"Dominus, the goddess of air lives in Lakhu," the cook said kindly. "And Biotus—"

"Anathrasa," Madoc interrupted, pressing deeper into the man's consciousness for answers the Mother Goddess had not already erased. "Where has she gone?"

"The Mother Goddess must complete the circle," he said. A woman behind him repeated his words. They nodded fervently, their belief unshakable.

"Stop," Madoc growled, using his anathreia to quiet them. It didn't matter; the other servants were all muttering the same thing. A dull roar rose in the hot, crowded room.

"The Mother Goddess must complete the circle."

"Stop!" he shouted, using his power to force their compliance.

They stopped and stared at him blankly.

Certain he would get no answers there, he stumbled back through the door. He tried to think of places he hadn't searched yet, but the gods could have taken Ilena anywhere in the city. For all he knew, they'd boarded a ship to Lakhu or Cenhelm, or headed north through Deimos.

He needed to check on Elias—maybe Ilena had returned while he'd been searching the grounds—but before he turned down the corridor that would lead to their balcony, he cut up the stairs to his own room. Perhaps Ilena had gone there to find him.

But his quarters were dark.

He raced past the bed, toward the open doors that led to the balcony, where a torch had been lit outside.

"Ilena?" he called. "Ilena!"

"She isn't here."

Spinning away from the balcony doors, he lifted his hands, ready to use the anathreia raging inside him to defend himself.

At the sight of the woman in white, his shoulders pinched together.

"Anathrasa."

"I like it better when you call me Mother." She stepped into the light beside his bed, her chin high and back straight. She was still wearing her gown from the party, a shimmering wrap of white, latched at the shoulder by a silver circle—an image he was coming to despise. Anathrasa was not a rebirth, not a fresh start. She was a hole humanity would fall into.

"Where is Ilena?" he asked, not yet lowering his hands.

She clucked her tongue in her cheek, and he was reminded of how she had once looked much older and would make that noise when she disapproved of the trouble he and Elias had gotten into.

"I'll tell you if you tell me how long you've been in contact with Ash."

Madoc inhaled slowly, lowering his arms but still ready for anything. Denying it would do him no good; it was clear she already knew the truth. Aera must have seen Ash before she'd left the library.

"She traveled through the fire like Ignitus," he said. "She wanted

Aera's power. I'd been trying to get it for you, but I couldn't. When Ash realized I was telling the truth, she left. Now, where is Ilena?"

Anathrasa sighed. "Aera seemed to think Ash was here longer than just a few moments."

His heart kicked against his ribs. Had Aera been spying on him? What had she heard?

Madoc weighed his options. If Anathrasa thought he was being dishonest, she could hurt Ilena. Control her, like she had the cook and the palace servants. Maybe do something worse now that she had more power.

If he told the truth, it could put Ash in more danger, or compromise her ability to kill Anathrasa—something he might already have done by linking himself to the Mother Goddess.

But Ash had Hydra, Tor, and the Water Divine behind her. And Ilena had only him and Elias.

"Aera lies," he said.

"Not to me." Anathrasa crossed in front of a table against the wall, glancing at her reflection in the basin of water he'd washed with this morning. He felt a sudden surge of hope that Hydra was listening through it—that she could warn and protect Ash.

Anathrasa must have had the same thought, because she casually lifted the edge of the bowl and sent it crashing to the floor.

Madoc's spine snapped straight. Sharp pieces of ceramic littered the floor, damp and shining in the light from the balcony.

"She and Biotus are plotting against you," Madoc said. "I heard them talking in the library."

Anathrasa smiled.

"You heard exactly what you were meant to hear," she said. "Biotus doesn't trust you—with good reason, it would seem. He wanted to test your allegiance. He thought that if you overheard his plans and reported them to me, we'd know you were on our side."

"And I have," he said, clinging to the hope that this could buy him some time.

Anathrasa chuckled. "Aera resisted, as we'd planned. You really can't stand to see a woman in distress, can you?"

He felt the blood drain from his face.

"You were supposed to comfort her," Anathrasa said, her smile growing hard. "Get her to lower her guard. And then you were supposed to take her energeia and give it to me." She pouted. "No, Aera and Biotus didn't know that part."

Anathrasa had planned this. She'd set him up to drain Aera, even to seduce her, maybe. He felt sick.

"But you were going to give the aereia to Ash all along, weren't you? That's why she came to meet you at the palace."

Tension laced Madoc's shoulders tighter together.

"Do you know what the punishment for treason is, Madoc?"

Anathrasa's mouth stretched into a thin line. She walked through the shards of pottery toward him, the muscles in her neck bulging.

"The prison guards are particularly creative, as Elias can tell you." Madoc flinched at her words, remembering the offhand comment about torture that Elias had made at the party. "But seeing as that would hurt me as well, we'll need a different strategy."

She came closer, and he found himself taking a quick step back.

"Don't hurt Ilena," he said before he could stop himself. "I'm sorry I lied to you about Ash. I can still get the energeia from Aera and Biotus and give it to you."

She stalked closer.

"You will," she said, "but not without more of a guarantee. I see that now."

He backed into the wall, scraping his heel against the plaster, which made her own eyes pinch in pained surprise.

"At first, I found this connection between us to be a nuisance," she said. "But then I could feel it—my anathreia returning with every tithe you made. I haven't felt so alive in hundreds of years."

What had he done? That lightness he'd felt, the high of tithing, it wasn't merely his own. It was her emotions, woven with his. He could feel it now. Her intrusion in his soul. Their energeias, braided together.

He'd been helping her without realizing it. Making her stronger with every breath of power he took. Dread mingled with panic inside him. He'd known that they had this link, and he'd continued anyway. Selfishly. Foolishly.

He wanted to tell himself that he would have stopped if he'd known what he was doing, but he couldn't say for certain. Tithing had felt so right. So necessary, so *useful*. For years he'd wanted to do something that had mattered to help the people of Crixion, and now he had the chance. But in doing so, he'd made Anathrasa stronger. Had he deliberately ignored the possible consequences? Looked only to the good he was doing, while he turned away from the bad?

He shouldn't have started tithing. He should have paid more attention to Tor's training, reached into himself for the power he needed.

Instead, he'd made Ash's fight more difficult. He'd put his family in danger.

He should have run with Ash and never looked back.

"It is a privilege to serve you," he said, trying to look earnest, but feeling his shoulders rise with each sharp breath.

He thought of the slap on Anathrasa's cheek. The cut on her hand. The way she hadn't been able to hurt him when he'd been with Elias.

He needed to be calm. To stay steady.

But she had Ilena.

"Of course it is," Anathrasa said. "And, I suppose, for me to be connected to you as well. It's nice, not being alone, isn't it?"

He didn't like the softness in her tone. The way she was looking at him like a son rather than a weapon. He could feel the anxiety rippling through his body, thinning his control.

Making him vulnerable.

"I'm sorry about Ilena," she said with a small frown. "I did like her. She possessed an impressive amount of fortitude for a mortal."

Madoc shuddered. "What did you do?"

"Be still," Anathrasa whispered. "I'll show you."

She placed her hand on his chest.

His lungs seized as they had when he'd kissed Aera, and his blood screamed through his veins. Her hand felt like daggers, pressing through his skin, wrapping his heart in knives. He gasped and fell to his knees, his arms too heavy to push her back.

"Let me in." Anathrasa's voice sounded far away. An echo in a tunnel.

He called on his anathreia to protect him, his body to defend itself, but he could do neither. He fought for calm, for the safety he'd felt with Elias. For focus. But it slipped through his fingers. He was frozen, choked out by the grip of her energeia.

Energeia he'd built for her.

"Let me in," she said again, and he couldn't help it. He felt as if his mind had been flayed, the walls around his thoughts sliced open. He saw Ilena, pressed against a door, her white dress from the party ripped at the shoulder, as if she'd been in a fight. A thin hand squeezed around her throat—

Anathrasa's hand.

"No," Madoc gasped.

He saw a dank cell, the bars corroded. Inside, a man scrambled against the far wall, a fighter—his legs were still coated with the golden dust from the arena. His back was sanded raw, blood running in streaks across his side. His matted black hair hung in his eyes as his blue gaze flicked up in terror.

Elias.

This was before tonight. After Madoc had fled the city with Ash and Tor. He'd left Elias to this fate. To torture.

Tears pooled in Madoc's eyes.

Let me in, he heard Anathrasa say in his mind.

No, he thought.

He was on a ship, gripping the siding, trying not to vomit from seasickness. He focused on the sound of Ash's laughter and couldn't help but smile.

He was eating smoked fish with Tor. Listening to a story about Char, Ash's mother. It was clear from the way Tor described her smile that he'd been in love with her.

Madoc looked down, and Ash's hand was woven in his.

No. He tried to fight Anathrasa off, to keep her out of his private thoughts, but any effort to focus his mind on other things—on the people he'd healed at the Temple, or even the battle in the arena—was in vain. She mined deeper into his memories, forcing him to see exactly what she wanted.

Ash was kissing him belowdecks. Leaning into him to watch the sunrise, her back against his chest. Under him in the tent in the Apuit Islands.

He pressed his lips to Ash's, and she had igneia and geoeia.

Hydra touched her, and she had hydreia.

Ash would be the greatest warrior the world had ever seen. Stronger than Anathrasa. Stronger than anyone.

He would fight for her.

He would prove to her that he was strong enough, and brave enough, and just *enough* to stand beside her.

He loved her with every fragile strand of his soul.

Inside his mind, Anathrasa sighed. *That wasn't so hard, was it?* He trembled at the sound of her voice, thundering through him.

Then, silence.

The pain was gone, but he couldn't breathe. He couldn't move. Was he dead?

He didn't have time for panic. An instant later, he rolled to his hands and knees, and then stood. His breath came in steady pulls. His eyes blinked, his throat swallowed.

He controlled none of it.

Through a stranger's eyes, he looked down at Anathrasa. She beamed up at him.

"You're truly mine now," she said.

He screamed, but knew he was shouting into a void.

Anathrasa knew everything.

When Madoc didn't return to check on Elias, Elias came to him. At the knock on the door, Madoc stood, a prisoner in his own body. He could hear with his ears. See with his eyes. But the movement of his muscles was dictated by Anathrasa. He knew, even without speaking, that his voice would say her words. It was as if everything that made him *himself* had been locked in a box in his mind, while the rest of him was used as a puppet.

He let his brother into the room.

"Did you find her?" Elias demanded, pushing inside. He'd changed his clothes from the party—a thick woven tunic and leggings. Travel clothes, Madoc realized, in preparation for a voyage.

He was ready to take the family and run.

Elias, Madoc willed. *Anathrasa did something to me. I'm trapped. You need to get to Ash. You need to talk to Hydra . . .*

"No," his mouth said.

Elias gave him a strange look. "Then did you find the other gods?"

"Yes," his mouth said.

Anathrasa had left an hour ago to meet with Aera and Biotus. There was something going on, something she'd hidden from him behind a screen of anathreia.

Run! Madoc screamed silently. *This isn't me. She's controlling me.* He didn't know what he was capable of. He didn't know if he could stop himself if his body attacked Elias. Why hadn't he stayed in control? Kept his guard up around her? Endangering Ilena had made him frantic. He'd practically opened the door to his soul and invited her in.

He blinked, and saw Ilena again, pressed against the door, her hands clawing at Anathrasa's fist around her neck. He didn't know where she was, or if she was okay. Anathrasa had attacked her, but it felt like *his* hands. His memories.

His fault.

"All right," said Elias slowly. "Do they know where our mother is?"

She's gone, and Cassia's gone, and you need to get Ava and Danon and get out of here!

"She's safe," he said.

He wanted to beat his own head against the wall.

"She's safe," Elias repeated, looking at him like he'd lost his mind. "So where is she?"

Madoc's head tilted. "Come with me. I'll take you to her."

Elias gave him a wary look. "I've got to stay with Danon and Ava."

"They'll be all right."

Don't listen to me. Madoc willed his body to move, his mouth to speak the words he was shouting inside his head, but all he said was, "Anathrasa won't harm them."

He walked out of his room, turning right down the open corridor.

"Oh, I'm fairly certain she will," Elias argued, hurrying after him.

The Madoc locked inside recoiled in pain, battered again by images of Elias in rags in a prison cell after he'd taken Madoc's place in the arena and fought Ash. Madoc could still see the terror in his eyes. The blood on his back. The way he'd scrambled into a corner like a beaten animal.

"—and Anathrasa is good and fair." His mouth finished, but the sound of his voice startled him. What had he been saying? He'd barely registered the words as his own.

But they weren't his own. They were Anathrasa's.

When he reached the stairs, he began descending them one at a time, ignoring the panic raging inside his own body. "She has my loyalty."

The words were flat, scripted by another consciousness—by Anathrasa.

Elias balked. "You're serious right now."

"I'm serious."

"You trust her."

"With all my soul," he said.

Madoc reached for anathreia, but it was unresponsive. He felt more pigstock than he ever had.

Elias slowed. When Madoc turned, he could see the lines of his brother's frown, deepened by the shadows from the flickering sconces.

"She got to you," Elias said.

Madoc's lips turned up in a smile. "I've just come to see reason."

Elias shuddered. A thought Madoc couldn't read slipped across his face and then was hidden by a guarded scowl. "If I resist, are you going to use your anathreia to make me go with you anyway?"

I don't know. Madoc could no sooner control the sun in the sky than his own body.

"Yes," his mouth said.

Tension stretched between them.

"If I go with you, will you leave Danon and Ava out of it?"

Madoc and Elias both waited for Madoc's answer.

"Yes."

"Then let's get on with it," Elias said. It was clear from the resigned look on his face that he knew this would end badly, but he couldn't risk leaving Ilena in the hands of Anathrasa. In that moment, Madoc both hated and loved him more than ever.

They descended the rest of the stairs in silence, and when they passed the guards in the main foyer, they met no resistance. Madoc's body led Elias toward the back of the palace, to where the old throne room had once sat. The damage there had been cleared away, leaving another stairway to the floors beneath that had been unearthed in the battle.

Down they went, one twisting set of steps at a time, until the green glow of phosphorescent stones became a beacon in the dark, and the smell of piss and death made even his controlled body gag.

"What is this place?" Elias asked, his voice echoing off the stone walls. It was too silent. Eerie and cold.

Madoc's voice answered, "The palace dungeon. Geoxus tithed his favorite gladiators here."

"You mean the ones Anathrasa used to suck the energeia out of," Elias muttered.

The stones lit two Deiman guards with a pale green. There was something wrong about their faces that shook Madoc within the confines of his own body. An unnatural paleness to their skin that highlighted the spiderweb of veins beneath. A blankness in their stare, as if they'd lived so long in the dark that they had lost the use of their eyes.

Behind them stretched a circular room, the walls lined with cells that were packed with people, all standing, all still. But Madoc's gaze was drawn to the center of the floor, where, between an elaborate wooden stretching rack and simple human-sized well of sand, sat a glass sphere. It was the size of Madoc and Elias's old bedroom in the quarter, and made of thick, marbled red glass. Two Air Divine guarded it on either side, watching carefully as Madoc approached.

Look inside, Anathrasa whispered. He could feel her excitement coursing through his veins.

Madoc leaned closer to the glass and found a boy inside, not much older than Danon. At first, he appeared to be sleeping on his back, but as Madoc shifted to a place where the glass was clearer, he was horrified to find that boy's blue-tinted lips were parted, and his small chest was rising in quick, shallow breaths. Strange clothes covered his taut body, a fabric woven of yellowed reeds and dead leaves, and dry, brittle branches seemed to sprout from his open palms.

The boy couldn't breathe, Madoc realized, revolted to the core despite his body's apathy. The glass box prevented air from getting in, or maybe kept it out. He glanced at the Lak guards, sickened by their now smug expressions.

She had her eye on Florus from the beginning, Anathrasa told him. *When they were young, she used to time how long he could stay awake while she siphoned all the breath from his body. See if he would faint when she thinned the air in the room. The case was her idea. There's something about the weak ones that excites her.*

Madoc did not have to ask the question to know who Anathrasa spoke of.

Aera.

She was not the flippant, carefree sister Biotus had abused. She was maniacal, creating a god-proof torture chamber for this boy—Florus—while she flirted and toyed with Madoc. She'd probably only targeted him because she had sensed the same weakness in him that she had seen in the plant god. The act in the library had been nothing more than a game.

He was disgusted. With Aera. With himself. A sudden rage burst in him at the thought that this small god had hurt Ash in Itza. He wanted to lift his own arms and shatter the glass cage.

He couldn't.

"The Mother Goddess has ordered the prisoners be brought to her and the other gods at port so they can be loaded onto the ships," one of the strange Deiman guards said. "Should we bring this one, too?"

Panic traced the edges of Madoc's control. He turned to find the guard standing near Elias. The man's posture was not threatening, but there was something terrifying about his detachment, and Madoc willed Elias not to do anything rash. Now that they were here, he didn't want to let his brother out of his sight. Not with a god locked in an airtight box. Not when he didn't know where these ships were going, or why these prisoners looked so strange.

You'll find out soon enough, my son, Anathrasa told him.

His gaze turned to the cells, taking in the prisoners in their silent lines. They were dressed in plain tunics—the kind that he had once worn beneath his gladiator armor. Pale sand dusted their legs and sandals, and bloody scrapes marred their exposed skin.

Not even the closest turned their head to acknowledge him.

Madoc trembled in the void. He recognized a woman in the cell to their right—her short hair shaved up one side, her hands as big as a blacksmith's. She'd been a champion in the celebration event. She was the one who had saved the boy who'd been shot in the shoulder.

These were all the winners from that event in the grand arena.

He didn't have to count the bodies to know there were a hundred people down here. Not just Deimans, but some Laks and Cenhelmians too. Judging by their blank expressions, their minds had been turned like those of the servants upstairs, but there was something more unsettling about them that he couldn't place. He longed to use his anathreia to reach out to their souls for answers, but it, too, was beyond his control.

"What is this?" Elias had regained his voice, and his tone was low and trembling. "Is she down here? Mother?" He pushed past the guard to Madoc's side. "Ilena Metaxa!" The words bounced off the hard ceiling.

No one answered.

"Keep him here until tomorrow's match," Madoc told the guard, motioning to Elias. "There's no time to turn him now, and we don't want the people thinking that we're fighting prisoners in the tournament."

Turn him? Madoc clawed his own mind for answers. *Where are these people going?*

Elias spun toward Madoc, but just as he was raising his hands, Madoc breathed a quiet "No," and Elias's arms locked to his sides. He looked down at them, baffled at first, as Tor had been on the ship when Madoc had finally controlled his anathreia. In a breath, his confusion slid into terror.

"Don't let Anathrasa do this," Elias pleaded. "You can fight her. We need you to fight her!"

The guard gripped Elias by the shoulders and dragged him toward the cell.

"You can't leave me here," Elias said, his feet pedaling over the damp stone floor. "Brother, please!"

Madoc felt as if a foot were pressing down on his throat. He could barely breathe.

"Don't worry," Anathrasa said through his mouth. "You will not be here for long."

SIXTEEN

ASH

DAYS AFTER ASH got back to the Apuit Islands, Hydra's palace was awash in preparations, littered with weapons and armor.

Tor arranged for a messenger to go to Igna in order to summon Kulan allies to supplement their ranks. He did it without Ash knowing, and when she told him she could have traveled there on her own, he said only, "It's done," and walked away.

He hadn't really spoken to her since the chamber in Florus's palace. There was too much going on for Ash to wonder why he was upset—in the wake of Florus's abduction, his Plant Divine army had converged on the islands too. Ash fought to ignore her kick of revulsion at having them here, but to the Itzans' credit, none of them seemed to wish her any ill will. Perhaps none of them even knew Florus had had her imprisoned.

Or maybe they did, and they all feared her now.

Ash reveled in that thought.

Whatever the truth, three different types of Divine mortals—

water, plant, and fire—were converging, and Hydra estimated they would be ready to attack Crixion within a week. The plan was that she would keep the Mother Goddess busy head-on while Ash, Tor, and a small group of Kulans infiltrated the city. There, they would find Madoc and hopefully get the aereia and bioseia Ash needed to complete her powers.

"What if Madoc hasn't been able to get the other energeias? What if we can't find him?" Tor stood at a table in the throne room with Taro, Spark, and a handful of Hydra's closest advisers, now makeshift generals. He angled the question at them, but it was truly for Ash and Hydra across the room, training.

Again.

Ash had been doing little but training for the past five days, both with Hydra and with various Plant Divine soldiers, to learn how to use her floreia. Ash was now deflecting attacks with stones, water, and plants almost as efficiently as she used fire.

Ash panted as the most recent swell of water dissipated into the ice floor, her hands on her knees, sweat sticking her Kulan reed armor to her back. "We'll find him," she told Tor. "*I'll* find him. I'll spy through every flame in Crixion if I have to."

"What if Anathrasa figures us out and hides him somewhere without flame or stone?" Taro added. "We know it's possible now."

The memory of Florus's prison box slashed into Ash, raw and visceral, and she channeled it into a spike of vines—because she could. Because she was *capable*.

She formed a wall of writhing greenery to counter a wave that Hydra sent toward her, the two crashing in the middle of their makeshift training ground.

Ash hated that she couldn't keep track of Madoc even now. Hydra had tried to check on him through a water bowl after Ash had gotten back, but Anathrasa had dumped it and it had been clear to Hydra that the Mother Goddess had sensed her presence.

They had to be careful. Cautious. They couldn't fling their energeias around Crixion until they absolutely needed to.

Ash lost her hold on the vine wall. The stems snapped in half and Hydra's water shot through, blasting Ash in the face with frigid spray and cutting beads of half-frozen salt water. She faltered backward and landed on her rear, sputtering in the shock of the water.

She wiped a hand down her face and eyed Hydra across the room. A sheen of sweat on the water goddess's face was the only sign that she was working as hard as Ash, her dark hair hanging in tangles around her shoulders.

"Teach me to listen through fire more strongly," Ash told Hydra. "I've done it a little, but if I can perfect it and listen through stones too, I can make sure no place in Crixion is out of my reach."

"Ash." Tor's voice was low in warning. "Don't stretch yourself too thin. I'm not sure I like the idea of you using these god powers *more.*"

"That's not really your decision, is it?" Ash shot at him.

The room hung for a moment in tense silence.

Hydra squinted between Tor and Ash. "Maybe we've trained enough for today, huh?"

Only then did Ash note the fading sunlight and how a chandelier had flared to life with bioluminescent algae. None of these days of training had left her tired—she always felt like she could keep fighting, and learning, and growing. It was as if floreia had given her limitless being. Or maybe it was the god powers in the igneia and geo-eia becoming more a part of her.

Making her more of a god.

A swell of frustration made Ash shoot to her feet.

She'd been suppressing these desires for days. She'd been training with Hydra in energeia over and over and *over* because she could see the tension in Tor, Taro, and Spark every time she mentioned what else she could do now.

"No. We haven't done enough. We won't have done enough until I'm a match for the Mother Goddess," Ash said.

Something unfathomably dark overtook Tor's face. Ash had seen pain like that from him before, just after Char had died, and Ash had become Ignitus's champion, and her life had been upended.

He was afraid for her.

This was different, though, couldn't he see that? She wasn't vulnerable like Char had been.

She couldn't *die.*

"All right," Hydra said slowly. "We can start with listening through fire, since it's more natural for you."

"No," Tor said.

Ash ignored him and faced Hydra. She eyed Ash, questioning, and when Ash prodded her along, Hydra rolled her eyes.

"Focus on any sources of igneia around you. Stretch your mind, shut off distractions, and open yourself up to it like when you travel. But it's less *active,* and more—"

"Like praying," Ash guessed. Like the times she'd prayed to Ignitus throughout her life, few though they were, or the times when her mother and Tor had frantically snuffed any candles to prevent Ignitus from hearing them. Praying was equal parts fear and reverence.

Hydra pursed her lips. "I suppose so. It makes sense, since that's what the mortals are doing on their end."

Ash was already closing her eyes in order to focus.

Fire. Fire like the ones that raged in temples to Ignitus, the orange flames flickering off the glass and obsidian buildings in Igna. The smell of the various fuels burning—sour, sweet, oil and wax and incense. She thought of the—

A scream seared through her mind.

She grabbed her temples, staggering, and felt Hydra's hands on her arms.

Another scream overpowered the first. The words were tangled and begging:

"Help us! Ignitus, hear us!"

"God of fire, save us—"

"Help me!"

And then a voice, strong yet quaking, one she recognized, whispering under his breath as if he was praying in between bouts of giving orders: Brand.

"Ignitus, I know you aren't here anymore. I don't know what else to do—yes, yes, send reinforcements to the southern harbor. Fire god, see us here. Protect us in your homeland and—not those! There are full storehouses of explosives off the main road—"

More screams. More desperate prayers for aid.

"Ash!"

Coldness washed over her body.

Hydra was standing before her—she'd clearly done something to the hydreia in Ash's blood to yank her out of the vision, and Ash came back to herself, gasping, nearly sobbing.

"Tor—Tor!" She whirled, but he wasn't across the room anymore—he was next to her, and he grabbed her outstretched hands. "Kula. Someone's attacking Kula."

Tor's face went gray. "What? Who?"

"Who else?"

Anathrasa. It had to be. That was why Ash and Tor had parted ways with Brand, so he could help restructure now-defenseless Kula. But clearly Anathrasa had wasted no time in staking her claim to Ignitus's country, just like she'd wasted no time in trying to abduct Hydra and Florus.

They should have foreseen this. Of course Anathrasa would strike out at Kula, even if it had no god. *Because* it had no god. She would strip the world of anyone who opposed her or she would force them into submission.

With Kula's Fire Divine warriors under her control, Anathrasa would have four of the six countries at her disposal. And Ash, Anathrasa's only weakness, would be helpless not to do anything the Mother Goddess demanded if she had Kula at her mercy.

"I have to go." Ash was already trying to refocus on traveling. "I have to—"

"Ash, wait!" Tor grabbed her arm. "You have to trust that Brand and the other Kulans can hold off any threat."

She wrenched out of Tor's grip. "What if they can't? Igna isn't equipped for all-out war. No city in this world is! They have no defense."

Hydra's eyes swam with concern. "Tor's right, Ash," she whispered, and Ash hated the sympathy in her voice. "Our armies move out in two days—you have to think of the bigger battle. But—" She glanced at Tor. "We could move out early. Go to Igna's aid."

"How long will that take?" Ash snapped. Her panic hadn't diminished, even as Tor and Hydra seemed to be settling into this plan. "Days, at least? I can be there instantly!"

"Ash." Tor lurched closer to her. He had rarely taken this voice with her, one of disapproval and command. "It's decided. Too much is at stake."

"I can fix this! I'm *immortal.*"

Saying it ached. Ash hated that it ached; she hated the fear that squirmed in her chest at the memory of Florus and his prison and his razor leaves.

And because of that fear, she would act. Goddesses weren't afraid.

"Your mother thought she was invincible too," Tor said.

Ash flinched, jarred out of her offense long enough to wheeze a gasping breath. "This is different. You *know* this is different."

"Is it?" Tor's voice had taken on a brittle quality. Was he close to tears? "Ignitus pushed Char just as ferociously as you are pushing yourself. You don't rest, Ash. You don't slow down. You don't let anyone help you."

"You mean I don't let *you* help me," Ash shot back. She couldn't acknowledge what Tor had said—was she just like Char? A plaything of the gods, trained to exhaustion, used as bait to foster bloodshed? "And what about you? You sent that messenger off to Kula without even consulting me. I'm supposed to save the world, but you still act like I'm a child who has to live with the decisions you make."

"Someone has to look out for you," Tor said through his teeth. His eyes shot to Hydra, accusing. "Someone has to make sure you take time to *breathe*."

"I can't afford to," Ash managed, a whisper. "This is my fate now. I shouldn't even be alive! Do you realize that? I should have died in that arena in Crixion. This life I'm living isn't *mine*."

That was where her fear was coming from. Her self-loathing. Her manic need to keep moving: her life, her body, her powers, weren't *hers*.

Tor was right. She was just like Char, a vessel used by gods. She would push herself, push and push, until nothing was left and the world was saved.

She spun away, pressing the back of her hand to her lips. "If we fail to defeat Anathrasa, I can at least fail knowing that Kula is secure enough to fend her off. This isn't—"

"*Stop.*" Tor barked the word. It echoed off the high, empty ceiling of the throne room, reverberating into silence when Ash just stood there, gaping at him.

"This is what I'm trying to prevent, Ash," he told her. "This war we're fighting will ask too much of you, but you don't have to bleed yourself dry, because you aren't the only one fighting it! Your mother never forgot that she had a team supporting her—you, and me, and

Taro and Spark, and others who were there to catch her and let her rest. She would be ashamed of the way you're behaving."

Ash jerked back like he'd struck her. Her eyes widened, shock falling over her like snow.

Tor's own eyes went wide. He could see he'd gone too far. "Ash—"

She fisted her hands, her body coiled. She wanted to attack him. She wanted to throw geoeia, hydreia, floreia, things she knew he couldn't control or deflect. She wanted to pummel him with all the fury raging inside, her frustration at how he could be so harsh, so cruel.

She whirled away, fists at her temples, and screamed. She screamed until fire swept up over her body, lighting her up like the sun, and she channeled her toxic feelings into one thought.

Igna. Find Brand, she willed, begging her strange new powers to comply. *Igna. Save my country.*

Other thoughts danced at the edges of her mind that she actively wrestled down.

Tor thought she'd changed. Had she? Was she wrong to want to help Kula?

No. Gods, *no*. She wouldn't let Tor make her doubt herself. Too many factors in the coming battle were out of their control—the least Ash could do was control what factors she was able to.

Ash's fire unfurled, and she was in Igna.

SEVENTEEN

MADOC

FOR THE SECOND time since his return to Crixion, Madoc found himself at the grand arena, only this time his body was not his own.

He could hear the thunder of stomping feet and the roar of the crowd as he waited in the tunnel along the northern entrance to the arena. When a servant handed him wine, he drank against his will, and felt the warm liquid slide down his throat. When one of Anathrasa's priests raised a piece of chalk to Madoc's face, he knelt, his legs ignoring his internal plea to run, so that white could be smeared across his mouth in honor of him spreading her word.

He could not stop any of it.

But a small part of him—an exhausted, beaten-down part—still fought. Still felt like *him*, locked in the prison of his controlled body. Maybe it was his soul energeia that shielded him. Maybe Anathrasa wasn't as strong as she thought he was. Either way, he was still *aware*, and could feel her presence creeping in on the edges of his consciousness, though he didn't know how to stop it.

The longer he was under her control, the weaker he was becoming. Stretches of time had begun to go missing from his memory. He knew Elias was somewhere in the palace, but he couldn't remember where. He couldn't recall where Danon or Ava had gone, or where the Metaxas' room was, though he knew he'd been there. He couldn't even say how he'd gotten here, to the arena.

He was disappearing, losing his hold on who he was. If he didn't figure out a way to fight off Anathrasa, he would soon be gone completely. Then Elias, and Ilena, and Danon and Ava would be lost. Ash would fail, because he had failed in his mission to get her the power she needed. And once Anathrasa used him to take the power from Biotus and Aera, and probably also Florus, locked in his glass bubble, the entire world was at risk. With the power of four gods, it was just a matter of time before she defeated Hydra.

A roar outside shifted his attention to the archway, and the gate, now opening onto the golden sand. Anathrasa took her position before him, her gown brushing his arm as she passed. Aera squeezed in beside her, and Biotus beside Madoc.

Hazy memories slipped through Madoc's consciousness of the previous day, when Anathrasa had made him kneel before the gods of air and animal life and tell them his escape from Crixion after Geoxus's death had actually been planned, and that transferring Geoxus's and Ignitus's powers to Ash had been an accidental side effect of trying to kill her.

Aera had been praised for reporting Ash's presence to the Mother Goddess, and it was decided that Ash's appearance in the palace only could have been an attempt at vengeance.

To show his loyalty, Madoc had kissed their feet.

The arena gates opened, and Madoc followed the gods onto the sand, before a crowd screaming their praises. His face smiled, his arm waved, but he controlled none of it.

Behind him, a red glass ball—the case holding Florus—slid into the light. The crowd hushed as it moved toward the center of the arena, carried by rolling grains of sand that the Earth Divine masters on either side manipulated with geoeia. When Anathrasa stopped and stepped beside it, Madoc's head turned, giving him a view of the youthful god and his wide, desperate eyes.

It had been almost a week since Madoc had first seen him in the dungeons. How long Florus had survived in his bubble before then, Madoc didn't know.

With a glance at the goddess of air, Anathrasa began to speak.

"People of Deimos." Her voice was not a shout, but barely a whisper. It came on a breeze, blown from the palm of Aera's hand. "And visitors from our beloved sister countries, Lakhu and Cenhelm. I have returned to guide you in Geoxus's absence. To unify our world, which has too long been at war."

Madoc's head bowed in reverence, along with the rest of the audience.

"But there are those who would oppose us."

A murmuring rose from the stands.

"Florus lured our allies from Cenhelm to join him in Itza under the guise of peace," she lied smoothly. "But along with the goddess of water, he attacked Biotus and his warriors." She paused as the murmuring grew to a dull roar and the wind carrying her words strengthened. "Florus is a traitor. A danger to our world. And I will tear down anyone who threatens to destroy our unified vision of peace and prosperity for both Divine and Undivine, be they god or mortal."

With this, the people cheered. *Madoc* cheered. But inside, he withered.

Anathrasa placed her hand on the red glass case. "As I speak, Hydra readies her army for battle. But whatever the goddess of water may bring to our shores will not be enough to withstand the fierce honor of Deimos."

Madoc's hands rose and clapped along with the spectators. His mouth shouted in approval that Anathrasa was their leader, the Mother Goddess, while his mind revolted at the words. Behind him, the Earth Divine knelt, pressing their hands into the ground and lifting the red prison to hip level on a column of sparkling sand.

"And let anyone else who might consider treason be warned what awaits them if they challenge the Mother Goddess. All energeia once belonged to me, and I will take it back from anyone who attempts to use it against me." She turned to Biotus. "Break it."

With a grin, he stepped to the thick glass and, with a roar, wheeled back and struck it with a hammering fist. The glass shattered in a spray of red dust, and though Madoc didn't move, he could feel a dozen pointed shards nick his face and arms.

The god of plants gasped, a horrible rattling sound, and his chest expanded with the first full breath he'd taken in days.

"Now," Anathrasa said.

Madoc didn't realize she was talking to him until his body turned toward the remains of the ball, and his hands reached over the jagged siding.

"Yes, my goddess," his mouth said, even as his mind screamed, *No!*

It was too late. Anathreia rose inside him like a torrent of wind, ripping through his soul, his flesh, his muscles. The hunger was sudden, absolute, and when he inhaled, he could taste earth and wood on the back of his tongue.

"Stop," Florus whispered, reaching for Madoc, but the god was weak from his days without breath, and the green branches that sprouted from his palms quivered, and then shriveled and turned black. With a guttural cry, Florus arched backward, chest lifted and toes pointed. Every muscle in his small body flexed to the point of snapping. His eyes bulged, staring desperately at the sky.

Madoc tried to shake himself free of his hold on the plant god. He tried to turn his shoulders, his head, any part of him away from the god of plants, but it was no use. Revulsion coursed through him, as potent as his own need. *I'm sorry,* he screamed silently. No one could hear.

Next to Madoc, Aera gave a quick gasp. From the corner of his eye he could see her hands fist. A wave of uncertainty peeled off her, but he couldn't make sense of it. She'd been the one to trap Florus in that bubble, breathless, in the first place.

She knows this could be her, he realized. Maybe he should have pitied her, but he didn't.

"More," Anathrasa ordered. "It was mine to begin with. It will be mine again, now."

Madoc reached deeper into Florus's soul, pulling at the twisting vines and roots of his energeia and yanking them free. Madoc could feel the pressure of the foreign power crushing him from the inside out—its heavy, living force sliding through his veins. His heartbeat pounded in his ears. His vision began to shake.

Florus collapsed in a heap, his breath shallow.

Madoc staggered. He blinked, and when he opened his eyes Anathrasa was before him. Her lips tilted in a smile as he took her hands, and maybe it was weak, but in that moment he longed for her help. Anything to ease this incredible burden.

How had he ever thought he was strong enough to help Ash?

"Complete the circle," she told him.

Her hands squeezed his, and when he exhaled, she siphoned the energeia out of his body. The screaming in his head quieted, the twisting of his joints released. He inhaled sharply, feeling a cool flood of relief. Too late he tried to cling to some small bit of floreia—enough to save for Ash—but it slipped away, drawn into Anathrasa's soul like a sprout opening to the sun.

Anathrasa sighed, her eyelids fluttering. When she smiled, not a single wrinkle lined her mouth. Her skin was flushed and smooth. Her hair was full.

"Thank you," she said quietly.

She released Madoc's hands, and he faced the crowd, disgusted with himself. Horrified by what he'd just helped her do.

"Itza belongs to Biotus now," Anathrasa told the people of Deimos, her voice carried again on the wind. The god of animals raised his chin and pounded his massive chest with one meaty fist. "The Itzan people are his, just as Hydra's Apuitians will soon be Aera's."

At this, the goddess of air lifted her hands and sent a blast of cool air across the stands, ruffling clothes and hair, delighting the crowd.

This was what Anathrasa had promised them, Madoc realized. This was why they sided with her—for power, for more people and more land.

They had no idea she intended to strip it from them the same way she had Florus.

"As for the god of plants, he belongs to Deimos now," Anathrasa finished. "Let's see how he fares among our fiercest fighters. The first one to bring me his heart will have their likeness cast in gold outside this arena."

No. Madoc glanced at the god of plants, so young and now so fragile, pushing himself to his knees in what remained of the shattered glass sphere. Madoc couldn't help thinking of the boy who'd been shot by an arrow at the first games—the child he'd healed at the sanctuary. He could offer Florus no such mercy now.

The Earth Divine who'd moved the glass sphere into the arena now exited the way they'd come, but Madoc and the gods did not follow. Before him, Anathrasa raised her arms, hands clenched, and the ground began to rumble. A moment later, dark roots burst from the sand, braiding together in a tightly woven staircase the stretched from the ground straight up to the viewing box.

The crowd screamed their approval.

Hand in hand, Anathrasa and Aera climbed, with Biotus just behind them, and Madoc trailing by a few steps, until they reached the marble ledge of the box and were helped down by their servants.

"Isn't that twig-armed grunt your brother?"

Madoc followed Biotus's pointing finger down to the sands, where more than thirty Earth Divine had emerged from the western gate to fight. Near the back of the cluster was a man in a red tunic, marked across the chest with an embroidered silver circle.

Brother—the word was only a whisper in Madoc's mind.

Madoc frantically realized that he'd nearly forgotten Elias. His brother was wearing the same clothing he'd worn to the party where Anathrasa had introduced Madoc as her son. How had Elias gotten here? The last thing Madoc remembered was searching for Ilena with him.

Ilena. Where was their mother now? And Danon, and Ava?

He couldn't lose his grasp on himself. He needed to hang on. To remember. To *fight*.

Elias wasn't holding any weapons, nor was he wearing any armor. His head moved, eyes roaming from his Deiman competition to the Air Divine filtering in from the opposite side of the arena and the horde of Biotus's warriors now spilling through the front gate. They'd brought more animals this time. Giant cats. Bears. Even wolves.

The ships from Cenhelm must have arrived, Madoc thought bleakly, remembering how few Animal Divine had fought in the last celebration. There were a hundred of them now, huge men and women with glinting steel weapons and leather armor.

In the center of it all, a small mortal who'd once been a god lifted a shard of red glass to defend himself.

Madoc looked again for Elias. *What have I done?*

"A Deiman not loyal to my mother is no brother of mine," he told Biotus.

The god of animals snorted, then gave a laugh. He slapped Madoc on the back hard enough that he nearly went over the railing.

"Then he'll be meat for my warriors," Biotus said. "But not before they take my brother's heart."

Madoc's consciousness trembled with what rage he could still muster. He hoped Anathrasa did use him to drain Biotus, just so the god would suffer.

Not yet, Anathrasa warned in his head. *We still need the loyalty of the Air and Animal Divine to defeat the water goddess and her little pet.*

When Madoc pictured Ash, he could feel Anathrasa's laugh rumble through his chest.

Below, Elias crouched, picking up a fistful of sand and rubbing it between his hands. He was passed by another fighter, who offered a quick word before moving on. He looked the part of a Deiman gladiator—his armor fit well, and he was big enough to fight off any of the Animal Divine.

Lucius, Madoc realized. He remembered the trainer's disgusted expression at the last fight. Maybe he'd decided he couldn't stand by and had entered the games himself.

Maybe, like Elias, he'd been forced into the ring.

"There's my little soul stealer." Madoc felt two hands slide around his waist, and a female body press against his back. He breathed in and was overwhelmed by Aera's floral scent as she rested her chin on his shoulder. "Finally learned your place, have you?" She giggled. "What you did down there was quite impressive. I'm glad you didn't get the chance to do it to me."

His eyes lifted to the shattered red prison, and disgust reeled through what remained of his soul.

"Never, goddess," Anathrasa said through his mouth.

Aera smiled against the back of his shoulder. "How about a wager? If a Deiman wins my brother's heart, I'll come to your room tonight. But if it's a Lak?" She nuzzled her nose against the side of his neck and, inside, he trembled in powerless rage. "You'll come to my room, lover."

Push her away, he told himself. *Tell her no.*

His body didn't listen. He covered her hands, splayed across his chest, with his own, and lifted his chin so she could kiss his throat.

She likes you, Anathrasa whispered. *That will serve us well when we drain her.*

The games began with the blare of horns and a wave of black and silver flags, and soon all the warriors were struggling to get to Florus in the center of the arena. The boy was fighting them off with handfuls of dirt and a spear he'd taken from someone, but the effort was weak and inconsequential. He disappeared beneath a crowd of bodies, only to be tossed into the air by a powerful, aereia-controlled burst of wind. When he landed, a Cenhelmian took him to the ground, but they both were soon knocked aside by an earthquake sent by one of the Earth Divine fighters. Madoc tried to follow Elias, but his eyes kept roaming, controlled by Anathrasa, who was seated on a white marble throne at the back of the viewing box.

The next time Madoc saw Florus's body, it was being thrown through the air, limp and bloody. A Lak fighter screamed that she had his heart, but she was immediately speared through the chest by an Animal Divine.

Soon Florus's body was forgotten, and the game became who could hold the heart of a god.

Biotus shouted for his warriors to draw blood, and they did not disappoint. Four Animal Divine warriors surprised a group of Aera's fighters, rallying around the bloody heart with a net, trapping them to the ground. Taking advantage of the move, Lucius buried them in a wave of gravel, only to be blown against the perimeter wall by another Lak man.

The fighters appeared to be attacking as though their lives depended on it. There was no sign that Anathrasa was controlling them, but if she could take over Madoc's body, she could do the same to others. Make divine men and women more skilled and powerful with their energeia than they'd ever been.

A new terror pressed down on the edges of his consciousness.

Finally, Madoc's gaze returned to Elias. His brother's back was against the wall—a choice, Madoc realized, that was serving him well defensively. Those who attempted to attack were forced to come straight at him, and Elias warded them off in droves with tidal waves of gravel and dust.

Stay standing, Madoc willed him. He didn't know if Anathrasa would end this battle before people died again, or if those who'd lost would be healed. He suspected Elias would not be so lucky. With another shock of helpless terror, Madoc remembered the first-round winners from the first games in the palace dungeon, and feared Elias would meet the same fate.

"My fighters still hold the heart," Aera sang. Her cool lips slid down the tendons of his neck, and he was revolted again by the pleasure she took in her brother's brutal death. "I think that means I'm winning."

Madoc could feel competitiveness take him by storm. It wasn't his choice, but rather Anathrasa's enjoyment whipping through his blood. He wanted nothing to do with these games, but as Lucius knocked down two Cenhelmian fighters in one battering swing of his spear and stole the heart for himself, his excitement grew, and soon he was cheering along with the other gods.

You're enjoying yourself, Anathrasa told him.

His body turned back to face the Mother Goddess. Smiled.

You're *enjoying this,* he wanted to respond. But she either didn't hear him or didn't care.

And after a moment, he didn't care either.

EIGHTEEN

ASH

IN IGNA, ASH was near the harbor. She faced the bulk of the city, its sprawling obsidian structures speckled with windows in a rainbow of hues. The sky was gray with low-slung clouds and the air had a twist of humidity, thick like a storm had come or was about to come.

She was relieved—only for a breath.

Then grief hit her, a piercing feeling of absence: Ash hadn't been to Igna since her mother died.

She had the sensation of being underwater again, her senses muted as though she was submerged, noises muffled to a dull roar, her breath a grating rumble alongside the thudding of her heart. Each blink was languid and painful, flashing with memories she had been able to ignore for several weeks.

Char taking her to Igna's markets. Idly shopping with her, whiling away time and money on trinkets and smiles to combat the horror of Char's life as Ignitus's champion.

Char and Tor arm in arm as they walked along the waterfront. Her mother, smiling, her teeth a blinding white and her face soft.

Char trying a dish at a tavern, then spitting it out and laughing through tears at how spicy it was.

Everywhere, Ash saw her mother. Everywhere, Ash heard her voice, her all-too-rare laughter.

She hadn't felt Char's absence so strongly since she'd watched her mother die.

Wheezing, Ash stumbled around and faced the sea.

Everywhere, Kulans were running. Innocent citizens were fleeing in terror; warriors, their bodies awash in flame, were positioned strategically around the bay.

And out in the water, charging through the surf, were half a dozen Deiman ships.

The breath went out of Ash's lungs.

Around her, screaming voices pushed through her fog.

"Ignitus!" They had seen her fire. They had watched her appear in a flare of blue and gold. "Ignitus! Our god has risen!"

But they turned, and they saw *her*, not Ignitus, and the cheers became confused cries, and Ash couldn't deal with an explanation right now.

"I haven't been to Kula in decades."

Ash glanced over her shoulder to see Hydra behind her, shifting out of her water form.

"I'm not leaving Kula with you," Ash told her.

Hydra locked eyes with her. "I know."

That was it. Just acceptance, and Ash realized with a jolt that Hydra had come to help her. Or at least to make sure Ash didn't get herself irreparably hurt.

Ash nodded, surveying her surroundings. She and Hydra were on the path in front of a naval building on the largest military dock. As she turned to leap up the steps, a man shot out of the doors and drew up short at the sight of her.

"Ash?" Brand's face contorted. Ignitus's former champion looked behind her, to Hydra, and his frown deepened. "How did you—"

"What is happening?" Ash demanded.

He took the steps two at a time to stand in front of her. The last she had seen the cocky champion, he had been gaunt and stricken by Ignitus's death. That, and his short time in Kula explaining Ignitus's fate, had seemed to mature him. The flighty confidence Ash had hated in him was gone. A rough line of stubble made him look unkempt and tired. He was wearing Kulan reed armor, but it was dented and well-used, not ceremonial in the slightest.

"Deimos sent a message ahead of their ships," Brand told her. "They've come to take the Fire Divine to fight in Crixion's arenas. It's a *privilege*"—he spat the word—"and the winners will become part of the Mother Goddess's circle. Whatever that means."

"She sent centurions to capture Kulans," Ash said, half to herself. Just as Anathrasa had sent Biotus to take Florus.

"Not just centurions," Brand said.

Ash frowned.

He pointed at the ships. "If you look through a spyglass you'll find rows of armed gladiators on those ships. If she's taking Kulans to fight in her arenas, and using the victors—"

"She's building an army of gladiators." Hydra was the one who finished the thought. Brand gave her an odd look, like he recognized her but couldn't place her, and nodded grimly.

"An army made of the fiercest fighters in the world," Ash said. She felt ill. "Such a force would quell any unrest."

Hydra blew out a breath. "Anathrasa would have complete control of the world."

Ash faced the sea, the coming ships. Anathrasa may have gotten Deimans, Laks, and Cenhelmians to obey her, but no Kulans would join her army.

Brand echoed her unspoken sentiment. "The Mother Goddess seems to think she can *make* Kulans bow to her, but after what Geoxus did to our god, any supporter of Anathrasa will find only bloodshed here!"

He shouted the last words and punched a fist into the air. All around him, frantic warriors and cowering citizens alike responded with a cheer.

But Ash watched Brand's face. His eyes showed none of the conviction in his voice.

He sobered and bent closer to her. "Many of our warriors deserted when they learned of Ignitus's death," he whispered to her. He kept his focus on the passing soldiers, the ones who were scrambling to set up a defense as the Deiman ships drew ever closer. "They fled the city, seeking shelter in the wilderness outside Igna. They think the world is ending."

He paused, eyes sliding to her in an unspoken question. *Is it?*

"We know how to defeat Anathrasa," Ash told him.

Some of the tension in Brand's face subsided. He cast his eyes to Hydra, this time with purpose. "Did you bring help from the Apuit Islands? Or Itza?" He looked down at her again, confused. "How did you know we were in trouble?"

"I heard you," Ash said. "And I did bring help. This is Hydra."

Brand's mouth fell open. For a moment, his body twitched as though he might drop to his knees in reverence.

But Hydra waved him off. "Ash is more powerful than I am."

Brand's jaw went slack. "What?"

Ash didn't respond. She was still watching the ships and could barely make out moving shapes, rocks shifting and lowering as centurions—gladiators—prepared their attack.

Such an army would destroy this city at Anathrasa's command and drag Kulans into her war, to be drained of their igneia if they refused to fight for her.

Ash would die before she let Anathrasa touch any of her Kulans. Because they were just that—*her* Kulans, *her* compatriots.

Anathrasa would not take anything else from her.

"Hydra," Ash said, taking slow steps toward the water. "With me."

Brand followed them. "Where is the army? Who did you bring? We have soldiers stationed around the—"

"Call them back," Ash told him.

"What? Are you insane? We can't leave the bay undefended."

"Call them back," she said again. She cut her eyes to him, and the strike of her glare rendered him silent. "Clear the bay. Now."

Brand faltered a step, but he nodded and started shouting the order. It caught, tentatively, and Ash watched the small specks of Kulans peel back from the water. Or maybe she just sensed it through her connection to them, the thrumming of her igneia beating stronger now that she was in Kula, surrounded by Kulans.

"You'll need to get closer," Hydra told her. "You'll have more control of your energeias if you can see what you're attacking and where."

Ash continued walking, closing the distance to the shore. When she reached the lapping water, she paused, whipping a look to Hydra. "*I'll* have control? You're not going to help?"

Hydra had matched her pace and was next to her. "You wanted to save your country? You're a god now. So get out there and act like the god of Kula."

Ash's hands shook. Blame was heavy in Hydra's tone. If something happened to Ash or Hydra—if Anathrasa captured them or injured them somehow—it would be Ash's fault, because she hadn't waited, because she was impetuous.

She was also a goddess, and Kula was hers, and she would defend it.

Ash started walking again. Small pillars of water lifted to meet each footstep as she headed out into the bay.

The lead Deiman ship had just reached their waters.

Ash stopped a few paces back from its bow. Hydra was beside her, hovering on a similar pillar.

A man onboard saw them.

"Turn around and sail back to Crixion," Ash told him.

The centurion laughed. "Not likely."

He noted their position, standing on the water. He noted Ash, especially, smoke like steam gathering around her and flames licking her face.

Fear broke his confidence with a flinch.

"Leave Kula," she said. "Now."

"We have our orders. Kula's god is dead. The Mother Goddess wishes to bring his lost children into the fold of her guidance—"

"I will kill the Mother Goddess," Ash promised. "Just as I killed your god of earth."

That made the centurion's unease shift into anger. "God Killer! We will not leave until all able-bodied Kulan warriors have surrendered to the superior might of Deimos. We will not leave until we have taken from you what you took from us tenfold!"

"Are you going to let him keep talking?" Hydra whispered. *"Attack."*

Ash felt the flames on her arms waver.

"High ground," Hydra prodded. "Rise up."

Attack. High ground. These were all things Ash knew from her arena training. How to fight. How to *win.*

She lifted her arms and a thrashing wave carried her into the air. The commotion on the Deiman ships paused as everyone watched her.

She saw the rows of immobile gladiators now. Their heads lifted as one, their eyes on her empty and unseeing.

Ash realized with a jolt of horror what Anathrasa had done. She was building an army of warriors wholly given over to her control. This was what she wanted from the world—utter, explicit obedience.

"The circle is unending," the gladiators began to chant. "The circle is unending. The circle—"

Panic swelled in Ash.

"She did this before." Hydra's voice came from the droplets of water on Ash's ears, the raging waves thrashing beneath her feet. "Forced people to obey her. It's disgusting."

"She's stronger than we thought." Ash felt sick.

"Steady. You can do this. They know you can control hydreia now. Attack where they won't expect it."

Yes. Ash could do that. The unexpected.

She called all manner of ocean plants up from the depths, and they squirmed and writhed around the thick hulls and up the wooden rails. The igneia was still alive within her, even as she used floreia. Fire sparked off the tips of her hair and the ends of her fingers and glowed from every muscle on her body. Water spewed foam and froth around her as it held her aloft, and the plants that scurried to do her bidding grew in great, powerful surges of green life.

"There are rocks on the ships," Ash said to Hydra, and she laughed. Didn't these stupid mortals know who they had come to fight?

"Get to them," Hydra told her, "before the Earth Divine can use them. Call on plants and fire also—I'll handle the water."

"I thought you weren't going to help?"

Hydra gave Ash a sardonic look. "Don't make me change my mind."

Ash laughed again. "Kula already has a god, Anathrasa," she told the Mother Goddess. She knew Anathrasa wasn't there, but she was listening through these people, and Ash's voice resounded out of the rocks onboard every ship. "And I am Deimos's god too."

Ash clapped her hands together.

The plants slammed into the wooden planks of the ships, snapping them like twigs. Hydra sent water gushing over the rails and pouring into the cracks. Ash called on flames to lick at rope and barrels, bright bursts of light and heat that singed hands and served as warnings. And when the centurions cried out and dived for their precious rocks, Ash used those, too; she lifted every stone into the air and crushed them to shards that she then showered down on the Deimans.

It wasn't enough. Ash pushed the shards of rocks outward, flinging them like projectiles. They met skin, dug deep; she pushed, the shards burying at her command as screams rose—

"Ash!" Hydra's voice pitched high. "Ash, *stop*! You don't need to kill them!"

"They'd kill my people!"

"Stop," Hydra pleaded. "Stop the bloodshed. Let them live."

Ash could so easily sink these ships to the depths of the bay.

But she felt Hydra, felt her intention tug gently on Ash's control of hydreia. The goddess would always control water, even while Ash manipulated it.

With a snarl, she relented.

The ships were damaged, not destroyed. The crews sprinted for order, but there was no order.

There was only Ash.

She had spared the crews' lives. She had given them a second chance. That was more than Geoxus had let his gladiator give to Char. More than Ignitus had given to Rook after his son had died. More than Anathrasa had given to Madoc. That was more than any god ever gave to any mortal, and for that, Ash would be known not only as God Killer, but Merciful.

"This world does not belong to you, Anathrasa," Ash said. "Ready your armies. I am coming for you."

She lifted her arms higher, pulling the wave she stood on up, up, up, before she dropped all her weight and plummeted into the water. The force of her surge propelled the Deiman ships hard and fast for the open, stormy waters of the Hontori Sea.

The bay churned and rocked. Ash hovered in it, watching the ships to make sure they wouldn't try to charge back. But their crews scrambled to turn sail, fighting the cracks Ash had left in their vessels.

Only the gladiators were not panicked. Ash thought she saw them smile.

Ash turned to Hydra, expecting to see the water goddess looking as triumphant as Ash felt.

But the water goddess scowled at the horizon.

"You look like you think we lost the battle," Ash said, gasping as her body trembled with the aftershocks of the fight. "Look what we did! We—"

Hydra lifted her hands. "We protected Igna, but at what cost? You were a threat to Anathrasa before, but you are deadly to her now. And with your Madoc currently in Crixion . . ."

Ash recoiled. Her body still hummed with the power she had unleashed, a ripe, resilient flurry that made her feel . . . *everything.*

Every particle of sand on the shore. Every thudding heartbeat in the crowds watching her. Every sparking flame in the hands of the Kulan warriors. Every splash of water.

Everything but the fear she should feel, knowing she had endangered Madoc even more.

It should have consumed her, that fear. She should have been frantic to talk with Tor and find some way to salvage it.

But all she could think of was whether or not Madoc had gotten aereia and bioseia yet. Had he given them to Anathrasa, or was he fighting her off to save them for Ash? She wanted those missing pieces. How much swifter would her defense of Kula have been if she had been complete?

"He'll be fine." Ash looked up at Hydra. "He'll get the other energeias for me—"

Hydra's eyes narrowed. "That's it? You just made your lover even more of a target, and you don't have any reaction? Any guilt?"

"I defended what's mine!" Ash whirled, a wave cutting up around her. Fire streamed along each arm, holding there in threatening flickers.

From the shore, a chant started. Ash thought she heard Brand's voice kick it up first.

"Goddess! Goddess!"

"Do you hear them?" Hydra snapped. "Do you hear what they're calling you?"

"Goddess!" the Kulans cheered. "Goddess!"

"How does that not terrify you?" Hydra's eyes teared. "Look at the gods of this world. Look at what has happened to them. All of them, all of *us*, are murderous and cruel. This is what you want to become?"

"Maybe it's what I already was," Ash said. "Cruel. Selfish. Untethered. Maybe this power just set me free to stop cowering and embrace that I've had this strength in me all along."

Hydra shook her head, tears clouding her eyes. "This isn't strength, Ash. There can be power in unbridled selfishness to a degree, but you need to learn those limits."

The water goddess sank into the bay, a ripple of sea-foam on the surface. Ash stared down at it, her shoulders heaving and her muscles aching while the crowd chanted *goddess* all around her and the sky raged a stormy gray above.

She screamed, and fire shot out from her hands into the roiling sky, and she fell into the flames.

NINETEEN

MADOC

MADOC'S CONSCIOUSNESS REVIVED in stages.

A breath of cool air on the balcony in his room.

A bite of sour yogurt with breakfast, Aera giggling with Biotus, all at a table together. Panic seized his mind when he realized he'd lost time—how long had it been since the fight? Where was Elias? Had he been injured?

The last he recalled, Aera had made a wager about whose people would win—a Lak or a Deiman—and whose room she and Madoc would later meet in. He prayed he hadn't followed through on that bet. That Anathrasa hadn't let him be used in that way.

Before he could find out more, he grew foggy and slipped away.

Days passed—he could feel them ticking down in his mind like notches in a wall, though he could never grab hold of any one moment long enough. He was so tired, drawn so thin.

He rested. He didn't know what his body was doing.

And then—the low light of a sheltered corridor, leading toward a stairway. He had to duck as he walked down the steps so he didn't hit his head on the ceiling. He felt as though he was waking from a long sleep and couldn't quite get his bearings.

He was following Anathrasa.

He became alert in a rush.

He was conscious. He would *stay conscious—*

Yes, stay awake, my son, Anathrasa told him. *I want you to watch this.*

He tried to lash out at her. He tried to fight—but fog overcame him and he started to slip away again. He relented, panicked.

She was still in control.

Where were they going?

"To prepare our winners."

Madoc didn't have to see Anathrasa's face to know she was gloating.

Would they tithe on them? He couldn't even summon the energy to be disgusted. He was so tired from fighting her. It was like standing in a room with Aera, feeling the breath pulled out of his lungs.

At the bottom of the stairs, they turned, the path twisting into a broad hall. The fighters were crowded in cells, lined with metal bars easily manipulated by the Earth Divine, but reinforced by a line of soldiers standing shoulder to shoulder. A quick glimpse told Madoc these people suffered from the same affliction that those in the palace dungeons had—their eyes were blank, staring mindlessly ahead. Their skin was paper-thin, showing shadows of sinew and bone beneath.

There was something very wrong with them, and Madoc

wondered if that's what would happen to his body should Anathrasa be left unchecked in his brain.

The winners were being held like prisoners. They'd suffered a few scrapes and bruises but seemed all right overall. Circle members in white robes tended to them, carrying jars of water slung over their shoulders.

Elias? He tried to look inside a cell, but his head wouldn't turn the right way. He could only catch sight of Lucius, sneering in his direction, arms threaded through the metal bars. Madoc could see the dark stains on his hands and remembered with another turn of his stomach that he'd last seen Lucius raising Florus's heart in his fist. Had he won? Madoc hoped not, now that he had seen what Anathrasa did to Deimos's fiercest warriors.

"Looks like you're a champion after all," he spat as Madoc passed. "How does it feel, son of Petros, to cheat your way into the company of gods?"

At the mention of his father, Madoc felt sick.

"Bring Lucius," Anathrasa said, without slowing. "The fight's victor will be the first."

Regret pinched the base of Madoc's neck.

"Or perhaps I'll be the last," Lucius tossed back, a clear threat to end the Mother Goddess's reign. "Why don't we meet in the arena? We'll see how your soul energeia withstands the power of an Earth Divine gladiator."

Madoc didn't watch the centurions beat the man, but he heard the grunts of pain.

"Madoc?"

He managed to turn toward the sound of his name and found Elias pushing through the winners to get close to the edge of the cell. Madoc's body didn't stop, so Elias had to keep moving to match his pace.

"Madoc, you have to stop her. She has—"

"That's enough," Anathrasa said.

Madoc lifted a hand, and Elias's words were cut short by a surge of anathreia. Elias scratched at his own throat, his eyes wide.

Panic strangled Madoc's relief at finding Elias alive. He focused all his energy on loosening his hold on his brother, and thankfully, Elias crumbled to the floor a moment later.

Had Madoc done that? Or had Anathrasa simply grown bored with hurting Elias?

They were escorted to the end of the hall, to a room like those Madoc had once prepared for matches in. Inside, the low light pulsed, and the decadent scents of meat and fresh bread wafted from a table against the far wall.

"Mother Goddess." One of Anathrasa's priestesses brought her a goblet of wine, the smear of chalk on her mouth already thinned by sweat. "Are you ready to begin?"

Madoc's consciousness rippled with horror as he recognized the woman.

Ilena.

She wasn't dead. She was here. She was . . .

"Mine," said Anathrasa. "Yes. She's mine, as are you, Madoc. You didn't really think I'd dispose of her completely, did you? She still has much to give."

Ilena didn't look at Madoc. She didn't look at anything. Her hands stayed slack at her sides as she awaited further instruction.

What will you do? Madoc's silent demand echoed through his soul.

"What I must," Anathrasa said, then patted Ilena's head and sent her from the room. "We need a suitable army to defeat Hydra and Florus's Plant Divine, do we not? The strongest fighters in Deimos?"

He thought of the people who'd been called to join the celebration games. It didn't matter if they'd been trained as gladiators—if they were strong, they were welcome, regardless of age or ability.

Two centurions appeared in the threshold of the door, carrying a limp Lucius between them. His head hung forward, his short hair matted with blood.

Despite everything, Madoc pitied him.

"You were right when you said I meant to take over the six countries," Anathrasa continued, stalking toward Lucius. She extended the goblet of wine at her side, and Ilena raced in from the doorway to take it. "But it's not as simple as sailing off and claiming them. As long as people have power, there will be those who mean to destroy me."

The gods, he thought.

"Not just the gods, Madoc. Those the gods created. The Divine."

Panic trembled through him. She meant to destroy the Divine?

Anathrasa glanced back at him, a patronizing smile on her lips. "Come now. You of all people should recognize the danger they pose. A god's power was never meant to live in a mortal body. I see now what a failure this Divine experiment truly was. They were always meant to be fuel for our own energeia, nothing more."

Madoc didn't understand what she was saying. She couldn't drain all the Divine in the world. There were too many of them. They would rally against her.

"They'll be too busy fighting among themselves," she said. "It's already begun. The most powerful Deimans, Laks, and Cenhelmians have already volunteered to join our cause. Look at how much happier they are to serve." She strode to Lucius, grabbed his hair, and jerked his head back. With a moan, his eyes blinked open, focusing unsteadily on Madoc.

Anathrasa was using her gladiator games as a way to rid the world of Divine. She pretended to honor them, raised them up in Geoxus's name, then she turned them into what Madoc had seen in the dungeons.

Empty soldiers. An army that would fight without fear, without emotion. Without their *souls*. She would tithe the entire world, becoming more powerful by the moment, and when all were shells, she would use them as she pleased—by controlling them with anathreia.

Anathrasa didn't just want to take over the six countries; she wanted to destroy them.

Ash. She had to hear this. She had to know.

He tried to focus on her in his mind, but he couldn't see her clearly. He couldn't remember the shape of her eyes or the sound of her laugh. He couldn't remember the last thing they'd talked about.

He couldn't remember anything they'd talked about.

He tried to hide his thoughts too late.

"Oh, she knows, my dear. The first wave of my army has already attacked Kula. I hear she mounted an impressive defense, but it did not save all her Fire Divine brothers and sisters. Aera tells me your Ash is gathering a sad little army, meant to face me." A smile. "She will find more resistance than she expected here."

This was bad. He needed to stop Anathrasa. He needed to . . .

"What?" she asked, dropping Lucius's head. With another groan, he attempted to stand, but he stumbled into one of the men holding him. "You need to what, Madoc?"

Help you.

He needed to help his mother.

"Yes," she said with a smile. "And soon, the Divine will be gone, just like you always wanted. You won't be that awkward boy fighting his way through the stonemason's quarter any longer. The Undivine will flourish. You'll be their champion, and I'll lead them all, a true Mother Goddess. The only one responsible enough to yield the power of energeia."

He watched as Anathrasa placed her hands on the sides of Lucius's jaw and sipped in a steady breath. Lucius struggled—quietly first, but then with the desperate movements of a man on the brink of death. He screamed and thrashed as he fought the guards.

Madoc did nothing to stop it.

The woman raced from the door, dropping to her knees beside Lucius. "He's ready, Mother Goddess."

Madoc blinked, and her face came back into focus with a sharp bite of clarity.

This was his mother. Not Anathrasa. *Ilena.*

"Complete the circle," Ilena said in a flat voice, controlled by Anathrasa's soul energeia. "Complete the circle."

He forced himself to focus, not to fall to Anathrasa's control. He willed Ilena to look at him. He reached for his anathreia, trying to force her to comply. Was she locked inside her body as he was inside his? The thought sickened him.

With a breath, Anathrasa lifted her hands, and Madoc could feel the surge of power in his own veins. Her mouth opened. Her eyes rolled back.

Lucius went still. He straightened. With renewed horror, Madoc watched as Lucius blinked and stared ahead with wide, blank eyes.

"Ah." Anathrasa lowered her arms. When she smiled, not a wrinkle lined her mouth. "Look at that. Isn't he wonderful?" She strode toward him, the use of her power not slowing her down in the slightest.

"Wonderful," said Ilena.

Madoc looked at Lucius again, at his pale face and slack mouth, and his head grew blissfully silent.

He couldn't remember where he'd seen this man before.

"Wonderful," Madoc said.

"They'll fight without fear," Anathrasa said. "The ultimate soldiers. Unafraid of death. Only willing to do what I ask."

"Wonderful," Madoc said again.

"This is how we win," Anathrasa said. "How we beat the Divine. By turning their strongest into true believers."

"The circle is complete," said Ilena.

"Go get Elias," Anathrasa told Ilena. "Bring him in next. He'll make a fine subject for Madoc's first attempt."

Elias.

Elias was his brother.

The last remaining shreds of Madoc's consciousness dug into his soul. He was losing himself, he could feel that now. There was little time left before he was completely Anathrasa's.

He had to protect Elias, but how? He couldn't move his body. His thoughts were betraying him. He was slipping into a black hole.

Ash.

Ash would pull him out of that hole.

He forced himself to rally. Ash was the goddess of fire and earth. She could help him.

But how? She was so far away.

The shame piled on him, weighing him down. Ash had always been a better fighter. Stronger. Smarter. She'd been able to hold the power of gods when it had nearly killed him. He'd thought that if he could help her, she'd see his worth. She'd keep him. But he'd always known it was just a matter of time before she'd see the truth.

He couldn't help her.

He couldn't even help his own family.

The things that matter live inside us, and we protect them as we protect any other part of ourselves, with the power we've been given. The words came from far away. An echo, already fading.

They lit one final spark of hope inside him.

He was still Deiman. Still that pigstock boy, fighting in street matches with lies and luck, fighting for Geoxus's blessing to keep him alive. Going to the temple. Kneeling before the golden statue. Touching the stones in the hope that the Father God would hear him.

Now Deimos had a new god.

With all his might, he wrenched his body toward the nearest wall.

Automatically, his hand lifted to brace against the stones. Then he did the only thing he had left to do.

He prayed.

Ash, if you can hear me, help Elias and Ilena. Protect them from me. Save them.

And then his grip faltered, and he lost his hold on brother and mother. On Danon and Ava. On the stone yards where he'd once been a mason and the arenas where he'd fought on the streets. On Petros, and Cassia, and Tor, and finally on Ash.

It all slipped away until there was nothing. Until he had no name but servant, and the shell of his body belonged to the Mother Goddess.

TWENTY

ASH

THREE DAYS AFTER Anathrasa's attack on Kula, Ash had actively shut her mind to the onslaught of prayers in her name. The city of Igna had embraced her as their new goddess and set her up in Ignitus's dormant volcano palace. Day and night, servants and staff and warriors funneled into the grand receiving hall to swear fealty to her. Brand, who had once been a champion devoted only to Ignitus and to bloodshed, rarely left her side, overseeing her transition as Kula's ruler with surprising skill and allegiance.

Her display against Anathrasa's navy had been more than enough to turn the country's loyalty to her. But by the time Hydra left to join the fleet of Water Divine and Plant Divine sailing into Igna's harbor, Ash felt no more ready to face Tor again than she had right after their argument.

She stayed long enough on the shore to let her Fire Divine warriors see her accept the fleet as friendly, not threatening. Then she nodded at Brand, who would organize the chaos of coordinating the

Apuitians' and Itzans' lodging. Not that they would be here long—they were all due to depart to attack Crixion at dawn.

Before Tor could disembark from the lead ship, Ash vanished in a flare of blue flame.

She reappeared in the bedchamber she had taken, a massive room carved into the dormant volcanic rock. The walls were roughly cut, following the natural divots and texture of the black obsidian, and the floor was covered with a vibrant orange-and-gold rug. The bed sat just next to an open balcony, letting in a salty breeze from the Hontori Sea.

Moments alone had been rare the past few days, but for each minute of solitude Ash had salvaged, all she could bring herself to do was lie on her bed, stare up at the canopy as it rippled in the sea wind, and ache.

Hydra hadn't really spoken to her since the attack, and her last words to Ash resonated as strongly as Tor's—all doubts and reprimands and horror at how Ash was behaving. She'd thought Hydra, of all people, might understand that Ash was simply accepting what she was now, but even the water goddess had pulled away.

So while armies converged in Igna and time ticked down to Ash's confrontation with Anathrasa, she was in a room in Ignitus's place, alone.

And she would walk into that final battle, alone.

And if they defeated Anathrasa—*when* they defeated Anathrasa—Ash would leave that victory alone too. She would still have this strange power inside her, and it would still cause a rift between her and Tor, between her and Hydra. Would Madoc see the same flaws that they saw? Would he cringe away from her?

Ash squeezed her eyes shut. She'd missed him every moment since he'd left, even when she'd seen him in the library and been in his arms. She felt like she was forgetting who he actually was, and all these worries would vanish if they could just be together without fear of attack or intrusion—

Ash.

She bolted upright, eyes darting around her room. But it was empty; even the sea breeze still for a moment.

Ash, the voice said again.

Ash stood. The scarlet gown she was wearing brushed her ankles, her black hair loose and curling against her shoulders as she tipped her head.

Maybe she *was* going insane. Because that voice sounded like . . .

It sounded like Madoc.

If you can hear me. His voice was rough and desperate and exhausted, as though he was using the last vestiges of his strength to speak to her.

Gods. He was *praying* to her. He was Deiman, and he was praying through stone.

"Madoc!" Ash didn't know how to talk back to him. The only reason she could hear him was because she *was* geoeia now, but there were no rocks in this room that obeyed geoeia—in any room in this palace, thanks to Ignitus's paranoia.

Ash spun in a circle. How had she listened through fire before? She hadn't practiced any more with stone—

—help Elias and Ilena, Madoc told her. *Protect them from me.*

"Madoc!" Ash stopped, eyes welling. "*From* you? What do you mean? What is she doing to you?"

Save them.

"Madoc!" Only silence followed. Ash gasped, tears sliding down her cheeks.

She said his name again. She shouted it, and she heard her warriors in the hall thundering toward her cry.

The door burst open. "Goddess? Are you all right?" one asked.

Ash drew in a shaky breath. She pressed the back of her hand to her lips and willed herself not to disintegrate.

Madoc had prayed to *her*. Not to Ash, who was the goddess of Kula—just Ash, who had powers he knew of but didn't shy away from.

And in that moment, that was all she was. The layers of her power stripped away, her destiny pooling at her feet. She was just a girl who loved a boy who needed her to save him.

She replayed Madoc's message.

If you can hear me, help Elias and Ilena. Protect them from me. Save them.

A familiar defiance almost had her launching away to help him right then.

But she stopped herself.

Breathed.

"Bring Hydra and Tor to the receiving room," Ash told her guard. "We're accelerating our plans."

There were only a few warriors and servants bustling about the receiving room when Ash entered through a side door that put her right next to the throne Ignitus had often sat on.

It was beautiful. Carved entirely of Kulan glass, the seat jutted out from a fanning back of opalescent scarlet, orange, and yellow. It looked like a fire that had been frozen somehow, each twisted strand of glass mimicking a shoot of flame.

Once, Ash had chastised herself for thinking anything Ignitus touched was beautiful.

Once, she would have scowled at the throne and ordered it shattered, as though doing so would avenge her mother.

Ash hesitated, her hands fisting at her sides. Through all the pomp and reception she had endured the past few days, she had stood, thanking everyone who swore themselves to her cause. She had purposefully put Ignitus's throne at her back so she didn't have to think about it.

But now Ash crossed the space to the throne and stood before it, looking down at the seat that had only ever held the god of fire.

The receiving room hung silent. Or maybe that was her own pulse deafening her, the rush and surge of blood through her veins making her want to run.

She turned and sat, hands on the armrests, back rigid.

Goddess.

Part of her reveled in the title, but part of her wanted to be exactly what she had been when Madoc had prayed to her.

Just Ash. Just a girl.

Sitting on Ignitus's throne, she couldn't help but wonder if the other gods ever wished for that. Mortals certainly dreamed of being godly; did gods dream of being ordinary?

Could she ever go back to being *ordinary* again?

The door at the far end opened. Tor rushed in, walking fast without quite running, Taro close behind him. The two of them pulled up short when they saw Ash on Ignitus's throne.

They said nothing.

A trickle of water cascaded down one of the obsidian pillars on the edge of the room, and Hydra materialized, leaning one shoulder against the glassy rock. She eyed Ash, her jaw tight.

Ash's fingers dug into the armrests. Tor, Hydra, Taro—they were all forced to look up at her on this raised dais. Forced to remember who she was now, as though they could forget. A god in a mortal body. A warrior who would save the world. An angry, violent girl.

"I'm sorry," she said, her voice cracking.

The servants and warriors must have felt the tension, because they dissolved into the shadows, giving her privacy.

Hydra pushed herself off the pillar, scowl shifting into surprise. "Are you?"

"I have become capable of more than I ever thought possible, but I was wrong to think that meant I was invincible." Ash could only look at Hydra as she spoke. Her chest ached with Tor's focus on her, and his final words to her still cored her out.

Your mother would be ashamed of the way you're behaving.

She swallowed and leaned forward. "I'm sorry I haven't been listening. That I've acted rashly. I don't—" She dropped her focus to her hands. The backs of her eyes burned. "I don't know how to do the things I have to do, but I'm trying. And I need your help."

"That's what I've been trying to tell you, Ash—" Tor started, but Ash snapped her eyes up to him.

"Madoc prayed to me," she said. "I heard him through the stone in Deimos. He said he wants me to protect Elias and Ilena—from *him*."

"What?" Taro's voice pitched. "What does that even mean?"

"Anathrasa is overtaking his mind," Hydra whispered.

Ash nodded. She knew her eyes were glassy with tears, but she was angry, too, and she let that anger build. "He wouldn't have asked me to intervene unless it was urgent. I think that prayer was his last attempt to contact me before she—" She couldn't finish. Her words fell and her eyes dropped too, landing on the floor. "We need to move. Now. Anathrasa is confident enough in her army that she sent them to attack Kula. She has Madoc under her control. We need to go to Crixion *now*."

There was a long moment of silence. When Ash looked up, Tor was watching her, frowning.

"Why didn't you go to Crixion yourself?" he asked.

Ash bristled. "I'm trying to think of the greater effects my actions have on this war."

Tor took a step toward her. "I meant it as a compliment. Thank you for coming to us first."

Ash ground her jaw.

"My people have barely started to disembark," Hydra said. "We can easily load back up and make for Crixion."

"Your Water Divine won't be too exhausted to accelerate the trip?" Ash asked.

Hydra gave a grim smile. "Who said they'll be giving us the fast trip? You and I will be traveling with them, and goddesses don't tire. Do we?"

Ash couldn't help but return Hydra's grin. "No. We don't."

"We'll get to Crixion and confront Anathrasa's army," Tor said, down to business. "If Madoc is under her control, how will we defeat her? We can't wage war indefinitely."

Ash pushed herself up off the throne. "Maybe we don't aim to defeat her with this attack."

Tor's brow furrowed.

"Maybe we just salvage what we can," Ash continued. "We save Madoc's family, and Florus too. We get as many innocents out as possible and we regroup. We take away her leverage."

Planning to do this without Madoc felt wrong. As though he was already lost.

But no—Ash would figure out some way to save him, too, once she got his family to safety.

"We'll need time to search for everyone." Hydra folded her arms. "Anathrasa could have Florus imprisoned anywhere—he might not even be in Crixion anymore. And I'm not leaving without my brother."

"We need a distraction," Taro offered.

"Something to keep Anathrasa diverted while we get Florus and the Metaxas out of Crixion," Ash said.

"And other innocents," Tor clarified.

"And other innocents." Ash worried her lip.

What would most distract Anathrasa? What would she *have* to respond to, for her own honor, for her own protection?

Ash paused. How had the gods been causing distractions for

centuries? By using their arenas.

"I know I can't defeat Anathrasa yet," Ash breathed. "But *she* doesn't know that."

She looked up, catching Hydra's eyes as a new thought formed.

"What if I appear in Crixion's grand arena and challenge Anathrasa?" Ash formed the words slowly. "We let Anathrasa think that Madoc already got me aereia and bioseia, and that I have everything I need to defeat her. We keep her occupied there while our armies free anyone still fighting her, and then we fall back to Kula. For now—"

"This is victory enough." Tor's face was a mask.

A wave of nausea surged through Ash's body. She nodded once. Again.

"Let's go to war," she said, the words tasting of dust and decay.

Hydra vanished, presumably to pass on orders to the Apuitian and Itzan ships. Taro whispered something to Tor before walking toward the door.

But Tor remained, hands at his back, staring up at Ash.

"You're not pleased with this plan?" she asked.

He flinched. "I didn't say that."

"But you're still here. So you must disapprove of something I've done."

A sigh, and Tor's shoulders deflated. He looked as if he might disagree before he shook his head. "Do you remember when we first met?"

The question threw her. She eased back to sit on the edge of the throne and shook her head.

Tor shrugged. "Not surprising. You were about four, maybe five.

Char and I had been together for a few weeks. Her mother had just died in an arena."

Ash shivered, not from cold, but from the mention of the grand-mother she couldn't remember. Char hadn't spoken much of her mother after she'd taken her place as Ignitus's champion, carrying the name of Nikau into arenas, fighting for him.

Char had hated it and did everything she could to keep Ash from the same fate.

A lot of good that did.

Ash shivered again.

"She brought you to my house the day after Ignitus declared she would be his next champion," Tor said. His voice wavered, warmer than Ash had heard from him in a long time. "You tried to pull a ball of flames from the fireplace and nearly set fire to my kitchen table."

Ash felt her lips twitch. "That sounds like me."

Tor smiled, his eyes gentle. "I showed you some toys I'd gotten for you, and while you were playing, Char asked me to take care of you if anything happened to her."

"What? She never told me that."

Tor took a step forward. "I have sworn many oaths in my life. Most to Ignitus, so they meant little. But what I promised your mother that day is the beacon I have lived by. To be someone worthy of being trusted with such a precious gift. It's an honor I would rather die than break, taking care of Char's little girl. I shouldn't have brought her into our argument when you heard Igna was in trouble. I'm sorry."

"I'm not that little girl anymore." Ash's voice was barely a whisper.

"No." His smile fell. "No, you aren't. I've been trying to come to terms with that for years."

Ash couldn't hold Tor's gaze. She looked at the obsidian floor, but it blurred in the tears rimming her eyes.

"I've been trying to do right by your mother," Tor continued. He was closer to her. She still didn't look up. "Trying to do right by you, not just as Char's daughter, but as"—his voice caught—"as *my* daughter."

Ash squeezed her eyes shut, but tears still fell. She stood and closed the space between them, throwing her arms around Tor's shoulders, burying her face into his neck. He caught her with a startled huff and wrapped his thick arms around her, holding her in Ignitus's empty receiving room.

Igneia burned in a chandelier high above them, and Ash wondered if, somewhere, Char could see them.

If she knew that Ash still had Tor to lean on.

If she had known, all those years ago, what an unshakable foundation she was leaving for Ash when she brought Tor into their lives.

TWENTY-ONE

MADOC

"VERY GOOD." THE Mother Goddess examined the woman before them, staring into her vacant brown eyes. The woman was empty. Soulless. Brought to this state by Anathrasa's command and by his own power. But even though anathreia swelled inside him, he was only vaguely aware of it. A fly buzzing in the corner of a room he occupied.

"You're getting the hang of it. She barely struggled," Anathrasa noted, pride in her voice.

He couldn't remember the woman struggling at all. He couldn't remember anything before this moment. If there'd been others. If he'd hurt them. If they'd suffered.

He felt nothing.

He saw only what his goddess wanted him to see. The four dusty stone walls of this room. The centurions with their dull eyes. A vaguely familiar woman in white standing at the back of the room holding a tray.

He did not know how long he'd been here, or where he was.

It didn't matter.

With a smile, Anathrasa sent the girl into the hall, and immediately another Deiman was brought in. A man with a gray beard and tears in his eyes.

"Please," he was saying. "Please. Not this."

The Mother Goddess sighed. "It's difficult to see their pain, isn't it? How wrong we were to give them such a wide expanse of emotions. Their soft minds clearly couldn't handle it."

"Please!" the man begged.

"You'll make an excellent soldier," Anathrasa said slowly, loudly, as if the man would otherwise fail to comprehend. "Find solace in the fact that you will soon do your part to take back my world from the selfish gods who would put you in this kind of anguish." As he trembled, she slapped his cheek lightly. "Your fear will be over soon. You'll be in my care, as you were always meant to be."

"I'll do anything," he begged.

"Yes. You will." Anathrasa waved a hand. "Now, if you don't mind, hold still. My son must tithe to stay strong, as he did with Florus. Hydra will be here soon, and there is much work left to do. Isn't that right, Madoc?" She grinned at him.

Madoc.

The name was familiar. He knew it, the way he knew water would ease a parched throat, and a gray sky meant rain. But he didn't know how he knew it, or why he was called it, or what kind of man this Madoc was.

His hands lifted. Again, his anathreia swelled. Fed. But he felt no relief as the man went still in the grip of the soldiers.

The man walked from the room of his own accord. His hands loose at his sides. His stare dull.

"I need some air," Anathrasa said, stretching her arms out to the sides. "Shall we see how the training is progressing, my love?"

He followed her out of the room, down a dark hall lined with cells filled with Deiman men and women. They called out in anger. In fear. Some cried.

He felt nothing.

Sunlight cut a sharp line across their path, and he followed the Mother Goddess through the stone archway onto the yellow sand. An arena stretched before him, an oval as deep as the palace, surrounded by empty stands.

Before them, lines of Deimans stared straight ahead, set in place like chess pieces by centurions in silver and black.

"One!" a centurion commander called from the front of the arena.

As one, hundreds of men and women lunged forward, extending their right hand in a thrusting punch.

"Two!" Their left hands followed.

"Three!" A hard kick.

An old woman in the front fell but continued to kick from the ground in silent compliance. A centurion righted her, but her hips buckled, and when she fell again, the soldiers dragged her off to the side. She continued to kick while they moved her.

"Four!" The lines returned to a ready formation in a cloud of dust.

"Impressive, isn't it?" Anathrasa asked. "Did you ever think you'd be capable of such great things?" She laughed as he stared forward.

"I did. To think that Ilena would have had you moving stones in the quarry, like some kind of Undivine animal."

At the name Ilena, he twitched, a reaction he didn't understand.

Anathrasa took his hand in hers and pet it gently.

"You are so much more than anything she could have seen."

A light flickered inside him, a tiny spark in the gloom. A question, outside the silence of his mind.

"What am I?" he asked.

Anathrasa looked up at him, her eyes gleaming, her mouth tilted in a smile.

"You are my servant," she said. "And that is all you need to be."

TWENTY-TWO

ASH

THEY LEFT IGNA before sunset.

Ash took one of the lead ships while Hydra captained the other, and together, they launched their fleet across the Hontori Sea. A journey that would normally take a week sped by in mere days, and their ship thrashed at the edge of Crixion's waters just as the sun was coming up behind them two days later.

She wasn't tired, but Ash panted all the same, sweat dampening her skin and sea spray sticking her hair to her cheeks. She was already wearing Kulan reed armor, the kind made for battle, not ceremony, and as the water stilled, she was grateful that she didn't have to worry about getting ready. If she paused, she might not do what she needed to do. She might just find Madoc and whisk him away and do something to force Anathrasa out of his head. Instead, she had to be steady, and patient, and careful.

The water around their ships solidified. Not ice, just Hydra holding them steady while they took stock of Crixion, spread out before them in the rising pink-gold dawn.

Anathrasa was ready for them.

All of Crixion's ships sat in a blockade before their harbor, waiting, laden with centurions and soldiers. Beyond, who knew what the city would be like?

A cold hand slid into Ash's. She met the water goddess's blue eyes.

Before they'd left Igna, Ash and Hydra had talked about how goddesses could fight differently than Divine mortals.

This was one large way.

Ash closed her eyes as Hydra did. Together, on the deck of their ship, as their people adjusted to being here and moments from battle, their two goddess leaders looked in on Crixion.

Hydra would take every waiting vessel of water—ponds and wells and pools. Ash would jump through fire. Together, they could make a feeble map of the city, who was where and what obstacles they might face.

Ash exhaled, let her shoulders relax, and widened her awareness. No one in Crixion was praying to her, unsurprisingly; a few Kulans on the ships were saying idle prayers for safety, but Ash pressed on, peeking through every flame in the city, every fireplace, every simmering coal.

There weren't many. Few houses had flames lit, few storefronts nursed fires.

Ash pulled back into herself, heart thudding.

"It's quiet," Hydra said beside her.

Ash nodded. "I didn't sense Madoc or his family. Or Florus. Did you?"

Hydra shook her head.

Worry made Ash go slack. Madoc's final plea had been to keep his family safe. What if she was too late?

"That doesn't mean anything, though," Hydra tried. "We knew Anathrasa would prepare for us. They're probably hidden somewhere—"

"Wait." Tor came up to them, hands slack on the jars of combustibles around his hips, things he could light with igneia and use in the attack. His eyes were on the line of Deiman ships, and he squinted in confusion. "What is that?"

Hydra and Ash turned. The lead ship in the Deiman blockade was in the process of raising something into the air. Two tall wooden poles, with a flag between them—

Ash retched, hand to her mouth.

Not a flag. A body.

A body with a gaping hole in its chest, rib cage torn open, gore and blood on display.

"Who is that?" Hydra asked the question that Ash couldn't bear. A hundred possibilities surged through her mind as Tor took a spyglass from a nearby sailor and lifted it.

He frowned. "A boy?"

Hydra snatched the spyglass.

The moment it touched her eye, she swayed.

"No," she said, and a wave arched out of the water in front of their ship. "*No*," she cried, and the wave rose, rushing for the Deimans. "*NO*," she screamed, and the wave blocked the ships and the city from view.

Ash grabbed Hydra's arms. "Stop! Who is—"

Hydra whirled on her, blue eyes feral, fury and agony ripe on her face. "Florus. It's *Florus*."

Ash went still. Her fingers turned to vises on Hydra's thin arms and she couldn't move as Hydra dropped the spyglass to the deck. It shattered at their feet, and Hydra screamed.

The wave slammed into the lead Deiman ship. Distantly, Ash heard centurions shouting, their cries buried in drowning garbles, but she found she couldn't care.

"Anathrasa killed the god of plants," Ash said, because she needed to see how that fact fit into this world now.

She hated that, selfishly, she felt vindicated. Her torturer was dead.

But if Anathrasa had killed Florus, then either she was strong enough to make him mortal on her own now, or she had forced Madoc to drain him as he had drained Geoxus and Ignitus.

In a final roar of foam and froth, Hydra made the sea swallow the ship whole, leaving the rest of Anathrasa's fleet unharmed, if horrified by what they would have to face.

Tor's head dropped to his chest.

Around Ash, their mostly Apuitian crew went silent, watching the wave decimate the Deiman ship. But on their other ships, the ones carrying Florus's Itzan warriors—the crews began to shriek. Not screaming in pain or wailing in grief; it was a screeching battle cry, a chant Ash couldn't make out, but the feel of it caught her chest like wildfire. The chant was agony, and it was power, and it was misery, and Anathrasa would regret having killed Florus and displaying his body in that vile, taunting way.

Ash pulled Hydra close. She didn't mourn Florus on her own, but she mourned for Hydra's loss. "She will pay for this."

Hydra sobbed hard, once. She pushed back from Ash, face red with tears, and growled. "I'm coming with you."

Ash inhaled as deeply as she could. Her part of the plan was to appear in the main arena and keep Anathrasa distracted. Tor would lead their fight here, keeping Anathrasa's army at bay.

Hydra had been meant to sneak through the city to find Florus and the Metaxas.

The Metaxas still needed saving. Ash eyed the sea where the ship with Florus's body had so recently sat, letting her mind calm, letting it calculate.

What other cruelty did Anathrasa have planned?

"All right," Ash said. She looked at Tor. "Hydra's with me. As soon as you break into the city, send groups scouting for the Metaxas and any other innocents who want to flee."

"Should the water goddess stay here?" Tor cocked his head at the remaining Deiman ships. "If you can so easily take down one vessel—"

Hydra shook her head. A grim smile twisted her lips and she nodded at the sound on the air, the chanting Itzan warriors. "You won't need me. The Itzans will be ruthless now."

Tor looked around. He met Ash's gaze and his own sobered, dark and purposeful.

"Be careful," he told her.

She smiled, but it didn't reach her eyes.

They would get out of this. They would survive to attack again.

And together, they would all see another dawn.

"Let's go," Ash told Hydra, and she burst into flames, one thought pulsing in her mind: *the grand arena.*

Last time she had been there, she had been dead on the sands from Elias's attack. Madoc had had to save her. Then Anathrasa had taken Ash's igneia, and her world had been chaos ever since.

So when Ash appeared in Crixion's main arena, she had a moment of painful nostalgia. The only thing different about it was the decorations. Banners fluttered from the high balconies, displaying an ivory circle instead of Geoxus's symbols. All signs of him were gone, his signature stones and gems, his onyx decor.

Ash stood in the center of the arena's fighting pit, staring up at the banners, and breathed.

The decorations were truly the *only* thing that had changed since she had been here last.

The stands were full. Full as though the audience that had watched her fight Elias had never left, waiting to see her bleed again.

Next to her, Hydra hissed in a breath. "What did we interrupt?"

Ash turned, eyes flicking from person to person, pulse roaring in her ears and sweat already dripping down her back. There were no gladiators midfight. And the crowd wasn't cheering or booing; they didn't even react when she and Hydra appeared. They sat in the seats, quiet, observant. It was eerie, as if the dead were watching them, and Ash's hands started to shake even as she pulled blue fire into her palms.

"I don't think we interrupted anything," Ash said. "I think she knew we'd come."

This was why the city had been empty. Everyone was *here.*

Hydra grimaced and matched Ash's fire with palmfuls of ice crystals. "Shit."

What had they walked into?

After a steadying breath, Ash screamed into the stands, "Anathrasa! Face me!"

The crowd didn't react. They looked like the gladiators on the ships that had attacked Igna.

"She's controlling them," Hydra whispered. She twisted so she and Ash stood back to back, ice and fire at the ready. "We're too late."

She felt Hydra deflate, just a little, just enough to spear Ash in the gut with panic.

"We are not too late," Ash told her. "We are not too late until Anathrasa rips the geoeia and igneia from my body."

She felt a rumble in Hydra's back—morbid laughter. But it gave Ash strength.

"Anathrasa!" she shouted. "I have what I need to defeat you. Come out and face me. You are not the only Mother Goddess anymore!"

As one, the crowd started to stomp. First one foot, then the other, a slow, thunderous build that wound the tension. It played the wrongness like a taut string.

Ash and Hydra spun in a slow circle, each eyeing the stands, searching for some sign that Anathrasa had heard her—

When a door opened in the wall ahead of Ash.

She stopped. Hydra turned, looking over Ash's shoulder.

A shadowed figure walked out, feet sliding through the arena's golden sands. The moment the morning sun's light caught on his face, his armor, the weapons at his sides, Ash went slack.

Hydra spun, grabbing Ash's wrist. "Ash, it's a trick."

"Madoc." His name slid out of her mouth and she almost sobbed. She lifted her hands, snapped the flames out. "Madoc."

When she'd seen Florus's body on display, part of her had been certain Madoc was dead too.

He was still alive. He was *here*, and—

"*Ash!*" Hydra shook her. "It's a trick. She's trying to distract you, like she did to me with Florus." Her voice cracked on her brother's name.

Hydra was right, and it broke Ash's heart. Anathrasa had planned this too.

Madoc kept walking across the arena toward them.

Ash took Hydra's hand. "With me." It was a question. A plea.

Hydra squeezed her fingers in unspoken confirmation, and they began walking, mimicking Madoc's steady pace.

He didn't look at Ash, didn't react to her being here. His movements were stiff and unnatural, and Ash wanted to scream.

Panic made Ash's chest buck.

Had Anathrasa overtaken him? Were they truly too late?

Ash almost collapsed on the sand, but she made herself stand tall. She wouldn't play Anathrasa's sick game.

She and Hydra stopped walking. Madoc did the same, close enough now that Ash could see his eyes. They were vacant and dark, his face void of expression, just as much a shell as the thundering crowd around them.

This was the world Anathrasa wanted: one she controlled in every way.

"Madoc," Ash tried. "I heard your prayer. I heard you, and I'm here now."

He didn't move.

Ash noted his armor. It was fighting armor, not ceremonial.

Her pulse sped up. "Madoc, please. I don't know how to help you. Give me some sign that you're still there. Let me—"

"Oh, he's not there, sweetie."

Ash's muscles went utterly rigid. Next to her, Hydra whirled around. Such a look of fury overcame her that Ash knew who had spoken before she even turned.

The goddess of air hovered a hand's width above the sands, arms behind her back, golden hair flowing in a gentle breeze. Behind her, shifting from eagle form back into a man, was Biotus.

Aera's round, childlike face twisted in a manic smile that only grew as she lowered all the way to the ground. "At least," she continued, taking delicate steps through the sand, "not the parts that matter to *you*. He's better now. Just as Anathrasa will make us all better."

"You killed Florus," Hydra growled. Her hands balled into fists. Spikes of ice flared up her arms, and Ash knew she should try to calm her, but she didn't. There was no calming this situation. No stopping this fight.

It was building and building, and they couldn't escape it.

Aera cut a wide circle around Ash and Hydra, then came to stand beside Madoc. "I did no such thing," she cooed. "My group lost. Yours did too, didn't they, Biotus? It was one of the Deiman gladiators who got Florus's heart."

Biotus hadn't followed Aera, putting Hydra and Ash directly

between them. It sent an uncomfortable itch up Ash's back.

Hydra went so still Ash thought she'd turned to ice. "What?"

Biotus folded his arms across his beefy chest and grinned wickedly. "Gladiators ripped Florus's heart clean out of his chest. After that one"—he pointed at Madoc—"made him mortal."

Hydra was now panting, shoulders heaving. Ash felt her fury on the air, electric and contagious, and she faced Madoc, wanting to burn this stadium to the ground. More than that, she wanted to run. To grab his hand and run and forget all the horrible things that had led them here.

That wish sparked from what felt like a lifetime ago, in Crixion's library. They should have run that night.

Ash's hands fisted, wrenching tighter when Aera traced her finger along Madoc's jaw. The only solace was that, while he didn't shove her away, he didn't lean into her touch, either.

"Anathrasa let Florus die," Ash said, more for Hydra's benefit, reminding her who the real villain was. "We didn't come to fight you. Where is she?"

"Are you sure you don't want to fight him?" Aera looked at Ash, ignoring her question as she wrapped her fingers around the tense muscles of Madoc's forearm.

"We're not playing these games," Ash growled. "Where is Anathrasa?"

"He's very impressive now," Aera said. "Unhindered. A real *champion*. The Mother Goddess has used this vessel for tremendous feats now that he's wholly given over to her."

Ash almost cried out. Aera's words struck like a knife to her soul, confirmation that Madoc wasn't himself. Not anymore.

"Shut *up*!" Hydra spun, flaring ice shards in the sand at Aera's feet. "Where is our mother?"

Her question echoed off the stands, the crowd still stomping.

Aera pouted. She'd launched herself up to avoid the ice but lowered now and put her hand on Madoc's shoulder. "Are you going to let her speak to me like that, lover?"

Ash called on igneia and had a ball of fire in her hand before she could think not to. Arm lifted, she aimed to hurl it at Aera—

But Madoc intercepted.

He grabbed Ash's wrist, twisted, and threw her across the arena. Ash went flying, only gathering her wits enough to vanish in fire and reappear on her feet before she hit the wall.

This wasn't him. She told herself that, held it against the agony that cut her.

Ash looked back at Madoc, gasping.

He was crouched for a fight. And then he was running at her.

Behind him, Hydra hurled water whips and ice shards at Aera and Biotus. Dark shadows of birds and hawks pinpricked the sky as Biotus called animals to his defense while the arena's sands caught up in funnels of Aera's aereia.

Madoc was closer. Closer still. The tendons in his neck stretched and he leaped at her.

Ash had no choice.

She wouldn't leave him. Even if it meant she had to fight him.

TWENTY-THREE

MADOC

THE GOD KILLER attacked with a vengeance. Blue flames spouted from her raised palms, a wave of heat searing his side as he dived to the sand. He coughed as his throat filled with dust. From the corner of his eye, he saw her lunge toward him, and he shoved himself back, sputtering.

"Stop!" she shouted at him, as if she hadn't just attacked him. "Madoc, can you hear me?"

Madoc.

He didn't know a Madoc. He only knew Anathrasa. His only purpose was to protect the Mother Goddess. He was her soldier. Her servant.

From the opposite end of the arena came a howl of manic laughter, magnified on the whipping wind. A tornado was ripping apart the southern stands, tossing bodies and hunks of stones into the air and over the ledge of the arena. Aera stood behind it, dress and hair dancing wildly. She shot another blast of aereia toward Hydra, who was fending off a giant lion behind a defensive dome of ice.

Anathrasa's servant shoved to his feet, then stumbled when the ground began to shake.

"I don't want to hurt you," the God Killer said, wiping the sweat from her brow with the back of her wrist.

He wanted to hurt her.

He needed to kill her.

With a roar, the servant sprinted toward the God Killer, knives bared. She threw another bolt of fire at him, but he dodged it, then dropped low to sweep her legs. She fell hard on her back, a huff of breath parting her lips, and when she screamed, the air hummed with a chilling vibration. He glanced up, searching for her next attack, only to find beads of water flying across the sands from all directions, congealing into a blast of hail that scraped his skin.

In his distraction, she leaped to her feet and charged toward him.

Drain her. The Mother Goddess's order resounded through his body.

He threw himself toward the God Killer, hooking her ankle. She tripped, but when he reached for her calf, a black root shot from the ground, snaking around his arm. Another hooked around his back. Instantly they tightened, cutting off his circulation, stifling his breath. He gasped, panic roaring through his blood.

"Stop fighting me!" The God Killer's voice trembled. Her eyes were glassy with tears. Her hair, pale with dust, was plastered to her cheek. A screech filled the air as a small black bird dived toward her. She batted it aside with a wave of water, but soon another followed, and another. An entire flock of birds sacrificing themselves at

Biotus's command, pelting her with sharp beaks and pointed claws. She raised her hands, blocking them with a weave of roots, and the pattering sound of their bodies bouncing off the hard surface filled the servant's ears.

Get up, the Mother Goddess ordered.

The order was not meant just for him. The ground began quaking as the bodies in the stands rushed to the edge of the arena, driven by Anathrasa's call. They jumped over the railings, landing on the sand, sprinting toward him, and toward the goddess of water, still battling her siblings.

He tried to peel off the vines, but they were too tight. His gaze shot to the God Killer fending off a wall of Anathrasa's soldiers. They fell in droves, then piled over one another to get closer to her. With a scream, she swung her arms in a wide arc, and a high wall of flames drew a hot, blue-tinged circle around her. The soldiers barreled into it, unafraid, but this was no ordinary fire. The moment a mortal body touched it, it burned them to ashes.

As the servant continued to struggle with the vines, some of the soldiers cut to the back, to where the circle of flames was not yet closed. The God Killer shoved them away with a blast of ice, but they were too many. A man fell against the servant's back. The soldier was broad-chested. Deiman. His eyes were like black coals, unfocused and empty, and the back of his tunic was still aflame.

A thought slipped through the servant's mind, too slick to cling to. A villa atop a hill. A sponsor shouting orders to his prized fighters. *Lucius.*

The thought was gone.

"Cut me free," he told the Deiman soldier.

The soldier, ignoring the fire that ate at his clothes, pulled a knife from his belt and hacked at the vines. Before he could sever them completely, a root tore from the earth and wrapped around his chest. It lifted him like a doll and threw him through the haze of smoke, out of sight.

Rushing to beat the God Killer's next attack, the servant ripped through the last threads of the vine holding him and hurtled toward her, tackling her to the ground.

Geoeia. Igneia. Floreia. Hydreia. He could feel it all raging inside her. His anathreia hungered for it, its sharp teeth biting at the shell of her soul. He would tithe it from her, split open her soul and drink its power like spilled milk.

"Stop!" She writhed beneath him, then twisted, her chest to his. He locked her hands over her head and dropped his forearm to her throat. Her lips parted on a gasp.

The heat was more intense now—sweat blurred his vision and made his grasp slick. The circle around them had been closed, a wall of flames blocking them from the war beyond.

He inhaled, drawing the power out of her like poison from a wound. His teeth bared with the effort. Blood pulsed in his temples.

"Madoc, please!" she managed.

Take her powers. End this. Beyond the flames, he could see a shadow rising at a dozen different points, and knew the army was attempting to climb over the barrier.

He pressed harder. Reached deeper.

"You know me," she wheezed.

Lies, the Mother Goddess hissed.

"We met here, in this arena . . ." She swallowed a breath, fighting harder. His muscles clenched as energeia surged through his body. It fought against the seams of his soul, threatening to tear out of him. Pain ricocheted down his spine and limbs.

Draining her would kill him.

It didn't matter.

"We fought just like this . . . ," she gasped. "No energeia. Which was good because . . . you didn't have any."

Pigstock.

He shook his head, the crackling flames warring with the thunder of his heart. That wasn't the Mother Goddess's voice. It had come from another place. A locked room in his memory.

"We danced," she said. "Do you remember? At the palace. The night we found Stavos."

He flinched, his arm loosening around her throat and wrists. He could see a body just as clearly as if he'd been laid out on the ground beside them. *Stavos.* The champion had stumbled through the palace gates, arrows in his back. Someone had murdered him.

"You remember Stavos," she said, blinking. "Do you remember Jann, too? You beat him here with anathreia."

He knew Jann—he could hear his taunts before their fight. Could see the gladiator curled into a ball, weeping, after they'd fought.

"And afterward, Tor and I told you . . ."

"Tor," he whispered.

The God Killer's powers sizzled across his nerves.

She nodded. "Yes. Tor. We told you we needed your help to take down the gods. And then we went to Petros's villa . . ."

He jerked his arm away from her throat.

He could see Tor, lunging across a ship's deck at him, knives and fire in his hands. *The things that matter live inside us, and we protect them as we protect any other part of ourselves, with the power we've been given.*

Lies, screamed Anathrasa. *End this!*

The shadows were climbing—the soldiers had nearly reached the top. One went over, but was seared by the flames on the way down, and with a stunted scream turned to ash.

"You called me," the God Killer managed. "You prayed to me through the stones to help you. To save Ilena and Elias."

He stopped pulling her energeia. His hands were shaking. The God Killer's energeia inside him was too much. Her words were illusions.

Don't listen to her, Anathrasa screamed. *She's nothing. She is no one.*

"I came back for you," the God Killer said. Her eyes were glassy, her fear thick. But there was more there. More he didn't want to feel. Hope and grief and longing.

Love.

He looked into her eyes, and he remembered.

The curl of her fingers over his on the ship's rail. The feel of her smile against his lips. She'd once said his name sounded like a bird call.

One memory returned at a time. One brick placed after another, and another.

Ilena. His mother. Scolding him for growing too fast. Kissing his forehead before he fell asleep.

Elias calling him brother.

Cassia bringing him home.

Him carrying Cassia home.

Brick by brick by brick, until he had a wall pushing back Anathrasa's howling screams in his head. Until he could breathe.

He was still there. He was still Madoc.

"Ash?" he whispered.

Tears spilled from Ash's eyes. Her nose scrunched as she gave a watery laugh. "Yes."

He gritted his teeth, more memories pouring back.

Home is here, Tor had told him, his hand on Madoc's chest.

Madoc forced his trembling hand off Ash's wrists and to his own damp chest. Screams from outside punched through the flames. He couldn't see Aera, but a burst of her power blew the flames in a sudden slant, singeing his skin. They went out in a hiss on one side, but before the wave of bodies, charred and burned, could press into the circle, he held out his hand and whispered, "No."

The soldiers went still. Watching. Waiting.

You disobey me? Anathrasa roared. *You are nothing without me.*

You're wrong, his own voice echoed inside his head, stronger than he'd expected. He was Madoc Aurelius, born of a goddess and a monster, survivor of the streets of Crixion, loved by a family whom he loved in return.

One brick followed another.

He was a champion of war, a gladiator trained in trickery and anathreia. A brother. A defender. A healer.

The walls rose until they became a fortress. He pushed himself back to his knees, holding Ash's stare as she rose on her elbows.

He loved her.

He couldn't remember the moment it had happened. All he knew was that he'd tripped when he'd first seen her in this arena, and after that nothing had been the same. She'd opened his eyes to the treachery of the gods, and the vastness of the world. She'd shown him the true meaning of bravery, and that honor could still exist, even in a city torn apart by greed and power.

"Ash," he said again. The name was familiar on his tongue.

Crawling to her knees, she took his face in her hands and kissed him. Her lips were soft but unforgiving, punishing him for forgetting, making him pay for every second they'd been apart.

He took it all. Her anger. Her fear. Her love. He breathed her in and remembered what it was like to be home.

Enough, growled Anathrasa. She wrenched Madoc's arm back like a puppet's, ready to drive his fist through Ash's chest like a spear.

No.

Madoc caught Anathrasa before she could follow through. His hand stopped, trembling over Ash's rib cage. He focused all his efforts on holding it there, forbidding his muscles from driving their full strength into her.

Anathrasa's scream filled the arena—not just in his head, but outside it.

The Mother Goddess was here.

"Go," he muttered to Ash. His arm was shaking. He wasn't sure he could hold Anathrasa off much longer, and he didn't want to hurt Ash.

She shook her head, rising to her knees. "No. You can fight her off. I'm not leaving."

She placed her hands on Madoc's chest, and his breath ripped free in a staggered gasp. The warmth of her fingers bled through his sweat-drenched tunic. His heart thundered against his ribs.

"Fight her off," Ash demanded again, a fierceness in her gaze that he'd come to know well.

Madoc closed his eyes, trying to drown out the fighting around him, trying to swallow the screaming voice in his own head.

He had a source of anathreia to pull from. He didn't need to tithe to use it—the well inside him was already full.

Don't be afraid, Tor whispered in his memories.

They were running out of time. Anathrasa was here—he could feel her consciousness punching through the synchronized pulse of the army she'd created.

The hunger inside him warred with the charge of the energeia he'd already taken from Ash. His anathreia was desperate, roiling like a shaken jar of wine. But the fortress he'd built around his soul held steady.

He opened his eyes and turned the hunger in on himself, giving it a source on which to feed: Anathrasa.

Do not—she began, but her demand broke off into a cry of panic.

His energeia swallowed her screams in his head, scraped her out of every crevice she'd lodged into—the gaps between his bones, the hollow of his throat, the spaces between his thoughts. It fed and fed, and it roared in satisfaction when she cried.

And when she was gone, before his hunger turned on the energeia he'd stolen from Ash, he pressed his hand to her stomach and forced it back into her body. Hot tendrils of fire. The solid strength of earth. Water slipping through her veins and the rootedness of living plants.

She gulped a breath, her head tilting skyward.

Then she fell into him.

He caught her, holding her tight. His chin dipped into the crook of her neck and he breathed in the warm, familiar scent of her skin.

"Are you . . . ," he started.

"Yes." She pushed back, wonder in her eyes. "You're back."

Her lips curled into a smirk as he pulled her up.

Again, the ground began to quake, and they braced against each other as a deafening hiss filled the air. The soldiers Madoc had stilled with anathreia were suddenly knocked aside by a slithering flash of red. A snake, as thick as the pillar holding up the palace roof and covered with glittering scales, circled them, strangling the flames Ash had raised beneath its massive body. It lifted its head, a black tongue darting out as milky poison dripped from two fangs the size of Madoc's arms.

A rumbling hiss echoed from its throat. "Traitors."

"Biotus," Madoc realized, horror flooding his veins as the snake's body coiled tighter, scraping over the sand. Before he or Ash could defend themselves, they were caught in the vise of his body, crushed together with a crack of bones and a gasp of breath.

With a scream of frustration, Ash tried to use her power, but was smothered by another rope of scales. Madoc struggled to move his arms, push them free with his legs, but his ribs were popping under the pressure.

His vision compressed. In the black smoke that rose around them, Anathrasa's army suddenly appeared, slack-jawed and single-minded. They stumbled toward Madoc and Ash, climbing over Biotus's coils, sending a new bolt of panic down Madoc's spine.

He couldn't breathe. Ash's knees dug into his thighs, her arms locked against his cracking ribs. They couldn't move.

His gaze lifted through the smoke to the stands, where a goddess in white stared down at him.

Anathrasa.

Fury rose inside him, hotter than Ash's flames and twice as potent. Anathrasa had done this—made this army, caused this war. Killed his sister and taken his mother.

He would not let her take anyone else.

He closed his eyes, drowning out the wind and screams and hisses, quieting even Ash's voice as she whimpered his name. Madoc drew on his strength again, on the power that made him *him*, and reached through the snake's thick skin with cool spikes of anathreia. Biotus's energeia was raw and bitter, and the taste of blood in Madoc's mouth made him gag, but he didn't stop.

The coils loosened, but he didn't stop.

Ash broke free, fighting off the army, but still, Madoc drank.

The snake shriveled. Writhed. It broke into the form of a human. Biotus's skin lost its luster. His muscles thinned. His mouth fell slack. He begged—*We can help each other, set me free.*

Madoc didn't listen.

Only when his power was completely gone did Madoc release his hold.

He staggered to one knee as Biotus crawled away through the waves of soldiers that were still pressing in. Madoc's vision was blurred by the thick, wild power inside him. He blinked, forcing his pounding head to focus, and frantically looked up to the box.

Anathrasa was gone.

"Madoc?" Ash helped him up. Touched his face. Blood was smeared across her cheeks. She cradled her left arm against her chest.

They were surrounded by a wall of rapidly crumbling stone—a fortress of Ash's creation. Already soldiers were knocking down the stones in a spray of dust.

He didn't have to ask if she was ready; she'd been born for this.

Trembling, he pushed Biotus's energeia into her the way he had Florus's power into Anathrasa. He sensed no resistance in her, only a welcoming warmth. She took it all, lips parted and eyes open, and when he was done, her teeth set in a vicious smile.

"One left," she said. "We still need Aera's power if we're going to beat Anathrasa."

"We don't have much time," he managed. The Mother Goddess had to have seen what he'd done. If Aera didn't know already, she would soon.

The goddess of air wasn't hard to spot. She had Hydra pinned at the top of the arena, throwing stones and sand at her with pummeling gales.

"Once she figures out what I'm doing, we won't have long," Madoc said.

Ash nodded. "I'll be ready."

"If you can hold her, I can drain her."

"We need to catch her by surprise," Ash said.

"No problem."

Madoc spun to find Elias. Dust coated the side of his brother's face, and his shoulder was weeping blood down his chest.

Madoc threw his arms around him, pulling him close. He'd never been so happy to see him in all his life.

When Elias pulled back, he was grinning.

"Did you know I can throw a dust wave across this entire arena?" Elias asked.

"Unfortunately, I did," Ash answered, making him cringe. He turned to Madoc.

"You know the sign," he said.

Madoc huffed. "You'd better be ready."

"I'm always ready." With a smirk, Elias grabbed Ash's forearm and dragged her away. They fought their way through the soldiers coming through the stones, leaving Madoc alone, clinging to hope.

He sprinted toward the side of the arena, pushing back those closest with a wave of soul energeia. He shoved off two of Aera's guards and one of Anathrasa's soldiers who attacked with a severed hand. When Madoc was close enough for a clear view of the goddess of air, he ducked low.

He focused on the strength inside him, and his anathreia surged and struck out toward Aera. Silver slivers of light cut across the gold sand. Her power darted away from him, the same uncontainable wind he remembered from the palace library.

She spun, fury painting her face. "Madoc!" she screamed. With a punch of her hand, she sent Hydra flying toward the far side of the stands, where she fell in a heap and did not rise.

Madoc aimed his anathreia at her again, but she spun, the wind whipping her a spear's throw to the left. He adjusted, tried again, but she was gone.

He heard her laughter behind him and twisted just in time for a breeze to cut beneath his knees and knock him to his back.

"Sweet Madoc," she cooed. "Did you really think it would be so easy?"

He scrambled up, and she jabbed a hand toward him. The air fled from his lungs in a hard cough, leaving him wide-eyed and gasping.

"It's a pity," she mocked, striding close enough that he could see the dark veins branching out like lightning beneath her eyes, and the jutting bones of her cheeks and bare shoulders. "I would have enjoyed playing with you for a few decades."

He tapped his fingers against his thigh.

"Sorry to disappoint," he rasped.

The ground shook, and twin waves of gravel three times his height rose on either side of Aera. They slammed into her with the force of two galloping horses, drawing a surprised scream from her throat.

"Now!" Ash cried from his left. To his right, Elias threw another wave of sand against the goddess of air.

Madoc couldn't see Aera in the cloud of dust, but he could feel the hum of her aereia, and struck out for it. With her power focused on Elias and Ash's attack, she couldn't siphon the air from his lungs or play her games. Cool fingers of anathreia locked her in place. Once he'd trapped her soul, he inhaled her energeia in gulps, the rise of wind rushing through his blood, raising the hair on his arms.

In a whirlwind, she broke free, forcing back the waves of dust that Ash and Elias struggled to throw at her. But before she could turn her attack to Madoc, she was lifted off the ground in a funnel of water, spinning and twisting against the self-contained current.

"Hold still, sister," Hydra growled, standing below her.

"Madoc, now!" Ash screamed.

He didn't delay. He pulled and pulled, teeth bared, feeling as though his skin would rip from the mounting pressure beneath. He drained Aera until she writhed in her prison of water. He drained her until her aereia was his, and her beating heart sounded no different than any other mortal's.

"That's enough," a woman ordered.

He fell to his hands and knees, dizzy with power. When his chin lifted, he saw Anathrasa standing beside him. Behind her stretched a wall of emerald vines, peppered with white flowers and bodies.

Ilena's body. Ava's. Danon's. Anathrasa had even managed to pull Elias away from the fight with Ash. They were held so tightly they couldn't even struggle.

Terror coursed through him.

Lunging forward, Ash struck out toward the wall with a burst of her own floreia—twisting ivy that shot toward Madoc's family. But before it reached them, the plants withered and ripped free from their roots in Ash's hands. With a shout of pain she staggered to one knee.

"You may know a few tricks," Anathrasa snapped at her, waving aside Ash's rescue attempt. "But you are not the goddess of plants."

"Finish this!" Elias shouted at Madoc, just before a vine twisted around his mouth to silence him.

"Give me the aereia, Madoc," Anathrasa said, carefully making her way toward him. "Give it to me, and they'll live. Drain the God Killer and give me the rest, and your family goes free."

He glanced at Ash, who was staring at Anathrasa, uncertainty in her eyes. At Hydra, who'd dropped the quivering form of her sister and turned her focus to the horde still closing in around them.

"The aereia," Anathrasa snapped. "Or Ilena is the first to die."

The vines pushed Ilena's body forward, revealing a thorned tendril that wrapped around her slender neck. She stared blankly ahead, still under Anathrasa's power, the white chalk on her mouth making her lips look pale and sickly.

Madoc quaked from aereia. From the terror twisting his soul. He could not lose Ilena. He couldn't lose any of them.

But he would if Anathrasa lived. She'd never let his family be free. As long as he was a threat, they would be used against him. He glanced to Hydra, fighting off the people still under Anathrasa's control. All of them had families too. All the world would suffer as long as she lived.

She would destroy the Divine and crush the Undivine into submission.

His gaze found Elias's, steady and knowing.

"I'm sorry," Madoc muttered. He tore himself away from Elias. From his mother, and sister, and brother, who he could no longer protect—who he never had been able to save.

He stumbled toward Ash. The last hope for his family. For Deimos. For them all.

"I love you," he said, and kissed her.

TWENTY-FOUR

ASH

ASH GRIPPED MADOC'S shoulders. The kiss was more pain than pleasure, his lips rough and insistent, bruising her mouth. Power poured from him into her, a whipping, violent tornado that thrashed from Ash's head down to her toes and sucked the air from her lungs. Air only surged back in as Madoc pulled away, transferring his breath to her.

He trembled, gasping, and Ash held him up as she felt him start to droop. His hooded eyes lifted to hers and he gave her a sad, aching smile.

"The last type of energeia," he said. His face darkened. "Get her."

Ash eased him to the sand. He knelt at her feet, one knee up and his forearm across it like he was bowing in reverence to her, not falling in exhaustion.

Ash looked down at him, shaking, her lips still hot from his. Her fingers splayed in front of her and she stared at them as though they would be different, some instructions scrawled across her skin as to what she should do now.

Aereia was the last piece. It fought for room in her body, churning winds and wild gales that were tempestuous and ever changing and never satisfied.

Bioseia was a constant growl in the back of her throat, an animalistic sharpness that took hold of her senses, heightening sight and sound and smell. The arena stank of body odor and metallic blood, of fear that smelled acidic and grief that smelled sooty and pain that smelled like bile. She could see everything, everyone, and hear the thrum of their heartbeats, a swelling whir like the agitated wings of a hummingbird.

Aereia and bioseia clicked into place with the floreia, hydreia, geoeia, and igneia.

Six energeias that had once been one.

Ash felt them unite inside her. She felt the aereia breathe life and the bioseia form it and the floreia grow it and the hydreia water it and the geoeia build it and the igneia detonate it. One energeia, one sprawling blanket that connected every part of her body and every person on this earth, Divine and Undivine and god.

Tor had worried this much power might kill her. Ash knew now that it was a foolish fear—this power was life. This power was death. This power was everything, and she understood now why a mortal had to die before holding such infinity.

A tear tracked down Ash's cheek. How had all the gods grown so far apart? How had they forgotten how much they needed each other?

How had Anathrasa corrupted the crystalline beauty of anathreia?

Ash turned. Barely a moment had passed in her revelation, all of time holding its breath as it waited and watched a new Mother Goddess form.

Off to Ash's left, Aera lay in the puddle of her water prison, screaming in fury. Hydra was fending off the soldiers.

There were no gods to worry about now.

Except one.

Anathrasa matched Aera's frustrated howls. "You fool!" she cried at Madoc. "You will watch your family die!"

She contracted her hand and the vines squeezed. Ava screamed in terror while Danon wept and Elias squirmed, his cheeks purpling. Only Ilena still didn't react, her face wearing that delicate sheen of controlled acceptance.

Ash lifted her hand. *Stop.*

The vines froze solid, the water deep in their pores quickly setting.

A flick of Ash's arm, and every vine withered, sliding Madoc's family to the soft, churned golden sands.

Anathrasa's eyes were wide and manic, a sign of how close she was to the edge even as she laughed. "You think you can challenge me, mortal? I am ageless. I am eternal. I will be here long after your bones turn to dust and you—"

Ash flared her hands palm-out and sent a whip of fire snapping into Anathrasa's chest. It threw her back against the swelling press of the army still bent at her command. Hydra was holding off the worst of them, but people poured in from every doorway, filling the arena, pulled by Anathrasa's call.

No more.

Ash closed her eyes.

No more.

She heard their minds. The same thought connected each soul to Anathrasa, like a tapestry fraying out its threads from a single point. Anathrasa's command fueled them: *Stop the God Killer.*

She had forced herself on these people. They were mortal and hadn't had a chance against a goddess.

Ash opened her eyes and released the hold Anathrasa had on them. *You are yourselves again.*

Instantly, raised weapons paused. War cries tapered to nothing. People blinked and looked around as awareness seeped back into them. Ilena was one of them, gathering her children into her arms.

Ash heard weeping from every direction, cries of confusion, pleas of surrender. But she smiled.

Anathrasa could not control these people anymore.

And now Ash would kill her.

Anathrasa righted herself from where Ash had thrown her. She bellowed in rage and the ground began to shake—great, mighty oaks burst up through the sand, pulled by Anathrasa's will. Their branches were jagged and sharp and skewered whoever happened to be in their wake, eliciting wails of pain and horror.

Ash punched her hands in two directions, one to push the floreia away from Madoc's family, and one to keep him and Hydra safe as well. She couldn't react fast enough to save everyone, and screaming dug into her ears, breaking past the battle-ready fog of concentration that was keeping her heart beating.

The roar of the growing trees settled, and where the arena had once been was now a deadly forest. Soldiers from the former army struggled to extract themselves from the twisted limbs and sharp branches. Blood dripped from the trees, falling like leaves.

Ash couldn't spot Anathrasa.

The screams of agony cut through the stillness that a forest couldn't help but bring. It was a nauseating contrast, peaceful floreia and so much pain.

"Ash." Hydra ran up to her and grabbed her arms. "Where did she go?"

"I don't—"

"Use the anathreia," Hydra coaxed.

Ash shuddered, wrapping her arms around herself. The trees blocked out the sun. They blocked out the sky. There were people impaled on their branches.

She couldn't break. She couldn't get distracted, not now.

She had to kill Anathrasa.

Eyes pinched shut, Ash pushed out the shouts and blood, the thundering of these hundreds of abused hearts and the fear in these innocent souls. She widened her awareness.

There was so much *pain* in this arena. It had already been a place of death, and agony was soaked into every particle of sand.

Ash grimaced and tore her eyes open. "I can't! We have to help everyone here—I can't see past the suffering."

She yanked her hand and sent a tree back into the earth, freeing the people stuck in it. Anathrasa had the bulk of Florus's floreia while Ash only had a small gift of it, but she would still be able to send this forest away, tree by tree.

Hydra grabbed her shoulders. "Not now. I need you to be

single-minded Ash again. I need you to be action-first-questions-later Ash. You can take care of this entire forest once you stop her. You need to find Anathrasa and eliminate her *now*."

Ash writhed, gasping. Anathreia was so much. It was all too much. The beauty in it was blinding, too bright, too expansive. There were thousands of people in Crixion alone, and they were hurting, scared, and Ash could feel it *all*—

"Let me."

A warm body pressed against Ash's back. Hydra released her as arms came around Ash's stomach, tightening, Madoc holding her to his chest.

His forehead rested on the back of her head and he looped one arm across her chest while the other kept her hips pinned against his. She could feel his anathreia, the essence at the core of him. He was scared, yes; he was tired; he'd been wounded somewhere on his side. But beneath all that, he was resolute, and he wasn't letting go of her.

She leaned into him, her body arching back so her head fell against his shoulder, and she knotted her fingers around his wrists.

"Breathe," he whispered. "Build a wall in your mind. One thought, then another, things you can use as anchors in the noise."

One thought. She just needed one to start.

She reached—and a searing pain came from one of the soldiers in the trees. She winced, shaking her head, whimpering. "No—it *hurts*, Madoc, it all hurts—"

"I know." He pulled her tighter, taking her weight. "Think about Tor. He's your anchor. Think about Taro and Spark. Think about Igna.

Think about—" His voice hitched, breath hot on the side of her neck. "Think about us, Ash. I'm not leaving you. I love you. Think about that, and anchor yourself to it, and use it to come back to yourself. Remember? We'll always come back to each other."

Ash reached up to touch Madoc's cheek, her fingers slipping down to hold his neck.

She loved him, too. She loved him, and that had saved her through this war, time and again.

It would save her now.

Ash stretched her mind. Anathreia swelled, bubbling up and out and scrambling across the arena.

Souls cried. People *wanted* and they *ached*—

Ash bit down on her tongue. Madoc. Madoc holding her, and his heart beating against her back.

Her anathreia searched and searched, scrambling through souls.

"When I find her," Ash started, her tongue dry and gritty, "what then?"

"Then you take the energeia in her body. Take it until there's nothing left. It's a hunger." She felt him swallow. "And it must be fed."

And then? Ash wanted to ask. What happened once she had Anathrasa's power? What did she do with so much anathreia?

Her awareness caught on someone behind her.

Ash's eyes flew open.

She whirled and shoved Madoc aside as Anathrasa charged out from behind one of her trees. A wave of vines carried her, one tendril licking the air ahead of her with a talon-like thorn at its head.

That thorn stabbed the space where Madoc had just been. Ash

spun her hands and cut the vine in half, letting the two pieces fall harmlessly to the sand.

Anathrasa kept charging. Ash braced her feet and planted her arms up so when Anathrasa reached her, the two of them slammed to a halt, Ash with her hands on Anathrasa's chest, Anathrasa snarling and spitting down at her.

"You will not take my victory!" Anathrasa shrieked, and then she *pulled*.

The energeia in Ash's chest rebounded, banging inside her as it fought against Anathrasa's incessant call.

Ash growled and fisted her hands in the collar of Anathrasa's gown. "This is not your victory," Ash spat back and scrambled through the Mother Goddess's body for the final remains of her soul.

Anathrasa felt Ash pulling at her energeia and redoubled her efforts. Her eyes strained, veins bulging in her face, sweat beading. Her smooth skin wrinkled and aged before shifting to become young again, a warring tangle of power and weakness as they each pulled the other's energeia.

An oily, horrifying thought wiggled into Ash's mind—she wasn't strong enough. Anathrasa may not have had her full power, but she was ancient and resilient all the same, and Ash barely knew how to use the power she had just gotten.

One of her feet slipped, sending her lurching back through the sand. She gritted her teeth and pulled at Anathrasa's energeia, harder, with everything she had—everything that still wouldn't be enough.

"Take it!" Ash heard a cry behind her. Hydra? "Madoc, take my hydreia and give it all to her, *now*!"

A hand touched her back, and water gushed through Ash's body. Cool and refreshing, it chased the other energeias in her soul and infused the hydreia already waiting there with extra power.

Something else came, too. Something still and sturdy and familiar.

Madoc was giving her his own anathreia.

She wanted to tell him not to. She wanted to stop him, but it filled her before she could protest, an effervescent burst of anathreia. It was small against the power Ash had—but it was enough.

Like the final surge of a wave against a weakening tide wall, Ash threw the extra power at Anathrasa.

A moment of tension, and then it gave. It gave and gave until Anathrasa's soul went limp and surrendered to Ash's grasp.

Ash stumbled back. Everything was sunlight. Golden rays cascaded over the arena, the forest, the world, threads of connection, pulses of energeia.

All she could see was golden power.

The knowledge came, sure and strong: no one had ever been this powerful. No being, no mortal, no god. Ash was something bigger than all of that. Something darker, and brighter, terrible and wonderful all at once.

She could rule it all. The world would bow to her, and those who wouldn't bow in honor would bow in fear. She was a goddess of goddesses and she was *everything*.

Ash breathed too fast and her heartbeat thundered.

Anchors in the noise.

Tor hugging her. Taro and Spark, smiling at her. Madoc, his lips on hers, his laugh.

Char.

Ash bent over with a cry.

No, Ash.

The voice came from a darkness. A space between spaces.

We are not meant for this power, the voice said.

An overwhelming embrace of love wrapped around Ash, softening her, warming her more deeply than any igneia. This wasn't like when she'd seen Char under Florus's poison.

This was *real.*

Ash wept. "Mama—"

Let the power go, said the voice. *Let it go, my fuel and flame.*

Ash screamed.

Anathreia was everything. And so Ash put it back into the everything that it had made.

She screamed louder and, as she had taken Anathrasa's soul out of her body, she pushed the energeias out into the ether. Floreia went into the trees, pulling them back beneath the earth and freeing the people trapped in them; hydreia went into the water; geoeia went into the stones and bioseia to the animals and aereia to the air—and igneia. Ignitus's fire flickered in protest, a scorching pulse in Ash's chest, and she sobbed as she pushed it out into the flames of the world. It was mingled now, one energeia made of six parts, and she had to break it all out of her soul.

When it was gone, Ash fell to her knees, sobbing, helplessly exhausted.

But she blinked, and the golden power was gone. The world was itself again, the fighting sands littered with the former army now freed from the floreia forest—

And Anathrasa was on the ground before Ash. The Mother Goddess gawked at her shaking limbs, her skin gradually shriveling, becoming old and mottled.

Ash could feel Madoc and Hydra behind her, pulling out of their own shock. But Anathrasa came to first.

"No," Anathrasa gasped, "*no!*"

She staggered to her feet. Ash didn't have the strength to retreat, her own body shaking as well, and she steeled herself with clenched fists.

But a figure moved behind Anathrasa, and Ash smiled.

Anathrasa took her grin as taunting. "How *dare* you!" she bellowed. She hobbled forward, aging more and more by the second. "You will pay for this, mortal. I survived this trick once, and I'll survive it again!"

"No." Ash shook her head. "You won't."

Before Anathrasa could respond, her body arched backward. The tip of a blade poked through her chest, blood glinting in a ray of sun.

Ilena's face appeared over her shoulder. "This is for my family."

She pushed, and Anathrasa's body toppled to the sand. Dead.

Ilena's eyes met Ash's across the space between them, and when they both smiled, it was exhausted, and it was relieved, and it was as many things as anathreia was. Everything all at once.

TWENTY-FIVE

MADOC

MADOC FELT WEAK, shaken. As if Anathrasa was still controlling his body. He didn't know where to look—at the Mother Goddess, lying dead on the ground, appearing more like Seneca, their old neighbor, than the ruthless goddess who'd captured Deimos—or to his mother, standing over her.

Ilena had done it.

They'd *all* done it.

He could hardly believe he was alive. He wouldn't have been, had he not channeled his anathreia into Ash. The link between him and Anathrasa would have killed him.

Ilena stepped back, instantly wiping her bloody hands on her dusty white robes. Long streaks of red lined her sides, but she didn't seem to notice them. She was staring at Anathrasa, her mouth, still marked with chalk, set in a tight line, her eyes hard with anger.

"Mother," he said.

Her gaze flicked up. Met his. Steadied.

She nodded.

Cassia's vengeance had been delivered by the one person who needed it most.

He stumbled toward her, feet pedaling through the sand. Behind her, the people who'd been trapped in the branches of Anathrasa's forest looked around, calling for help and searching for a way out. The remaining Laks and Cenhelmians looked to their gods for answers, but Biotus was dead, pulled apart by the crowd, and Aera, as powerless as any Undivine, was kicking in rage at the sand beside his body. Voices were raised in confusion, yet Madoc couldn't feel their panic or their pain. He could feel nothing but his own battered body and the wonder and relief that they were still alive.

His anathreia was gone. He didn't have to call on it to know. The power that had been growing inside him since the war between Geoxus and Ignitus was silent now. It demanded nothing—not to tithe on emotion or injury, or feed on another's energeia. Without his intensified intuition, he felt untethered, unable to gauge the intentions of those around him. Unable to truly grasp their victory.

But he also felt . . . free.

"Madoc," Ilena said as he approached. "You're all right?"

"Yes." He took her hands, finding them cold and shaking. He pulled her close, remembering the way Cassia had fit against him. Wiry. Small.

Stronger than stone.

"Madoc! Mother!" Elias was running toward them, and with a sob, Ilena pulled him into their embrace. Danon and Ava weren't far behind—Ava shoved her way between their legs to be in the middle of the huddle, while Danon kept pointing at Madoc, brows drawn in confusion.

"Did you just—to a *god*?" he was saying. Madoc just laughed.

"My children," Ilena said, over and over, and somewhere, Madoc knew Cassia was smiling.

Over Ilena's shoulder, he spotted Ash embracing Hydra. Saw Hydra laugh and wipe away a tear. Tor had arrived as well, and was running toward them, and when Ash leaped into his arms, he let out a holler loud enough to make Madoc laugh even harder.

She smiled at him then—the warrior who could kill gods and hold six energeias inside her. The girl with the fist around his heart.

He moved toward her, but she was already coming to him. He didn't know whether to pull her into his arms, or kiss her, or tell her the hundred things he'd been wanting to say since they'd last spoken. In the end, when they stopped toe to toe, he said, "Thanks for bringing me back."

She bit her lip. "You brought yourself back. I just reminded you what you were missing."

"Keep reminding me. Every day."

She blew out a slow breath. "That sounds like a lot of work."

"You won't regret it," he said. She laughed, and he cupped her cheeks in his hands and drew her close. But he paused a breath away at the drop of her gaze.

"What is it?" he asked.

"It's gone," she said. "The igneia. The hydreia. All of it. I pushed it away."

He swallowed, feeling, even without anathreia, what an enormous effort this must have been. She'd had the power of gods. She'd been stronger than Anathrasa herself, and she'd given it away.

He was in awe of her all over again.

"Are you all right?" he asked.

Her mouth quirked in a smile. "I will be."

When his lips touched hers, the sounds of the arena quieted beneath the tandem boom of their hearts. Her hands found his waist, then his back, and as her body aligned with his, a new wave of emotion shook through him—pure, and strong, and entirely his own.

He loved her. He would love her all his life. And if she let him, he would proudly stand beside her.

Her kiss was steady and strong, warm and growing. Even if the energeias that she'd held were gone, they echoed inside her. And in answer, he felt a cool breath lift his soul. A whisper of a power he thought was gone.

She loved him back.

He never wanted to let her go again. But he did stop kissing her when someone cleared their throat.

"There is a time for these things," Tor said gruffly.

The old gladiator was right. There was much to do. Hydra was already barking orders to her people, breaking those who'd fought in the arena into groups of healers and injured, and directing teams of survivors into the city to calm the citizens before any new riots could ensue.

Anathrasa was still lying on the sand, half her army of fighters strewn across the arena. Those who'd voiced dissent against the

Mother Goddess were waiting in jails across the city, and others she'd locked in their own minds were rousing, as Madoc and Ilena had.

A weight settled between Madoc's shoulder blades. The coming days would be difficult—Deimos hadn't fully recovered from the loss of Geoxus, and now had lost Anathrasa as well. Lakhu, Itza, and Cenhelm no longer had gods, Kula was still suffering, and those who'd perished under the Mother Goddess's reign had to be buried and mourned.

But Crixion, and the world, would be all right. They would rebuild. They would survive. And he and Ash would do what they could to help.

"What happens now?" Elias asked, taking Ava off Danon's hip.

Ash glanced up at Madoc. Her fingers wove through his.

"We try something new," she said. "Not fighting."

"I like the sound of that," Madoc said.

Ash laughed, and when he pulled her close, he could feel the warmth pulsing through her, soft and gentle.

Maybe it was his old exaggerated intuition, but it felt like hope.

EPILOGUE

ASH

Three Years Later

COUNCIL MEMBERS LINED either side of the meeting room's long glass table. The tall ceiling and wide windows made the volcanic rock walls look open and airy instead of dark and closed in—not that any of the mostly Kulan councilors minded, but visiting ambassadors always preferred light.

"We have preliminary numbers in from the wheat farmers," Brand said, flipping through correspondence. His eyes widened. "They expect a full crop this year."

Tor looked up from where he was making notes on a parchment. "A full crop?"

The other councilors, busy taking their own notes or sorting their own papers, paused. The ambassadors cut their eyes between Tor, Igna's lead councilor—and Ash, his second.

Brand nodded, eyes sparkling, his lips stretched in a grin.

At the opposite end of the table, Ash eased upright from where she'd been going over a list of Kula's exports. There had been many adjustment pains these last few years—Aera, now Undivine and mortal, was a furious prisoner in Crixion, while Deiman ambassadors had been dispatched to oversee the beginnings of mortal rule in Lakhu and Cenhelm—but overall, the world was healing.

And now Kula was producing *crops.*

Ash smiled at Tor. It rose, breaking her lips open, and she put her fingers to her mouth.

"Well," Tor breathed, leaning back in his chair. "How about that?"

Ash sniffed and rubbed her tingling nose.

The Deiman ambassador moaned heavily from his seat near the middle of the table. But when Ash looked at Elias, he was smiling. "Gods, it's just wheat, you sentimental fools."

It was still so odd to see Elias in this role, but he had leaped at the chance to remake Deimos and undo the system of poverty that had strangled his family.

Next to him, Brand rolled up the correspondence and thwacked Elias on the shoulder. "*Just wheat.* Like you don't cry at every small victory Deimos has."

"I don't know." Hydra, across from them both, folded her arms on the table. "I'm still not convinced Deimans have that wide a range of emotion."

Elias put a hand to his chest in mock offense.

Ash let out a bark of laughter. "Cruel, Hydra! Don't bait him."

"I am the goddess of water. I do not *bait* people."

"Ehh." Elias bobbed his head. "Can you really say that anymore? *Goddess.*"

It was true that Hydra was no longer a goddess—when she had

given all her power to Ash to defeat Anathrasa, she had given up her immortality too, and all but a weak use of hydreia. But she was still the ruler of the Apuit Islands, and now Itza as well.

A movement drew Ash's attention. The door swung shut in Madoc's wake and he leaned against the wall, arms folded, his lips playing at a smile.

Ash thumped the table. "Bickering means we've done enough for today," she said. "We'll reconvene tomorrow and decide where all this sentimental wheat will go."

Brand smirked as though he'd won something. Elias grinned back at him, making Ash wonder, not for the first time, if there was more between the Kulan councilor and the Deiman ambassador.

"Are you mine now?"

Ash smiled before she'd even turned to Madoc, who was standing next to her at the end of the table now, a playful grin on his face.

The room was emptying. Brand, Elias, and Hydra left, calling back that Ash and Madoc should join them at one of Igna's taverns. A few other councilors still talked with Tor.

Ash put her supplies into a satchel with exaggerated slowness. "I thought I'd stay here."

Madoc sat on the edge of the table. "Oh? And do what?"

Tor glanced back as if he'd left something. He caught Ash watching him, saw Madoc, and gave an exasperated shake of his head that told her he knew she was waiting for him to leave.

He shut the door behind him, and finally, the room was empty.

"Chart import projections for next month. Unless"—Ash stepped in front of Madoc and threaded her arms around his neck—"you have something more exciting to entice me with?"

Madoc hooked his fingers into the top of her orange skirt and yanked her hips flush with his. She fell against him, her laugh turning to a little gasp of pleasure that he covered with a kiss.

His lips were familiar now, full and soft, and he tasted of mint and smelled of musky sandalwood, and everything about him made her drunk.

They were free to do this. Be together in this palace, in this country, in this world. And they could take their time, linger over each careful touch and each fluttering kiss, because there were no arenas waiting for them or uncertain futures beckoning with bloodstained hands.

A knock came from far away, and the door to the meeting room opened.

Taro peeked in. "Tor said to knock. Loudly. He also said I should give you a disapproving lecture on what should and shouldn't take place in the meeting room before I tell you that Ilena wants to see you both."

Ash instantly dropped her eyes to Madoc's, sharing a sober look.

Taro waved her hands. "She said it's nothing bad. She's in your apartment."

But Ash and Madoc were already halfway to the door.

They had rooms one floor beneath the meeting area so Ash could be close during late nights. Madoc spent much of his time fostering relationships between the Undivine and Divine populations, so he worked throughout the city and traveled abroad, but he hadn't minded lodging in the dormant volcano palace at Igna's center.

Ash suspected he'd agreed to live here because part of him still felt guilty that he hadn't returned her own igneia all those years ago. What he'd given her had been Ignitus's, and when Ash had pushed the anathreia out of her body in the final fight against Anathrasa, she'd lost all traces of her god's former powers, too.

She was Undivine now. Then again, so was Madoc.

Ash beat him to the door of their apartment and pushed it open. The main room had a full wall of pale glass windows that brightened the whole space. A small brazier with smoldering coals sat off to the side, warming the woven rugs on the floor, the scattered lounges and chairs, the table stacked with books and scrolls and notes.

Ilena sat on the floor beside one of the lounges, her legs folded under her on a butter-yellow blanket she had knit. She looked up when Ash barged in and instantly held up her hands. "I told Taro to make sure you knew nothing was wrong!"

Ash scrambled around a chair. In front of Ilena on the yellow blanket, gnawing on a wooden block Tor had bought for her, Ciela stared up with big, dark eyes.

When she saw Ash, the baby extended her arms with a demanding squawk.

The tension in Ash's chest eased. She dropped to her knees and lifted Ciela, putting the girl's weight on her feet. She surveyed her more closely—her curling black hair, her full golden cheeks, her three small white teeth, the plump belly Ash loved to press kisses to.

Ciela squawked again, stretching for Ash, impatient that her mother hadn't hugged her yet.

Madoc lowered next to her. Ciela saw him and screeched merrily. In return, Madoc gave her a smile Ash had never seen from him until eleven months ago. Now she saw it daily, a softening around his lips and his gaze. Adoration. Obsession. *Love.*

"She's fine," Ash told him as she settled Ciela on her lap.

Ciela clapped and gave a happy chirp.

"I know," Ilena laughed. "I told you, it wasn't *bad.*"

"Then what—"

"Ash." Madoc put a hand on her knee. "Look."

She looked down.

Ciela clapped her hands again. A small spark burst out of her fingertips, and Ciela squealed, delighted, and clapped again. Another spark, another squeal.

Ash's entire body went stiff. "She has igneia."

Ilena made a soft hum of agreement. "I'll give you some privacy," she said gently.

When his mother was gone, Madoc blew out a breath. "Igneia. She's Fire Divine."

"We knew it was a possibility." Ash's throat was dry.

Madoc fell back against the lounge. "A Fire Divine baby. A Fire Divine *toddler.*" He cast a look around, horror graying his face with every new thing he saw. "We have so many flammable things in this room. And *I'm* flammable! I'm not Kulan! What are we—*how* are we—"

"Madoc." Ash balanced Ciela against her chest and put a hand on his leg. "It'll be fine. We're in the best place for her. We'll be all right."

"Blankets. Every blanket could catch fire. And what about—"

He twisted, arms stretched wide, but he stopped. His eyes drifted through Ash's.

"Are *you* all right?" His voice was a whisper.

Ash wanted to say she was. But she looked down at Ciela again and watched her laugh at her own small sparks, sheer joy in every beautiful giggle.

Her daughter had igneia.

Tears filled Ash's eyes. She tried to wipe one away as it fell, but Madoc saw.

"Ash." He wrapped an arm around her shoulders. "It's all right if you're . . . upset."

"Upset?" Ash smiled, the movement pushing more tears down her face. "She has *igneia*."

Madoc's eyebrows lifted.

"She has igneia," Ash continued, "and she can be a dancer. Or she can be a glass maker. Or—or *anything*. Madoc—she can use it however she wants to."

He smiled. "Yeah. She can."

Holding Ciela, feeling her little body's warmth and watching the orange lights flicker in her hands, Ash thought of the future her daughter could have. She wasn't locked into one fate because of her bloodline or deranged gods.

Every day with Ciela brought memories of Char. Ash understood her mother now more than she ever had before.

Ash leaned her head on Madoc's shoulder, letting Ciela play with her hair. "She's perfect."

Madoc pressed his cheek to the top of her head. "Of course she is. She's your daughter."

"Your daughter too."

"We won't hold that against her."

Ash smiled. Madoc pulled a blanket off the lounge and the three of them bundled into it on the floor of their sunlit apartment, together.

Happy.

ACKNOWLEDGMENTS

Every book is a labor of love, but when a book is cowritten, we get double the amount of love in every step.

As always, the first thank-you goes out to our agents, Mackenzie Brady Watson and Joanna MacKenzie.

To Kristin Rens for helping us wrap up Madoc and Ash's story with such flair.

To Jenna Stempel-Lobell, Chris Kwon, Johannes Voss, and Martina Fačková, for giving us a deeply gorgeous cover. To Gillian, Lindsey, Michael, Sabrina, Aubrey, and the entire HarperCollins US team. To Simran and the whole team at HarperCollins UK.

A special thanks goes out to everyone who loved *Set Fire to the Gods* and followed us over to *Rise Up from the Embers*. We are so honored to close out Ash and Madoc's story with you. Know that this journey would not be possible without your dedication and encouragement, your love and excitement, your support and strength. We are overwhelmed with appreciation for you!

From Sara: Kristen, thank you for enduring this story with me. There is no one else I would rather share this experience with, and I am so grateful we got to ride it out together. I will never look at rocks without thinking of you.

From Kristen: Sara! My fuel and flame! We did it, my friend. I have learned so much from you and would be honored to fight by your side in any arena. Especially if it involves cupcakes.

TWO GODS ARE DEAD.
THE MOTHER GODDESS HAS RETURNED.
WAR IS RISING.

"COMPLETELY ENTHRALLING."
—Kendare Blake, #1 *New York Times* bestselling
author of the Three Dark Crowns series

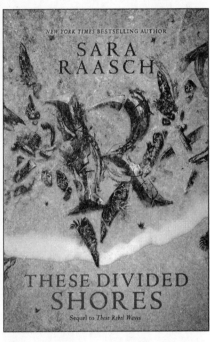